EVERY SHAPE,
EVERY SHADOW

a
pale horse
production

Cover design: Mark A. Clements
Maps: ArstSmart Media (artsmartmedia@yahoo.com)
Author photo: David Kinney

EVERY SHAPE,
EVERY SHADOW

Roger L. Conlee

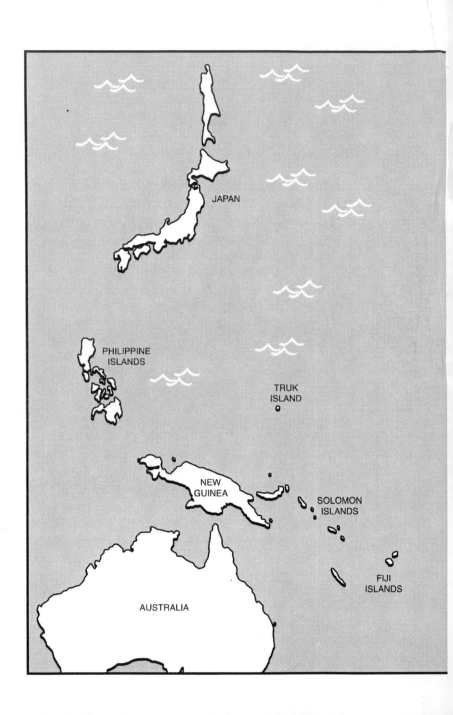

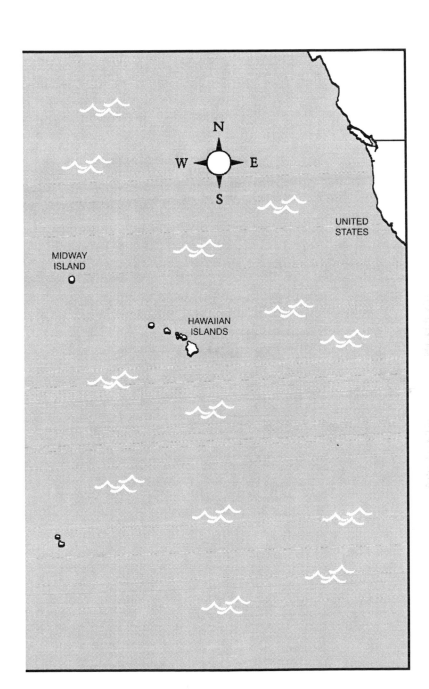

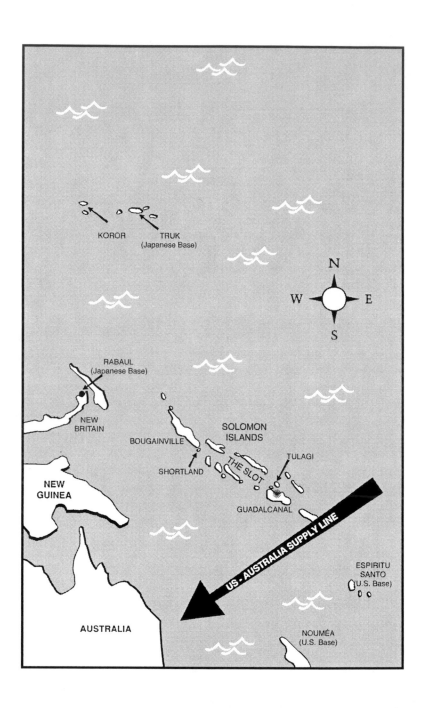

Going into battle with an infantry company is
not the way to live to a ripe old age.
-Ernie Pyle

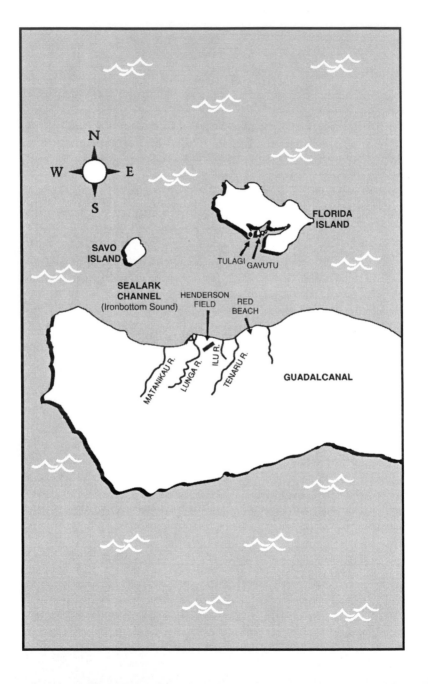

CHAPTER 1

"KEEP THOSE SMELLY feet out of my face, Harris," he told the kid.

"Christ, Kenny, I ain't got any more room than you. Ain't my fault they packed these bunks so damn close together."

Kenny Nielsen's bedroll reeked. So did his clothes. Steamy tropical air and the body heat of hundreds of Marines filled the troopship's cramped hold. Everybody on the *McCawley* was ripe. Kenny's temper had been short for days. Whose hadn't?

The Old Man's up there—what?--twenty, thirty feet above us, Kenny thought, and I'll bet he's cool as lemonade in those sea breezes. Wish to hell they'd let us sleep on deck.

All around him, on bunks stacked five high, other guys played poker, shot dice, read or wrote letters, argued, sharpened their Kabar knives, slept. Elegant chords drifted from a strumming guitar.

Beneath all this, like the muffled drums of a funeral cortege, came the ba-rum, ba-rum, ba-rum of this old bucket's drive shaft. Or was it the propeller? *Ba-rum, ba-rum, ba-rum.*

Is that what this voyage was? A funeral procession? Sometimes Kenny hated the thoughts that sneaked into his mind.

He put his book aside when his platoon leader plopped down next to him. The huge North Carolinian had a face like a brass knuckle. From the start Kenny had been smart enough to get on Sergeant Had Plunkett's good side.

Plunkett's Christian name was Hadley but Kenny never called him that. He'd heard that back in school some kid had called him Fat Hadley and within seconds had a busted nose and a shortage of teeth.

"Whatcha readin' now, Corporal?"

"*Of Mice and Men.*"

"Which one you gonna be tomorrow?"

What a question. Kenny slowly shook his head, then slapped at a persistent fly. "Hey, Sarge, is it true what I heard about those rebels down in Nicaragua? When they ran out of ammo for their French rifles, they'd use smaller caliber and wrap 'em in goatskin so the cartridges wouldn't fall out of the chamber."

"How the hell old you think I am? I wasn't in no Banana Wars. Ask Butch Morgan, the Old Man's cook. Morgan's been in the Corps two years longer than God."

"Anyhow, you figure the Japs might be kinda like that? We keep hearing these stories about their bad eyesight and bad equipment."

"That's all bullshit. After they stuck it up our ass in Guam and Bataan, I figure the Japs are tough little bastards who got plenty of the right ammo. Thinkin' we're better'n them ain't gonna get us nowhere."

"Where you think we're going, Sarge?" Kenny asked for the hundredth time. He knew the *Wacky Mac* had slowed down in the last five hours. The word had gone out to get their gear combat-ready. He'd heard all kinds of scuttlebutt.

"We're gettin' the dope at eighteen-hundred. Prob'ly hittin' some Jap beach tomorrow morning. Gotta stop them bastards someplace, 'fore it's too late. Wherever it is, I hope there's some good-lookin' native gals to jump."

Kenny knew that was barracks talk, that Plunkett was married to a good woman to whom he was more or less faithful.

"Yeah, me, too." Kenny didn't mean it either but didn't have as good a reason. He was twenty-two, single, and had been a Marine for four years, right after finishing high school in Galesburg, Illinois.

"How come us?" he said, swatting at that damn fly. "We were supposed to train our butts off in New Zealand before fighting. A whole Army division's been in New Caledonia for months. How come they weren't sent?"

"Ain't ready, that's why. You need somethin' done fast, it's always the Corps can do it. We been road-tested. If the brass figure some Jap island's gotta be taken right now, we're the ones. Like last year when we occupied Iceland to free up the Limeys for Africa. Who could do that in a jiffy? Us."

"Sounds like a snow job to me."

Plunkett grunted. "Iceland. Snow job. Good one, Nielsen."

A few feet away, Scupper Harris was mumbling again. "Tomorrow I get me some Japs, tomorrow I get me some Japs."

Kenny had coined the nickname Scupper because he thought Harris' mouth looked like a drain hole. The one his brains had gone down. He frowned at the strange eighteen-year-old and snarled, "Ah, shut your warped face. We're sick of that stuff."

Scupper Harris pushed past three guys, his face scrunched up in fury, and got to Kenny. The short little twerp grabbed Kenny's collar and shouted, "You'll pay for that, you son of a bitch."

Kenny squinted at the boy-man trying to be all grown-up and tough. "Get your meat hooks off me or I'll throw your ass clean off this boat."

Sergeant Plunkett seized the Harris kid by the scruff of the neck and lifted all 140 pounds of him like a basket of flowers. "Save it for the Japs, assholes."

Being included in the rebuke pissed Kenny off, but he let it go. There was no way he was going to mess with Plunkett.

He and Harris gave each other dirty looks, the eye contact broke, and the squall passed.

Kenny crawled in his bunk and stared at the slats beneath the bed above. The mattress bore a stain the shape of Texas.

Wonder what they're doing tonight on North Prairie Street, he asked himself. But it's not even tonight in Galesburg, it's last night or yesterday afternoon, something like that. It was hard to grasp that it was yesterday back home--right now.

The little Illinois city between Peoria and the Mississippi River would always be home to him although he'd only seen its maples and elms and brick streets four times since 1938. Lying there, he pictured the square in the middle of town, the big Victorian house on North Seminary he used to think was haunted, and the Mail Pouch Tobacco ad on the side of a barn on the hard road to Monmouth.

Joining the Marine Corps in the depths of the Depression had been his way of avoiding the breadlines. Before Pearl Harbor, the Corps was small and only the best volunteers were taken. Kenny figured he'd been lucky and tough. Now eight-balls like Scupper Harris were getting in.

As Kenny closed his eyes he could almost hear a train whistle from the Burlington tracks and the clatter of a horse-drawn milk wagon. He could see the red brick walls of Old Main, a stone's throw from where South Cherry entered the campus at Knox College. He knew he'd never go to Knox--"hard Knox" was his school--but he still liked the place.

A funny thing happened. From his mind's eye, Galesburg began to shrink, fading away as if he were high above it in a balloon. The town floated farther and farther away, the church steeples growing smaller and smaller.

Hell, he thought, I might be dead by the time it becomes today in Galesburg.

Kenny felt he was well-trained and a good Marine. He was sure he would be brave enough to do well in combat. Pretty sure. Hell, to be honest, he had no idea. *Ba-rum, ba-rum, ba-rum.*

Topside, the commanding general stared at the dark, secretive sea. He thought about the monumental foul-up in the Fijis. If things didn't go a damn sight better this time, those stars on his collar wouldn't be worth the metal they were made of.

When Major General Archer Vandegrift's 1st Marine Division practiced this amphibious invasion at Fiji, davits and winches hadn't worked. The coral reef made it impossible to land the boats. The element of surprise--if there'd been a real enemy--had been shot to hell.

Leaning on the railing, he noticed that the ship tossed a curious glittery white wake in the dark water. The transport

McCawley had been the passenger liner *Santa Barbara* in its peacetime incarnation. Though not a big ship, it glided smoothly on the Solomon Sea. Old King Neptune was being kind this night, he thought. No storms, no rain squalls. Even the swells were docile.

Vandegrift rubbed his hands against his temples. This reminded him of another night on another ship, more than thirty years ago. That vessel had been the *Summer Girl*, which made regular runs from Port Royal, South Carolina, and the island had been Parris Island. From the deck of that old mail boat, Parris Island hadn't looked at all inviting to the frightened young officer candidate, and now in the summer of 1942 neither did this island in the Southern Hemisphere, which few Americans had ever heard of.

Vandegrift knew in his gut that this place would turn out to be much tougher than Officer School had been back in 'Ought-9. Parris Island. Where he'd had those run-ins with Colonel Cole. Vandegrift had wondered then if he'd ever make a Marine officer. It seemed like an eternity ago, and it was.

The distant island pushed higher above the horizon. It usually felt and smelled good to approach a tropical island after a long time at sea, the offshore breezes perfumed by jasmine, plumeria and other tropical flowers with their message of "welcome sailor." Not now.

He thought this one smelled evil, malignant. It couldn't, not yet, he corrected himself. We're much too far away to actually smell the place. Just some mischief of my old mind.

Still, despite the heat, the island made him shiver. He told himself it wasn't just because the place was occupied by an enemy who would do all they could to kill him. There would still be something ominous about that lump on the horizon even if this was a peacetime pleasure cruise.

With each passing minute the island code-named *Cactus* grew a little, a destiny he could not possibly evade. He felt his brow wrinkle. Cactus was an unlikely place to fight. An obscure island nobody ever heard of at the bottom of the Solomons chain. But a convergence of military necessity with a fluke of geography meant that fight for it they would, these two great powers of the Pacific. A big, hellish, no-quarter-asked fight.

You're a 55-year-old man, Vandegrift told himself, with a bum knee and failing eyesight, and you're going into the biggest, ugliest war mankind has ever turned loose on this planet. And leading your country's first counteroffensive against Japan.

Vandegrift had maps he couldn't trust, those that hadn't been lost. A complete set of aerial photographs, taken by Army reconnaissance fliers in General MacArthur's command, had been assembled and mailed. Mailed! They'd never arrived. Damn that MacArthur.

Better get some sleep. We'll be climbing down those cargo nets into the Higgins boats in a few hours and you won't do your men any good if you're exhausted. Gol' darn it, you stayed out here too long. Your night vision's terrible. Blind as a bat. Never find the hatchway. Got yourself into a heck of a mess and the invasion hasn't even started. Some general.

He glanced up at a blurry sweep of stars and wondered what the devil he was doing here off this black island, whose fragrance still hadn't improved. He'd learned that its Japanese name was *Gadarukanaru*.

In English it was Guadalcanal.

■

CHAPTER 2

KENNY NIELSEN had explored almost every inch of the *McCawley*--anything to get out of that hot, smelly hold. Now he was visiting the young communications officers in the radio room.

"Thanks for letting me sit in, gentlemen."

"Sure thing, Marine. Glad to have the company."

They huddled around a receiver, listening to a woman's voice.

"Where are the United States Marines? They're supposed to be such great fighting men, but where are they? The Japanese army would like to meet them."

Kenny said, "You won't have long to wait, lady," and the Navy guys laughed.

"We'll find you," the woman teased. "Come out, come out, wherever you are. I'll close my eyes and count to twenty."

"This gal speaks surprisingly good English," said an ensign.

"I'll bet she studied communications in Berlin under Goebbels," Kenny threw in.

"This song is for all you brave Marines, hiding in the Fiji Islands or wherever you are. Enjoy your beer while you still can. Here's Count Basie with *One O'Clock Jump.*"

Kenny said, "She plays good music, I'll say that. Tomorrow, lady, tomorrow you'll find out where the Marines are . . . Some day we'll throw you a necktie party in downtown Tokyo."

Still night-blind out on the weather deck, General Vandegrift took stock of the situation. World War II in the Pacific was only nine months old and the Japanese had not once been beaten on land. Despite their loss of four vital aircraft carriers at the Battle of

Midway, they still controlled the seas around Guadalcanal and the air above it. These were enemy waters.

The Japanese army had overrun Malaya, the Indies, most of Southeast Asia, and the islands of the western Pacific in a scant six months. Now they were building an airfield on Guadalcanal. A base in the southern Solomons could cut the supply line between Australia and the United States, and threaten Australia's very survival.

Although preoccupied with what was considered a greater threat from Nazi Germany in Europe and the Atlantic, the Joint Chiefs couldn't tolerate this. They ordered Vandegrift to take the 1st Marine Division, well, most of it, and capture and hold Cactus. And with too few supplies because of a shortage of ships. He was also to take Tulagi, the Solomons' capital a few miles across Sealark Channel, and destroy the seaplane base the enemy had set up there.

Vandegrift remembered observing Japanese army maneuvers at Tokyo in 1927--could that possibly be fifteen years ago? He'd been impressed with the regimental formations and tactics and the obvious hard training. He had a high regard for Japan and had made friends there. Now he had to fight them.

He'd provoked an incident in Wellington two months ago when most of the division had been transferred there from New River, North Carolina for "six months of training." When he found the New Zealand stevedores working at a slow peacetime pace, he ordered his Marines to unload the ships themselves--the Navy needed them back fast. That embarrassed the U.S. Embassy and the prime minister but by God it had needed doing.

Vandegrift and his force had been ashore in New Zealand only five days when Navy intelligence discovered the enemy was building an airfield on Guadalcanal. Six months for training, ha! So much for that. His troops soon made rendezvous at Fiji with other Marine Corps units rushed from San Diego, Sydney and Nouméa, the former French base on New Caledonia. After their amphibious landing practice had turned into a Chinese fire drill, Vandegrift tried to console himself with the old saying that a bad rehearsal means a good show.

That night his men crammed themselves back aboard their nineteen transports and sailed for the southern Solomons and tomorrow's appointment with history.

Seldom was an army so stripped for action. At least seven more transports were needed to ship the troops and their supplies but they simply didn't exist in the Pacific at this time. So he'd issued the battle order: "Take only that which is necessary to fight and to win." They didn't even have tents or electrical generators.

The enemy airfield was on the north coast, near the mouth of the Lunga River. His troops would land at a spot designated Red Beach, too far east of the airstrip to be defended in force. He hoped. This was near a river a supposedly informed Australian planter said was the Ilu. But one of the general's maps called it the Tenaru, showing the Ilu farther east. See what great dope he had.

It was a scratch team but his Vandegut, as he called his intuition, told him they had a good chance of surprising the enemy and taking the place. Holding it, well, that was another matter.

"General, what in the world are you doing out here?"

Thank God, thought Vandegrift, hearing his aide, Captain Ray Schwenke. Rescue from the black deck.

"Oh, I was just vain enough to think my landing force needed me. Would you show me to my quarters?"

Back in his cabin, before trying for a couple hours' sleep prior to the pre-invasion bombardment, he finished a letter started earlier in the day to his wife Mildred:

"... Long before you read this, you will have heard about Operation Watchtower. Whatever happens you'll know that I did my best. Let's hope that best will be enough."

It was almost sack time in the ship's torrid hold.

"You got an idea a minute, don'tcha, Nielsen," Sergeant Plunkett said. "What'cha you workin' on now?"

Kenny said, "Well, Sarge, back in Wellington, I saw one of those new wire recorders. Pretty swell gadget. Recorded your voice clear as a bell on a thin little filament. That gave me an idea.

Hook one of those up to your telephone and record a message when you're not home to take a call."

Plunkett grunted. "Huh. A robot contraption to answer your phone?"

"Sure. Think it'd catch on?"

"You'd need two spools. One for you to tell the caller what to do, the other to take down what he had to say."

"I think engineers could work it out. Telephones are sound-powered."

"Might work at that. You oughta try'n patent that idea."

"Yeah, the Nielsen Tele-Messenger." Kenny grinned. "You know, I sure miss those clean sheets in Wellington."

"Yeah, me too. I can guarantee ya, there ain't no clean sheets where we're goin'."

"The bedding on these bunks feels like crinkly paper."

"Don't bitch. Them's the best you're gonna see for quite a spell. Startin' tomorrow, you'll be sleepin' in holes an' livin' like a groundhog." Plunkett gave a wicked grin. "Nighty night now."

"Gee, thanks, Sarge."

Kenny turned in, but had trouble getting to sleep. He tossed and turned and figured most everyone else on the ship had the same problem.

Eventually, though, he must have drifted off, for this had to be a dream. He saw an elegant, creamy white building, two or three floors, with archways, fancy balconies, a tiled roof, and high, shuttered windows. Italian Renaissance or French Colonial, something like that. Palm trees flanked the entrance, and trim pathways, paved with white rock or shells, criss-crossed a lush green lawn. The French Tricolor rippled from a flagstaff.

■

CHAPTER 3

COMMANDER KIMI OTOMO of the newly formed 11th Air Fleet stood under silent tropical stars in the sky above Rabaul, the big base on New Britain Island. The constellations in these latitudes, splashed outrageously across the heavens, were unfamiliar to him.

The Japanese had established this post in January and quickly made it the axis of their South Pacific operations. With its strategic location and two excellent harbors, Rabaul was the essential base that could dominate the entire New Guinea-New Britain-Solomon Islands region.

Otomo flew a single-engine Aichi D3A dive bomber, Type 99. He knew the Americans called it a "Val" and there were thirty-four of them at Rabaul. When it first came out in 1940 it was the world's best all-metal, low-wing dive bomber. In Otomo's opinion, its only weakness was its obsolete, non-retracting landing gear.

Otomo was a 29-year-old squadron leader. He had seen action against the British over the Malayan Peninsula and Singapore, and against the Dutch in the East Indies. He had a daughter of six and a seven-month-old son he had never seen. As he gazed at the wonder of the night sky, stars seemingly scattered to infinity, he whispered a soft prayer to his wife Kaneko, hoping the gods would carry it to her. Surely part of her soul was hovering nearby.

"How nice it will be when this great war is over and our family circle again can be complete. I miss you more than you can know.

"I see your face in the stars and in the clouds. I kiss your face. I I caress your body. I pray for your soul and hope that you are praying for mine. You ride with me in my plane always. Sleep in peace, my love."

* * *

The rumble of the big guns jarred Kenny awake. He hadn't had much rest, dozing in and out of troubled dream-slumber for five hours. Like everyone else in the platoon, he'd slept in his combat utilities so he wouldn't have to dress. When he'd first joined up, Kenny had thought "utilities" was a pretty odd name for combat clothing, but now it was just familiar old jargon.

Sailors brought around tin plates of warm--not hot--breakfast: reconstituted eggs, damp biscuits and mysterious lumps of something masquerading as meat. "Probably mutton," Kenny grumbled. "Sure sick of that New Zealand mutton, but hell, it's probably the best we'll get for quite awhile at that." He dug in and ate most of it.

Before long, Sergeant Plunkett said, "Git to the head an' shave, girls, in groups of four. Count off now." When it was his turn, Kenny ambled in there and managed to shave, although his hand was a little unsteady. But when he pulled out his tube of Ipana, he could hardly brush his teeth. Now his hand didn't want to obey at all.

Back at his bunk, he checked to make sure his Thomas Wolfe novel and collection of James Thurber short stories were stashed in his field pack. He and Skinny Wade were the company's "librarians."

Everybody was unusually quiet, adrift in the sea of their own thoughts. How was Dad? Kenny wondered. Will I live? Will I ever see Galesburg again? He thought about his mother and the shirts she used to make for him on her foot-powered sewing machine using patterns clipped from magazines. Depression clothes, she called them; those were tough years. How courageous she'd been during her illness. He had the feeling her soul was lingering around here somewhere, that she knew her boy was about to go into battle.

Sitting there, he noticed his right hand resting on his seabag was trembling again. He couldn't quite remember the term, but he knew that when a ship or plane reached a certain speed far beyond its design capability, it would just fly apart. Critical speed, was that it? His growing anxiety about combat, grinding doubts about his ability to be brave, the fear of being in some yellow rifleman's crosshairs--was he reaching that point?

He looked down at his hand. Still shaking.

■

CHAPTER 4

THE SHOOTING BEGAN exactly eight months after Pearl Harbor. At 4 a.m., August 7, 1942, General Vandegrift watched intently from the bridge as the cruisers' and destroyers' eight- and five-inch guns opened up, red pencil lines searching out the enemy airfield on the dark mass of the island. It took them awhile to get the range--he'd heard that the U.S. Navy wasn't as good at night gunnery as the Japanese. But at last the shells hit home. Small blazes splotched the jungle and then a big fireball gushed up. Must have hit a fuel dump.

Vandegrift was thinking that this was America's first amphibious invasion since Cuba in 1898. He lowered his heavy black binoculars and said to Captain Schwenke, "This is the first time the Corps has ever taken the field against an enemy at division strength."

He flexed and unflexed his fingers as the boats circled in the water, waiting to load Marines for the run in to Red Beach. He raised the binoculars again and refocused. The thing he was looking hardest for, he didn't see: answering fire from the beach on Cactus. "No tracer shells coming this way. The enemy's not shooting back. Thank God for that."

He tried to think of something else. He conjured up visions of his wife Mildred and of Charlottesville, Virginia, where he'd grown up amid tales of the Civil War from his uncles and grandfathers, Confederate veterans all. He remembered the first time Grandfather Carson had seen him in his new dress blues with the fancy red stripes on each leg, signifying the bloody Battle of Chapultepec. "You look mighty fine, Archie, but I never thought I'd live to see a grandson of mine in a *blue* uniform."

Vandegrift hadn't seen much of Charlottesville since his 21st birthday--about an Ice Age ago--but it was still a great place to remember. Beautiful town in the foothills of the Blue Ridge Mountains.

Archie, you've finally got your war, he told himself. How bad can it be? You know the jungle--you cut your teeth on Nicaragua and Haiti.

Down below, the *McCawley's* klaxons screeched. Loudspeakers emitted a scratchy crackle, then Kenny heard, "Now hear this, land the landing force."

He shuddered. So this was it. Did he have the guts to do this? To kill Japs? Would he live through the day? Well, he'd find out soon enough. He wiped the sweat from his forehead, but it was no use. It was back again in seconds.

Able Company of the 1st Battalion, 5th Marines, was the fourth unit called, so Kenny didn't have long to wait. Good. He was glad to escape the hot hold and get on with it.

As the three preceding companies were called, Kenny watched men in green dungarees, battle packs slung on their backs, struggle down the swaying cargo nets into the Higgins boats, carrying World War I rifles and machine guns. The nets swung out from the ship, then slammed against it as the *Wacky Mac* rode the swells.

Then it was his turn. Damn, he thought, was the rope net this wobbly at Fiji? All around him, guys struggled and swore. Like most of the battalion, Kenny wore a modern helmet, but some still had the old "steel derbies," inverted soup bowls that protected only the top of the head. Their leather leggings dated from the Banana Wars.

He finally got his skinny frame aboard. His loaded field pack weighed half as much as the 160 pounds of his six-foot-one body. Sergeant Plunkett had said that if he was a bear of a man, Kenny was a buck deer--slender, mischievous, sturdy.

Kenny remembered how seasick he'd been during the

screwed-up amphibious rehearsal in the Fijis.

Surprisingly, he wasn't woozy this time--yet--even though the flat-bottomed boat bucked and jerked like a bronco, jarring his bones. Sea spray soaked his dungarees.

Kenny liked making up nicknames, and he quickly labeled the boat the Flying Carpet. "That what you call sarcasm?" Plunkett shouted over the din.

Through the clanging and splashing, Kenny heard explosions. It looked like the shelling was all inbound. He hoped he was right. Soon the dim shape of planes materialized in the faint predawn light and the artillery barrage from the ships stopped.

"Hope those are ours," Kenny shouted, looking up and clutching his rifle a little tighter.

"Hell," Plunkett said, reading his mind. "If we're gonna get hit, we're gonna get hit. Nothin' we can do about it. But I got two bucks says we'll all be alive tonight, diggin' foxholes an' heads. But don't be worryin' 'bout those planes. Them's Dauntless dive bombers from the *Saratoga*, 200 fucking miles away, along with the *Wasp*. Scuttlebutt says Admiral Fletcher's scared to death of losin' another precious carrier."

The gruff sergeant seemed to know everything. Kenny liked him even better than his father. He deserved some of the spankings he'd got when he was little, sure, but not all of them. Not by a long shot. Kenny's father, a laborer in the garage-door factory, had shown little interest in his son's writing--he'd been on the school paper at Galesburg High--or anything else he did. A tough pill to swallow. It was too much trouble for Dad to take him to a Cubs game. Kenny's only two visits to Wrigley Field had been made with high school buddies.

Now he saw the dive bombers attacking the island. The tracer shells of the strafing planes fascinated him, etching straight red lines as they hunted the enemy, then skipping into check-marks as they ricocheted.

He was more afraid that his nerve might fail him than of getting killed. Not knowing whether he could be brave when the time came. Oh God, he said to himself, don't let me cringe behind a tree or piss in my skivvies.

The run to the beach seemed interminable. He looked about at other members of his platoon packed into the 35-foot-long boat. Moon Whitely from Chicago Heights, his squad leader; John McKenna, a Bible-quoting Virginian who'd been dubbed John the Baptist; machine gunner Del Cranker, a husky farmboy from Iowa; Skinny Wade from Dearborn, Michigan, his fellow "librarian"; Billy Ninetrees, a Pawnee Indian whom Kenny had taught to read and write; Clint Carmichael, who'd had two years at Marquette and who outran them all in foot races; Desmond Sweeney, a brawling Irishman from South Boston; and the screwball Scupper Harris, from Fort Smith, Arkansas.

Kenny was sure they were all just as scared as he was, lost in thought as they hunched in the lurching boat, loaded down, extra clips of ammunition hooked to their web belts. Except maybe for glassy-eyed Scupper Harris, who was testing the sharpness of his bayonet with his right thumb and index finger. Kenny worried about that eight-ball. A lot.

He tried to evoke an image of Galesburg, but it didn't work. Instead, he silently recited the Cubs' lineup--the lineup of a month ago when he'd last had word on his favorite team.

Dom Dallesandro in center, Lou Stringer at second, Bill Nicholson in right, Phil Cavaretta at first, Stan Hack at third, Lou "The Mad Russian" Novikoff in left, Lenny Merullo at short and Clyde McCullough behind the plate. He wondered where they were in the standings. Last he'd heard they were battling the Reds and Pirates for fourth.

He wished he had a sweetheart back home or even a mother to care about him and pray for him but he didn't, only his father and a 14-year-old brother. Kenny's mother had died six years before after a brave and uncomplaining battle with cancer.

He'd always been envious of the other guys' snapshots and the sappy, faraway look in their eyes when they read letters from their wives or girlfriends. He had a girl in high school for two years, but Jacqueline Lundquist and her mother moved to Chicago after an accident at the brick factory killed her father. After four months, Jacqueline stopped writing. Nothing ever seemed to work out. Even his cocker spaniel Nathaniel Hawthorne ran off. Nathaniel the Spaniel. Okay, so he was feeling sorry for himself. Why not? He might be dead in the next ten minutes.

The Flying Carpet ground to a halt in the shallows thirty yards from the beach. "I thought the Navy was gonna get us in close," he muttered.

"B'lieve this is our stop, Fourth and Main," Plunkett yelled. "Saddle up, children."

Kenny cringed when the first man over the side fell on his face into the surf. God, he got shot.

■

CHAPTER 5

THAT BLACK ISLAND over there would either make or break him, Vandegrift knew as he watched the boats through his binoculars.

His superiors in Operation Watchtower were Richmond Kelly Turner, who commanded the amphibious unit and the transports, and Frank Jack Fletcher, skipper of the covering carrier task force. He didn't regard either admiral as a military strategist. He knew damn well he would be their scapegoat if the invasion flopped.

In New Zealand he'd found an *Encyclopaedia Brittanica* and studied up on Guadalcanal. It was 100 miles long, 35 miles wide and 10 degrees south of the Equator. Discovered and named by a Spanish explorer in 1568. Inhabited by about 15,000 black-skinned Melanesians; a handful of Australians and Britons who maintained coconut plantations near the north shore; lethal snakes, spiders and crocodiles; and clouds of malarial mosquitoes. A joint British and Australian possession, Guadalcanal was a place of wild contrast, not all jungle. Besides miles of thick rainforest, there were grassy but treeless knolls, swamps, towering inland mountains and dusty, igneous stretches unable to support vegetation.

The plantations, primitive even by South Seas colonial standards, were the island's only signs of civilization, except for a trading post, a couple of Christian missions and a few native villages.

And, for the last few months, Japanese troops. Troops he'd been ordered to wipe out.

Relief puffed from Kenny's mouth. Del Cranker, the guy who'd fallen in the surf, had only stumbled. These early Higgins boats had no bow ramps so Kenny and his buddies dropped from the gunwales and began sloshing through the waves.

The surf soaked his utilities up to his waist. He held his rifle high. The water was blood warm.

He scrambled onto the beach, where the rainforest almost reached the shore. Sand clung to his pants and boondockers. He jogged up the slope and under a canopy of mangroves and palms where the company CO, Captain Charlie Brush, was rushing around in a crouch, quietly telling sergeants do this and do that. Kenny went to where Plunkett was assembling his platoon. They hunched and peered into the eerie forest darkness. Del Cranker shook drops of salt water off his rifle.

Good for me, Kenny thought. I've made it this far alive.

An hour later, staff officers helped General Vandegrift into a boat and it chugged toward the beach. He'd sent a smaller attack force across the channel to capture the Japanese seaplane base at Tulagi and the small nearby islands of Gavutu and Tanambogo, which the enemy also occupied. The heart of that force was Merritt Edson's First Raider Battalion. I hope they have an easy time of it, Vandegrift was thinking.

Captain Schwenke yelled above the throbbing engine that Red Beach on Guadalcanal had been undefended. "The report said that only a few scattered enemy riflemen were encountered. Maybe the Jap troops and construction workers were driven into the jungle by our pre-invasion shelling."

"I hope you're right, Ray. So far so good."

He knew the big challenges this day would be the sweaty, back-breaking work of unloading supplies onto the beach, hacking a trail through the jungle, evading the scalpel-sharp kunai grass, and a tough crossing of the Tenaru River which some fool Australian plantation manager named Widdy had assured him could be easily forded. But Widdy, who supposedly knew the island, had struck Vandegrift as a lazy, dreamy sort.

"I was afraid that a lot of blood would be spilled the first day,"

Vandegrift said. "I fear it still might, before long."

At Lakunai Airfield at Rabaul, Kimi Otomo was hurriedly stuffing himself into his bulky flight suit. Nearby, ground crews rushed to arm and fuel eight dive bombers, including his own, and thirteen Zero fighters. They hadn't been scheduled for combat that day, but now they were being sent to catch up with a flight of twin-engine bombers already airborne.

An urgent message had come in from the 3rd Special Naval Landing Force at Tulagi. They were under attack by American Marines. A fierce firefight raged. The Americans had also landed on *Gadarukanaru*.

On receiving the message, Rabaul's commanding officer had immediately diverted a flight of Mitsubishi bombers that were in the process of taking off for a raid on the Australians in New Guinea. These medium bombers were loaded with bombs instead of torpedoes, but someone had to attack those enemy ships right now!

Kimi Otomo got a sketchy briefing from his 11th Air Fleet CO. "Lead your squadron to *Gadarukanaru* and attack the American transports and warships."

"How far is *Gadarukanaru*?"

"Between 500 and 550 air miles."

The roundtrip would be more than 1,000 miles! Otomo knew it would be one of the longest combat missions ever flown by fighters and dive bombers. He wanted to say, "but this plane's range is presumed to be 900 miles," but didn't because it would be rude.

As if reading his mind, the briefing officer said, "Auxiliary fuel tanks will be added to these Type 99s for your next mission. There is no time now."

Otomo silently asked Kannon, the Shinto Goddess of Mercy, for help.

■

CHAPTER 6

HOT? KENNY FOUND it hard to believe that a month ago he'd been shivering in New Zealand's winter rains. He was soaked from head to toe long before the first rain shower pelted down. A soggy uniform takes on weight. He felt as if he'd taken a hot shower while fully clothed.

Some of the birds and plants reminded him of the San Diego Zoo. Even though they'd come from North Carolina, there hadn't been enough ships on the East Coast for the whole division, so his regiment had crossed the country by train. Before shipping out from San Diego, Kenny had taken a trolley to Balboa Park and idled away a day of liberty gawking at the polar bears and giraffes.

There'd be no idling this day. The 1st Battalion spent it hacking a trail through the jungle from the landing beach to the airstrip. Southwest of the river they called Tenaru, Marines ran into a stench-filled rainforest their intelligence officers hadn't known existed. The jungle floor lay slimy with rot. Instead of a few hours' hike, it took them all day, stumbling, slashing and hacking with machetes, pushing branches out of faces. And they still hadn't reached the field.

Kenny continually slapped at mosquitoes and flies. In some places the trees, vines and strange thorny shrubs were so thick and the jungle floor so slippery underfoot that it took them an hour to make a hundred yards. On the other hand, they occasionally encountered a well-kept coconut grove and made good time.

Gazing at the incredible foliage, Desmond Sweeney said, "This reminds me of an Irish folk song, *Forty Shades of Green*. Hell, there must be twice that many."

Kenny was at the bottom of a huge green world. It wouldn't have surprised him to see Johnny Weissmuller come swinging from a vine, wearing his Tarzan loincloth.

Kimi Otomo adjusted his goggles and fingered the cloth headband that bore the red Japanese insignia. The white *hakimaki* circled his flight cap above the goggles and bore several Japanese characters pertaining to courage and duty. He'd been wearing the same fur-collared flight jacket for two years and its brown leather was badly frayed. He'd bought the rakish white silk scarf at his neck after seeing the American movie, *Hell Divers*.

He looked back at the rest of the dive bombers following behind him, each carrying a 900-pound armor-piercing bomb. He was leading his squadron on a course of one-two-zero, straight down New Georgia Sound, the narrow body of water in the central Solomons now being called the Slot. Although his Type 99s could fly much faster, they were cruising at an air speed of 190 miles an hour to save fuel.

Otomo's squadron had been ordered to strike enemy ships at Guadalcanal and turn back immediately with no strafing or scouting. Even then, they might not reach base.

Kenny suddenly heard gunfire crackling up ahead. He hit the deck, then looked around sheepishly, glad to see everybody else was hugging the ground, too, as scared as he was.

After a few minutes of sweating it out, word was passed down the line that a two-man sniper's nest had killed a Marine before being wiped out. Kenny wondered who the dead guy was. He caught himself feeling relieved it was the other fella's bad luck and not his own.

The first U.S. casualty on Cactus! Captain Brush ordered that instead of burying him on the spot, he'd be carried along to the airfield.

"He'll be pretty ripe time we get him planted," Sergeant Plunkett observed.

Some of the men whacked each other on the back and

complimented themselves on surviving the sniper attack, thinking they'd had the true test of fire. Kenny figured they hadn't. Not yet.

Like his comrades, he was in good shape but he still grew weary picking up one foot and then the other with all that gear on his back. Sometimes he walked in blinding sun, at other times under towering trees so thick the daylight reached the spongy jungle floor only in sporadic patches. How did Plunkett keep that barrel-chested, thick-legged body of his going? he wondered. That's one tough son of a bitch.

Even after the excitement of the sniper attack it was hard to stay alert. Several times Kenny's mind, in a kind of floating delirium, wandered off and left his body to trudge mechanically on its own. Not even going over the Cubs' lineup helped. He doubted nightfall would ever come.

General Vandegrift knew the Navy would get out of these enemy waters as fast as it could. On the landing beach west of Koli Point, he looked in dismay at mountains of supplies that had piled up in chaos, turning the clogged beach into a logistics nightmare. He'd have to use combat troops to hump supplies through the thickets to the airfield. Fortunately, several trucks had been off-loaded and there was a colonial track along the beach that didn't quite deserve the name road but at least avoided the worst of the jungle.

But Vandegrift's frown vanished when informed that an advance patrol had reached the crushed-coral airstrip and raised the Stars and Stripes on the Japanese flagstaff. The enemy had fled its base camp at Kukum Village, a native settlement near the airfield, leaving a big supply of rice and canned food, plus all its construction equipment, including a grading machine. The patrol reported that the airstrip wasn't quite finished--the Japanese had been working from each end and the middle section was incomplete.

Shielding his eyes from the blazing sun, Vandegrift stared in disbelief at Mount Austen, the peak behind the airfield. The briefing had said Austen was "a grassy knoll your men can easily reach on the first afternoon."

"That mountain's a lot farther off than we'd been told," said Colonel Jerry Thomas, his chief of staff.

Vandegrift nodded. "And higher. That planter who advised us on this island must be a drunkard."

"Based on terrain reports from our forward patrols, I doubt we can reach that mountain for three or four days," Thomas said.

"We'll do this one step at a time," Vandegrift answered. "Tomorrow we'll have a look at the airfield and set up a defensive perimeter. This may become an unorthodox operation, making up the rules as we go along. After we've had a good look, I may decide it's not necessary to take the whole island--let the other fellow have the jungle as long as we control the airfield. If we can hold and keep an air base, we can win. That's a mighty big *if*, Jerry, with the Navy pulling out quick as they can, along with our air cover. We'll be lonely fellas here for awhile."

■

CHAPTER 7

KIMI OTOMO had flown thirty-eight combat missions in this dive bomber, including one over the great British base of Singapore on December 8. The rudder bore a bullet hole, a souvenir of that attack, and he refused to have it patched.

He felt a great attachment to this aircraft and he smiled slightly as he led his V-formation over the vivid waters toward Guadalcanal. He listened to the throb of the Kinsei radial engine's fourteen pistons. It was running perfectly.

Leading his column of powerful bombers gave him a sensation of spiritual strength. Thirteen thousand feet below, the sea sparkled a bright blue under the tropical morning sun. In the distance, creamy cumulus clouds formed weird shapes and towered to great heights.

For a moment he felt very alone, forgetting even the existence of his radioman-gunner, Takai Asakawa. He watched, fascinated, as a single drop of water, pushed by the propeller blast, crawled across his windshield like an earthworm.

Otomo hadn't seen his wife and daughter since before Pearl Harbor. His son had been born a month after that surprise attack. He longed to see his wife and little family and hoped he would get some leave soon.

They had crossed the green-carpeted mountains of Bougainville Island and now the Slot led them like a great watery dagger straight to his first encounter with the Americans. He had no way of knowing that coastwatchers--Australian planters who'd taken to the hills upon Japanese occupation--had counted his squadron's planes, noted their course, and radioed the information to the enemy.

Otomo knew these equatorial waters seemed to have their own climate. Almost every day the combination of sea, humid air, hot sun and mountainous islands cooked up localized but turbulent convectional storms.

He was sidestepping one of these above Florida Island, just minutes north of Guadalcanal, when his squadron and the accompanying Zeros were jumped by F4F Wildcat fighters from an American carrier.

It was the first time he'd ever seen the plump, sturdy little fighters with the white stars on their blue wings. Knowing it was suicide for his Type 99s to dogfight with fighters and that the American ships were his assignment, he signaled his squadron to follow him in a right turn into a layer of cumulus, letting the Zeros tangle with the Wildcats. Even so, one of the Wildcats shot away part of a wing on one of his dive bombers. It plunged to the sea, flaming like a Roman candle. That left Otomo with only seven planes. And an ache in his heart.

He saw the twin-engine bombers that had left before him drop their bombs from 15,000 feet on U.S. Navy ships between Savo Island and Guadalcanal. From that altitude, they appeared to be causing little damage, creating only spectacular, harmless splashes.

Now the tiny scattered ships just off Guadalcanal presented themselves before Otomo. It was time to fight the mighty Americans. He formed up his remaining seven planes for an attack on transports near the mouth of the Lunga River.

At 10,000 feet he pushed over and began his dive. He glanced back and saw the others following him down in precise formation. The air-speed indicator jumped well past the 300 line. As they screamed down, a few American Wildcats tried to interrupt their attack, but his diving speed was too great for them.

Otomo picked out a fat black transport. He concentrated intently as it grew in his bombsight. He forced himself not to think about the orange globs that were tracer shells floating up toward him from the ships' antiaircraft guns.

The altimeter spun counterclockwise as the bomber hurtled

downward. G-forces thrust at him. He called back to gunner Asakawa to get the camera ready. He wanted good pictures of the attack.

At 1,000 feet he squeezed the bomb release, freeing the 900-pound canister. He leveled off just above the waves and looked back to see an explosion. A hit! Flame and debris boiled up from the afterdeck of the transport. Asakawa clicked the shutter and got his picture. "*Kouotsu! Chokugeki!*" Otomo shouted. Excellent. Bulls-eye. Hitting a ship from a diving airplane was not easy.

Enemy fire popped and burst all around him. He swung to the left and pulled back on the stick to climb. The engine screamed. Within minutes he was in a rain squall that hid him from the American fighters.

He was proud of hitting that enemy transport, and suddenly exhausted, but he knew he had two and a half more hours to fly. Doing a head count, he found another plane from his squadron gone. He thought about the sudden loss of four cherished comrades, the heavy antiaircraft fire and the stubborn resistance of those rugged little American planes. The simple war I had known is over, he told himself. It will be much more difficult from now on.

Seventy miles out, Otomo was relieved to hear the radio voice of his direction finder, giving him a steer toward base.

When he landed in twilight at Rabaul, having been aided by fortuitous winds, his gas tanks were bone dry.

Kenny had heard the bombs exploding and felt the concussions thudding at his ears, but the thick cover of trees had kept him from seeing any of the raid. It had taken hours to cut through the vines, cross the streams and get Able Company this close to its objective. Plunkett said they would reach the airfield before noon tomorrow.

Kenny had experienced just that one nasty moment, when small arms fire had burst out of a green nowhere. It had been silenced by machine guns and a couple of lobbed hand grenades, with the loss of that one Marine. His body must be lying around here somewhere, he thought.

After sundown, less than a mile from the airstrip, the company made bivouac in a grassy area.

"I wanted to kill them Japs, but the guys up on point got 'em. Wish I'd been on point." It was Scupper Harris, the crazy private from Arkansas. Kenny knew Harris' father had been killed aboard the *California* at Pearl Harbor on December 7 and that was a big part of his problem. Then only 17, Scupper had enlisted in the Marine Corps the next day, lying about his age. He'd told the story many times. He had idolized his father and, in the serious manner of teenagers, he'd become obsessed by one thing: hatred of the Japanese.

"Don't worry, there's a few left on the island," Plunkett said. "You'll get plenty of chance to pay 'em back for your pappy. Hell, they're out there now, gettin' squared away, puttin' your name on their bullets." Plunkett gave him an evil grin.

"Those bastards' names are on *my* bullets," Harris retorted.

"Winnin' this war and helpin' keep your Marine buddies alive is the best way to avenge your daddy," Plunkett said, but Kenny felt the sergeant was wasting his breath.

Kenny sympathized with Harris' loss, but he knew that tenacity and motivation were bad when carried to extreme. He'd seen Harris' fanaticism grow and he hoped the boy wasn't near the breaking point. He might really screw up in combat.

Sopping wet, Kenny undid his bedroll. It had rained twice and he'd waded through streams. Just pulling his boondockers and socks off and wriggling his toes felt indescribably good. Even the cold rations didn't taste so bad after the day's hard march. The soggy clothing and the constant whacking at mosquitoes was the worst of it. The best of it: he wasn't dead.

Mosquitoes buzzed around his ears. Horrible sound. He slapped and slapped. How could he ever sleep? Those devils were everywhere.

Scupper Harris started to undo his bedroll beside Billy Nine-trees, but the stolid Pawnee said, "Not here."

"Why the hell not?"

"You're possessed of the dark spirit."

Laughter erupted from several nearby Marines but Ninetrees' icy stare cut it short.

By a freak of atmospherics, they heard the occasional distant "crumph" of an explosion. Plunkett said it must be artillery fire at Tulagi, rumbling the eighteen miles across the sound.

"Wonder how those candy-ass Raiders are doin'," Del Cranker said.

Night came on fast. Unlike northern Illinois, there was no lingering twilight here, close to the equator. Moods changed as darkness fell. Kenny saw their skipper, Lieutenant Gates, huddle with Plunkett and the platoon's other noncoms. Sentry assignments were made, passwords and countersigns arranged, and the men turned in.

Nightshade brought no relief from the heat and mugginess, but in darkness the jungle took on a new aura. The trees had secrets. Sounds and shadows were full of menace. Kenny imagined danger lurking everywhere. He'd been right as a small boy after all. Goblins do inhabit the night.

"You scared?" Plunkett asked.

"Yeah, I guess."

"Good. Me too."

Kenny pulled an hour of sentry duty. Strange night-blooming flowers opened up like the jaws of death. He almost jumped out of his utilities when a jungle bird screeched.

Finally, he turned in. Somewhere around oh-two-hundred, just as he was about to fall into a deep sleep, an airplane droned overhead. It didn't just pass by, it stayed there, flying in big, sluggish circles. The plane clattered like an old Ford with a blown muffler. It sure wasn't one of the American Wildcats or Dauntlesses with which they'd become familiar. Then it dropped a flare that illumined the whole area with a sickly greenish light. The flare floated downward beneath its parachute.

"Sumbitch Jap reconnaissance plane," said Plunkett. "He's takin' pictures."

"And screwin' up my sleep," Desmond Sweeney grumbled.

"Hey, Washing Machine Charlie," Kenny shouted, "take the rest of the night off."

"Washing Machine Charlie, perfect," said Plunkett.

Washing Machine Charlie hung around for another half hour and dropped a second flare while Marines cursed him.

Kenny felt naked under that ghostly light, as if the whole Japanese air force could see him.

■

CHAPTER 8

MAJOR GENERAL Kiyotake Kawaguchi had become a hero in Japan for taking Borneo and then the big Philippine island of Mindanao. But his 35th Infantry Brigade had been cooling its heels for two months now in the Palau Islands. He was about to explode, angry at how the army was waging the war and the navy was keeping him in the dark.

"Some of the young extremists in the army think it is clever to go around lopping off the heads of conquered civilians," he told Major Kai Suzuki, his chief of staff. They nibbled on rice and dried squid at a camp table under a tropical sun. "I abhor the practice. It is a black stain on Japanese honor. And the navy, those aloof rogues, think they are too good to cooperate with mere soldiers."

After taking Mindanao, Kawaguchi had been ordered in June to regroup in the Palaus and await orders. Now it was August. He was still there. Rumors had come and gone that they might occupy Midway Island. The Battle of Midway had been announced as a great Japanese victory, but Kawaguchi knew better. "It could not have been much of a victory," he told Suzuki, "since the enemy possesses the island as before. It is nonsense that as a general officer I have not been informed of the results of the sea battle at Midway, but I understand the navy's need to save face."

He put aside his rice bowl, stroked his long gray mustache and speculated about his next assignment. An order to occupy the New Hebrides had been mysteriously rescinded. He suspected the Americans had got there first.

Kawaguchi willed himself not to think of home, the island of Kyushu, and family. Melancholy will not do, he thought. Many of my boys are lonely and homesick--it is my duty to make a good example. Where will I lead them next?

Somehow he knew he wouldn't have long to wonder.

Arriving at the airfield, Kenny met a guy from one of the advance patrols, who said he'd been there a whole day.

"How'd you get here so fast?"

"We found out the regiment could've made it from the beach in about three hours by hiking west on the government track, then cutting inland short of the Lunga River near that little settlement, Kukum Village they call it. You skip a mile of thick jungle that way."

"Is that the straight dope?"

"Scout's honor, Corporal."

"What other screwups are we gonna have," Kenny crabbed, "if our maps and intelligence are this bad?"

Marines found a steamroller, bulldozer and cement-mixer in good working order and also an ice-making machine, which already bore a new hand-lettered sign, "Tojo Ice Company. Under New Management."

Kenny and his buddies discovered a box of strange rubber sandals with little straps separating the big toe from the others, too small for most of them to wear, and two gasoline-powered electrical generators, a windfall since there had been no room on the transports for generators. They'd been disabled. Until they could be repaired, Marines would have only flashlights for electric light--if the supply of batteries held out. There wasn't even a kerosene lantern to be had.

They also unearthed a large supply of rice, tea, soy sauce, canned fish, sake and beer. His buddies sneered at all but the beer and sake, but Kenny, who always had an appetite, thought they'd change their tune in a few days.

The command post cook, Butch Morgan, didn't wait for his field kitchen to be set up. The burly veteran of the last war had brass to feed. Not one to let a fire go to waste, Morgan hauled a kettle of beans over to the open-air blacksmith shop left behind by the enemy and cooked them on top of a hot forge. His olive T-shirt revealed Popeye arms lined with tattoos that rippled as he stirred. He looked as if he could handle an enemy squad with his bare hands.

Stripped to their waists and dripping sweat, Kenny and the rest of the 5th Marines buried their one casualty in a shady grove near the sea, squared away their gear, dug heads, and then proceeded to clean up a small administration building for the general's use. Its roofline had that strange Asian uptilt. Kenny labeled it the Pagoda, and that became its name.

"The Pagoda's perfect, Nielsen," said Plunkett, "but there's one thing on this damn island you ain't gonna name and that's the airfield."

"How's that, Plunk?"

"Already been done. Henderson Field. One of the brass named it. They say a Marine flier named Henderson bought it at Midway. Can't think of a better name myself."

"Me neither, Sarge."

Kenny could see that the airfield had been built on the plain of the Lunga River, just east of Kukum Village, the only native settlement within the Marines' new perimeter. Already the bulldozer was grinding away as the engineer battalion began finishing the airstrip and also making a short Japanese rail line operational. It led to a pier at Lunga Point. Kenny quickly dubbed the ancient steam engine the Toonerville Trolley.

Plunkett had the platoon dig foxholes to sleep in. "Ain't gonna have no tents for quite a spell, so let's make do, dig us a home for ourselves."

When the work was done, amid grumbled obscenities, they covered the holes with mosquito nets.

"Okay, girls," Plunkett said, "let's get some rest." Cheers. "We're goin' on patrol tonight--"Boos."--to recon the perimeter, see what the hell's out there." The sergeant put his head against the base of a palm tree and was snoring within minutes despite the heat, the bulldozer's clamor, and Scupper Harris sharpening his bayonet.

* * *

That night, General Vandegrift lurched toward the *McCawley* in a whale boat from the cruiser *Australia* with Rear Admiral Victor Crutchley, the leader of the cruiser screen. They'd been summoned to a council of war aboard the *Wacky Mac* by Admiral Turner, the amphibious force commander.

Vandegrift told Crutchley, "I'm not happy with the intelligence we got from the planters. Terrain and distances were badly misrepresented."

"Pity. Some of these colonials grow barmy after a few years in the tropics. But how do you stand overall?" Crutchley, a British officer serving in the Australian Navy, commanded a mix of U.S. and Australian cruisers and destroyers.

"All things considered, Vic, we're in pretty fair shape. Despite the interruption of the air attack, we have maybe fifty percent of our supply and eighty percent of our troops unloaded."

When beckoned by Turner, Crutchley had pulled his flagship, *Australia*, out of line and sailed it across Sealark Channel in search of the *McCawley*, instead of going by small boat. Vandegrift knew that Crutchley was a veteran of the Battle of Jutland twenty-six years before, but thought that hauling his flagship out of the screen was absurd. He was using the heavy cruiser as an officer would have used his horse in earlier years, a wasteful practice in this age.

Vandegrift glanced off to the left, where the bombed transport *George F. Elliott* still burned. Darkness had fallen and its flames flickered over the water like candles at a wake. The *Elliott* had been beached and abandoned, the only serious loss during the air raid.

"My men are moving equipment in from the beach as fast as they can. It's being offloaded in a jumble." Vandegrift noticed the gleaming white wake that leaped behind the boat.

Through his red beard, Crutchley said, "One of the Aussie lads at Port Moresby, flying one of your Hudson bombers, sighted a force of Japanese destroyers in the Solomons Slot about noon today, coming this way. Mind you, I don't mean to steal Turner's thunder, but that may be what he's going to tell us. I shouldn't think our yellow friends will come in force straightaway. I doubt they can react that fast. Probably just nipping down here for a look-see. They shan't be keen on your pinching their air base. I've put my force in its usual nighttime alert, the lot of them. We shall be quite all right tonight."

In fact, Crutchley hadn't even appointed an interim commander of the cruiser force to serve in his absence.

A Japanese naval force bearing down on Guadalcanal already! And his transports only half unloaded. This was a surprise the general's Vandegut--that instinct of his--hadn't anticipated. Some of his troops were still on those ships.

It was nearly midnight when they boarded the *McCawley*. After his arduous day, Vandegrift was exhausted. Soon he got another jolt.

Over wardroom coffee, Admiral Turner's eyes looked tired and hollow behind his wired-rimmed glasses. He grumped that the carrier commander "is leaving us bared-assed, pulling out his flattops."

Vandegrift thought, Fletcher promised two days and now he's running out even twelve hours short of that? He can't leave us in the lurch now. But what the courtly Southerner said aloud was, "Fletcher is leaving now?"

"Says his fighter strength is reduced by twenty planes and he's got to skedaddle," Turner said. "Furthermore, we have a report that an enemy force of three cruisers, three destroyers and two seaplane tenders is heading our way."

"Cruisers?" Crutchley blurted. "Not just destroyers?" This night was full of surprises. At last it must have dawned on Crutchley that being here was a mistake--he should be with his battle line.

"They won't be in striking distance tonight," Turner said. "In my opinion, this force will go to Santa Isabel Island, northwest of here, and try to attack us tomorrow. I'm sorry, Archie, but I've got to pull my transports out in the morning. I'll work my men all night unloading. It's the best I can do for you."

Trying to subdue his anger over being abandoned like this, Vandegrift said, "Please, admiral, have them unload like the dickens. It's a good thing our Japanese friends left us some supplies. Also, my division surgeon says their medical kit was superior to ours. He says our doctors will gladly use the surgical instruments they secured . . . Been quite a humbling year for we Americans, hasn't it? Underestimated the Japanese in many ways."

Now came the next surprise. Turner said almost no supplies had been unloaded for the Raiders across the channel at Tulagi. Guadalcanal had received almost everything.

Vandegrift felt the blood drain from his face. "Then I must get to Tulagi tonight and meet with Bill Rupertus and Mike Edson about their needs."

"You're exhausted, Archie, we all are. You need some sack time."

Though he himself would never speak ill of a flag officer, Vandegrift remembered his operations chief, Colonel Bill Twining, calling Kelly Turner a horse's ass. Others called him Terrible Turner. His Dutch temper fuming again, Vandegrift said, "No, it's the first day of a battle and I belong with the men."

"Okay then," Turner acquiesced, "I'll get you over there. I've a minelayer alongside." He turned to Crutchley. "Vic, it will also convey you back to your flagship."

"I say again, admiral," Vandegrift implored, "have your men unload like the very devil tonight, get everything ashore they possibly can."

Going down the Jacob's ladder a rung split. Vandegrift wrenched his bad knee. Pain surged. He felt like a very old man as he struggled aboard the minelayer *Southard* with Crutchley.

"I shouldn't blame Turner for what he's doing, old boy," Crutchley said, trying to sound comforting.

They hadn't even reached the wardroom, Vandegrift limping, when they saw ominous flashes in the distance.

"Commodore, all sodding hell's broke loose," a sailor shouted.

"They mustn't attack tonight," Crutchley said, his voice desperate. "Bloody hell, it won't do."

Kenny went on patrol beyond the perimeter south of the airfield. Sergeant Plunkett led two squads out there. The lavender twilight was beautiful, and brief. The men moved slowly in the dark, crouching and whispering, someone occasionally reaching out to touch a comrade's sleeve.

Kenny thought of playing hide-and-seek on hot summer nights in Illinois. He couldn't remember a night this hot, not ever. Almost all the Marines had stripped off their shirts during the day, but Plunkett had ordered them back on before taking the patrol out. Kenny's was soaked through. His damp right hand clutched the trigger guard of his twenty-year-old Springfield rifle. Again he wished he had a sweetheart waiting somewhere for him.

The nighttime sounds were a strange mixture of insect buzzings, birdsong and other noises Kenny couldn't even guess at. Probably something ghastly and poisonous. He took comfort from the nearness of his buddies but figured they were just as scared as he was.

When one of them tripped and fell, it seemed to Kenny that every Jap on the island must have heard the clang of that rifle and helmet hitting the ground. To his relief, no gunfire broke out, no searchlights flashed on.

A familiar clatter overhead. Washing Machine Charlie was back.

Desmond Sweeney lit a cigarette. "Douse that thing, asshole," Plunkett snarled. "Our friend Charlie can see that, and there might be Japs all around us."

Sweeney, the Irishman from Massachusetts, had had a tough day and this was the final straw. "Go shit in your hat," he barked, and took a drag.

The sergeant was on him like a dart, quick and light on his feet for a big man. He slapped the stocky Sweeney so hard across the cheek that he moved him over a foot. The cigarette went flying in a spray of sparks. Plunkett's other hand drove a bolo punch to the solar plexus. Sweeney was on the ground, vomiting. He hadn't even been able to raise a fist. Kenny figured there wouldn't be a mark anywhere on him, but he would be sore for days. This was exactly why he didn't mess with Plunkett.

Fortunately, Washing Machine Charlie didn't stick around

long and the only flare he dropped was nowhere near the patrol.

Plunkett led them up a ridge, running north and south, a mile from the airfield. The going was easier here, wide clearings providing relief from the tangle of jungle. Sweeney lagged behind, limping.

They'd actually walked 300 yards or so without having to push through any bushes when Plunkett stopped them with a hand signal. He looked around and studied the terrain under the light of a quarter moon. He took a few steps this way and that, taking note of two spurs that ran off to the west of the ridge, surrounded by ravines.

"Here," Plunkett said softly, returning to his starting point near the center of the ridge. "Here," he whispered again. Kenny wondered if the sergeant was cracking up.

"This is perfect ground to defend. Look at the fields of fire you got on all sides. We're just south of the airfield, surrounded by damn near impassible jungle on both sides. I can already see 'em, long columns of Japs, waving them old-fashioned battle flags, snaking across this ridge. This here leads right to the field. The Japs'll have to come this way. I'll tell Lieutenant Gates to pass the word up--we gotta secure and strengthen this ridge."

Kenny already admired Plunkett but his esteem for the sergeant just went up a notch. He'd observed something important none of the others had. He was always learning from this man.

Just then he heard the thunder of distant guns. He looked to the north and saw flashes over the water beyond the island.

"Navy battle," Plunkett said. "Sure didn't take them Japs long to get here." He motioned his men to sit, then assigned a picket to each end of the little unit. The rest of them proceeded to watch the spectacle.

Kenny was reminded of a Fourth of July fireworks show at Lake Storey. He'd been unable to go, so he'd watched from the front lawn on North Prairie Street and all he'd experienced were distant flashes and the "crumph" of explosions, much the same as now. The rumble of the big guns, sound traveling far slower than light, were all out of sync with the flashes.

Now and then a small slice of sky was splashed with a greenish glow that drifted downward for a few minutes before vanishing. Parachute flares.

"Hope we're creamin' the bastards," a voice said.

An extremely bright flash burst on the horizon. "Got 'im," someone muttered. "Must be a magazine goin' up," said another.

"Wonder how the *Wacky Mac*'s doing?" Kenny said. He'd complained bitterly of the *McCawley* for a week, had hated how the crackly sound system invariably bawled "Now hear this" just as he was falling asleep. But now, on this alien island with a great battle raging on the horizon, he felt a sudden fondness for that rust bucket that had been his home at sea.

■

CHAPTER 9

THE SUDDEN THUNDER of a big naval gun rolled through the humid night air and across the minelayer. General Vandegrift's head jerked. A flare brightened the channel.

The approaching Japanese force obviously hadn't waited till the next day to attack the Americans. Terrible Turner had made a very bad guess about that. Enormous explosions pierced the black horizon with vivid red and orange flashes. With each blast, the American sailors on deck cheered.

"I trust your boys are throwing their Sunday punch, Vic," Vandegrift said.

"Let us hope so."

Crutchley said he had ordered his cruisers and destroyers into nighttime defensive alignment and to stand battle ready. With his radar destroyers out in front, what could go wrong?

Just before dawn a distant hellish scream woke Kenny. It came from somewhere off to the right. It reeled through the jungle, rising and falling like the angry surf at Wellington during a storm. Finally the sound strangled on itself and died.

Later, the unerring grapevine delivered the word. Over in Charlie Company, a Marine woke up to find his foxhole mate stiff as a rock, his throat slit, a gruesome calling card left by some Jap infiltrator.

Jesus, nights were bad enough already. The incessant insect buzzing, strange bird screeches, sinister scuttling sounds made by land crabs, the fearsome shadowy rainforest itself. Now this. Silent murdering Japs creeping around in the dark like savage Indians. Captain Brush would have to post even more sentries.

Kenny didn't have long to think about it. Pretty soon, Brush ordered his squad and two others to the beach to pick up some ammunition.

Work parties were still trying to sort out the jumble of supplies along the shore when Kenny and Plunkett pushed through the last of the trees.

"Damnation, will you look at that," Plunkett said as Sealark Channel came into view. Dead in the water, four wrecked cruisers leaked greasy smoke into the sky.

Kenny's mouth dropped open.

"We musta got ourselves royally clobbered last night," Plunkett said. "How the hell could that be? Looks like Pearl Harbor all over again."

Kenny felt sick. "Sarge, I've got a feeling we're going to be on this island a long, long time."

General Vandegrift was only a hundred yards away, looking out on the ugly scene. *Vincennes*, *Astoria*, *Canberra*, and *Quincy*, each low in the water, burning, oozing oil, about to sink.

Colonel Thomas, his chief of staff, said, "It was unbelievable, sir. A horrible defeat. I heard that one of the cruiser skippers under attack actually signaled the enemy to douse his searchlight and cease firing. He was sure it was Americans shooting at him; couldn't believe the Japs were here."

"It's hard to comprehend, Jerry, so many Allied skippers caught with their pants down. Poor old Crutchley."

"Sir, scuttlebutt says a fifth cruiser, *Chicago*, survived because the captain ran off, sailed right out of the battle zone after taking a hit."

"Apparently what we've heard about Japanese torpedoes and night gunnery was correct. Capability superior to ours in both categories."

"Damn that Fletcher, running off with his carriers. With air cover, sir, this might've been prevented. Now the transports are sitting ducks. Turner's pulling them out."

"And with them go my sandbags, my barbed wire, and even some of my men," Vandegrift said wearily. "Twelve hours ago it seemed we might pull off a clean victory. Now we're all alone." His heart ached as much as his knee. "Our whole operation has become a roll of the dice."

On Koror Island in the Palaus, General Kawaguchi finally got his orders. They couldn't have surprised him more. At last he and his men would be on the move, but not to any place he'd expected. He was ordered to load his brigade on transports and ship out immediately for Rabaul to join the main body of the 17th Army. From there they would embark on "a very important mission." To *Gadarukanaru*.

Kawaguchi had never heard of the place. He looked it up on a map and quickly saw its importance. U.S. control of the lower Solomons would prevent Japan from isolating Australia. Yes, this island had to be recaptured.

He'd ordered three months' pay distributed to the soldiers, so a lot of them were hung over the next day when the transports steamed under a blazing equatorial sun toward the big base at Rabaul.

Kawaguchi smoked a Kinshi cigarette along the scalding rail and watched the Pacific glide past endlessly. Never overconfident, he nonetheless was certain he would succeed in his mission.

"The Americans are still not capable of mounting a major counteroffensive," he told his chief of staff. "We will beat them as we did in the Philippines. But this is a serious business. It will not be easy."

Kawaguchi flipped the remains of his cigarette into the wind and turned to watch his men doing calisthenics. Despite the heat, he had them trotting and exercising each day. Superior fitness was one of the keys to the success of the Japanese army.

He wanted to move faster than the eighteen knots which was the best the old *Sado-maru* could do.

∎

CHAPTER 10

AT ABLE COMPANY'S bivouac Skinny Wade said, "Let me read some of those Thurber short stories, Kenny."

"Sure. What have you got for me?" Kenny handed him a book, then glanced up at the clouds that had been building, turning from white to steely gray with more than a hint of rain.

"What I've always had," Wade said. "*Of Mice and Men, The Great Gatsby,* and my set of Shakespeare's plays. You want *Mice and Men* again?"

"Yeah, I'm about halfway through that."

"Readin' books again?" Plunkett scoffed. "Ain't you guys smart enough already? Why'n't ya get into a poker game, really improve your mind."

When the rain began to fall, Plunkett and Wade pulled ponchos over their shoulders. Kenny pushed his books inside his seabag while raindrops pinged on his helmet like buckshot. He took the helmet off and raised his head, letting the rain wash sweat from his face. He licked beads of water off his upper lip with his tongue. The warm shower was just like summer rain back home, except for the absence of lightning and thunder. In Illinois, lightning crackled from the clouds and thunder rumbled over the prairie when cold fronts collided with warm ones. Apparently Guadalcanal didn't have cold fronts.

Still exhausted from his long bombing mission, Otomo perched on a small hill overlooking Rabaul's Simpson Harbor. Threads of red veined his eyes as he watched a transport unloading at a pier down below. The soldiers, clad in dun-colored fatigues with leg wraps that were one war behind in fashion, were making fast work of it.

Sweat blotched the underarms of his shirt even though it wasn't yet 9 a.m. Tomorrow his squadron would fly the impossible distances to the far end of the Solomons again and attack the Americans. Otomo's Type 99 dive bombers would have extra fuel tanks, but still it would be a difficult mission and he was glad to have a day of leisure. He looked skyward, where a single white cloud foretold the mountains of cumulus that would build up later as they did every day.

Images of home crept into his mind. The rice paper-and-wood sliding doors to their sleeping room that he'd made himself. He'd taken the measurements with meticulous precision, and carefully selected the cherrywood. His wife reclining in that room in her silk kimono, her dark moist eyes welcoming him to their sleeping mat.

The new arrivals down below Otomo were the men of General Kawaguchi's brigade, just in from the Palaus. Within thirty minutes of stepping off the *Sado-Maru*, Kawaguchi was in the office of his superior, Lieutenant General Harukichi Hyakutake, army commandant for that part of the South Pacific, to plan the brigade's transshipment to Guadalcanal. A slowly turning overhead fan whispered in the damp air.

Some people take an immediate liking to one another. Not these two. They were stiff and ill at ease. Kawaguchi knew his reputation as a rebel had preceded him.

The agenda contained but one item: reinforcing Guadalcanal to recapture the airfield. Kawaguchi would command the attack.

A detachment of 1,000 men just in from Guam was leaving that very day by fast destroyer, or Rat Patrol, as the Japanese called it. After spending the next day at Shortland Island to evade enemy scout planes, they would speed down the Slot at night and land east of the captured Guadalcanal airfield, beyond the Tenaru River. Kawaguchi would follow a few days later with his 3,500 men. How would they get there?

"Transports are out of the question," Hyakutake said. "They are in short supply here and vulnerable to American air attack."

"In that case," Kawaguchi said, "I prefer to go by Ant Patrol. Island-to-island troop movement by barge served me well in the Philippines. I will be able to land with all my equipment and food stores."

"Barges are too slow," Hyakutake barked, his hands stabbing the air. "I need you there soon after the first detachment."

"But by day we can hide from enemy airplanes in the little islands and be assured that the men and supplies will land safely. These are not the Philippines. Enemy air is very active in the southern Solomons."

"You can clean up Guadalcanal easily," Hyakutake snapped. "There are 2,000 U.S. Marines there, maybe 3,000. The Americans are in no position yet to start a major offensive. I need you to handle that island quickly, so we can get on with the more important New Guinea operation. We cannot deal with the Australia problem until we take southern New Guinea."

New Guinea still more important than Guadalcanal? Kawaguchi couldn't trust his ears. He believed the entire war could swing on this Guadalcanal operation and that retaking it--while he could surely do so--would not be easy. He believed most of his men would die in the effort.

The ranking officer won the argument, of course. "Kawaguchi, you will go by Rat Patrol, fast destroyer."

On his sleeping mat that night, Kawaguchi used force of will to push angry thoughts about Hyakutake from his mind. He also found himself worrying about the restless young officer who commanded the detachment already headed to Guadalcanal, Colonel Kiyono Ichiki. As he fell into a troubled sleep, Kawaguchi tried to picture the island and the fate that awaited him there.

When the rain stopped, Kenny's squad leader, Moon Whitely, said that tomorrow most of the platoon was going on patrol all the way out to the Matanikau River. That was about four miles, most all of it jungle, and it was well behind enemy lines.

This was it then. Action at last. The patrol's mission was to see what was out there, how many Japs, find and probe their strongpoints. There'd be shooting for sure.

All of Kenny's doubts and fears resurfaced. He started to clean his rifle, which he did every day. Squirted oil on a patch but had trouble getting it down the barrel with his ramrod. His hand was shaking again.

Damn, he'd be worthless out there. Death would be lying in wait in that dark green stinking hell. Yellow men would be shooting at him. Shooting *at him*. Trying to kill him.

And to think that he'd voluntarily joined the Marine Corps. Walked right in there and signed his name. Was going to see the world. Exotic places he'd read about, places like Panama, Honolulu, Manila, Shanghai. All he'd seen was a smelly old steamer and a rotting jungle.

Suddenly he was back in the fifth grade at Silas Willard Elementary. In big trouble. A few sixth grade toughs had taken up hazing helpless little kids after school and it had gotten out of hand. They'd started "pantsing" first and second graders. Take them down, strip off their pants and hang them in a tree. Humiliated, the kids would run home crying rivers of tears and pissing their skivvies, their poor little heads messed up good.

One afternoon he came on one of these sixth grade bullies in a vacant lot north of school. He had ambushed little Tommy Eriksson, a neighbor of Kenny's and a nice kid. The big bastard was going to pants him. Kenny waded in to break it up and it became a wild slugfest. Dempsey versus Tunney. Schmeling versus Sharkey. Without gloves. Kenny got a black eye and a bloody lip, but he sent the bully home with a broken nose and one less tooth.

At home that night, while his mother held a cold cloth to his face, he knew he was in very deep Dutch. His hand was shaking.

Just like now.

He was afraid to go back to school, would have to report to the principal, maybe get a whipping. Maybe he'd be expelled for fighting, sent to reform school. Maybe the police would be there.

He didn't want to face tomorrow, didn't want morning to ever come.

Just like now.

General Vandegrift moved into his interim command post, the Pagoda, near Henderson Field. He was grateful to the engineers for doing a good job of fixing it up. He described his lodgings in a letter home to Mildred:

"My temporary home is near the airfield. This morning at sunrise white and red parrots and macaws were all around. I have some Japanese wicker furniture. The mats by the bed are Japanese too, and likewise some of the mess gear. So you see, they did well by us. The situation is not an easy one, but thus far we are accomplishing our mission.

"Please don't worry about your old boy. Butch Morgan, our cook, feeds me well, forever performing miracles with what little he has. The other evening we literally had nothing for supper, but old Butch sent a private out to a fallen palm tree with a machete. What in the world he was up to? An hour later Butch served us hearts of palm salads as elegant as you'd get in the best restaurant. My D-3, Twining, calls it a 'millionaire's salad'."

Even better than comfortable Japanese furniture was the news that the Marines had taken Tulagi and the surrounding islets. Colonel Merritt Edson's 1st Marine Raider Battalion and the 5th Battalion of the 2nd Marines had run into a hornet's nest. Against overwhelming odds, tough Japanese troops had resisted from caves and well-placed concrete dugouts with interlocking fields of fire.

"The Japs fought like madmen, sir," the intense Edson reported by radio. "But the bastards also employed some very dirty tricks. Snipers hiding in trees behind our lines were bad enough, but there was worse. Their wounded would cry out and when our corpsman reached down to help, the yellow crud would stab him in the back with a hidden knife or pull the pin from a grenade."

Edson said they'd faced about 400 Japanese in the bitter two-day fight for the islands across Sealark Channel from Guadalcanal. When it ended, there were none. No prisoners taken.

"I'm afraid this is developing into an ugly racial war," said Vandegrift, a gentleman so proper he didn't like hearing the word "Jap" even after Pearl Harbor.

"If so, sir, we didn't start it. We tried to take prisoners and help their wounded, play by the Geneva rules, but the Nips have a different system. From the sneak hit on Pearl Harbor right down the line, they play it differently. They're fanatics who think it's a great honor to die. We've got no choice but to honor them, know what I mean? Fight fire with fire, sir."

"I suppose you're right, Edson. Apparently the only answer is war without quarter. Well then, get as many of your men as prudent over here for some well-earned rest. And, Mike, good work!"

That wasn't easy for the general to say. Vandegrift didn't particularly like "Red Mike" Edson. Back at New River, Edson, a Vermont Yankee, had come in and stripped the division of many of its best young officers when forming his Raider Battalion. It wasn't Red Mike's fault, of course, and the general knew he wasn't being fair.

Vandegrift was most at home with the Wide Water Gang, his Southern buddies from the old days, who used to congregate at the Potomac River plantation next to the new Officer School at Quantico. Edson had never been a member of the Wide Water Gang.

Vandegrift believed it was wrong to form elite outfits within the Marines; the Corps was already an elite outfit, damn it. But President Roosevelt, an old Navy man, loved to tinker. Besides Raider battalions, he had the Corps form beach-jumper, paratroop and war-dog units.

Although Vandegrift scorned the term "crack Marine outfit" as redundant, he'd had to go along when Colonel Edson had been ordered to form a Raider battalion in Virginia, and Evans Carlson to do likewise in California. The cocky Edson eagerly shanghaied the officers and men he wanted and there wasn't a darned thing Vandegrift, who outranked him, could do.

But he was glad to have Red Mike and his Raiders here and back under his authority. He needed everybody he could get. And there was no denying what they had accomplished on Tulagi.

Vandegrift wrote out a report to be read to the men on Guadalcanal and there were about 11,000 of them. It said in part:

"The Commanding General wishes to transmit to all hands the good news that has reached us from Tulagi. Our Raider comrades have added the name of a splendid victory to the long roll of battle honor of the Corps.

"The fight was carried to the enemy at all times and all places by resolute men who were not afraid to die."

■

CHAPTER 11

SHE SAT IN a closet-size room at the Japan Broadcasting Corporation in Tokyo. Having several minutes till air time, Iva Ikuko Toguri D'Aquino, a pretty young Nisei woman, ruminated on the incredible recent changes in her life.

She thought, I guess I should be mad at myself for what I'm doing, but I kind of like it. I loved listening to the radio back in L.A. *Fibber McGee & Molly* and *The Shadow*. Great shows. And the guys who played dance music; we called them disk jockeys. Whoever would have thought I'd get to do that kind of work? A woman like me?

Iva, a U.S. citizen, a Christian and a zoology graduate of UCLA, had reluctantly gone to Japan before Pearl Harbor with her husband Philip, a Portuguese-Japanese she'd met at UCLA, to comfort an ailing aunt. Her mother, too ill to visit her sister, had insisted that Iva make the trip on her behalf. Then, marooned by the outbreak of war, Iva was asked to take a radio-announcing job for six dollars a month. If she refused, the alternative was to work in a weapons arsenal.

Of course I'm homesick as heck, she thought. I miss my folks and my friends. I hope they understand I don't have much choice in this. If I don't do as I'm told, there's no telling what the authorities would do to my aunt or my husband. I'm not worried for myself but for her and for Phil.

The things I'm told to say about the war are mostly true. Japan does have an overwhelming military. I've seen the army marching, part of the powerful fleet, and the clouds of warplanes that fill the sky. Japan has not been defeated in 3,000 years and certainly not once since this war began. If I tell American boys they're foolish to fight, I'm just telling the truth. I love America--I'm an American myself--and I don't want our boys to die. I didn't know anything about the politics of the Pacific before I came here, but for Japan to be the economic master in this part of the world makes sense, just as it does for America to be the same in the Western Hemisphere. There's good logic in that.

Reminding soldiers and sailors how lonely they are and about their sweethearts back home--I admit, Lord, that's the part I don't like. But talking to them and playing music for them gives me a kind of power. I don't know if it's a sin to enjoy that feeling, but I do. Forgive me, dear Jesus, if I'm wrong, but I do love it.

She checked her play list of recordings and went over the copy again. She would talk about the terrible pounding the inferior U.S. and Australian navies took the other night off Guadalcanal. Don't they know they can't stand up to Japan's Combined Fleet? What a shame that so many fine young sailors lost their lives. So unnecessary. And all those cruisers that went to the bottom. *Astoria, Quincy, Vincennes, Canberra.* Admiral Turner must be very unhappy.

Iva called herself Ann on the air. She didn't know yet that American servicemen called her Tokyo Rose nor had she given much thought to what would happen after the war.

She figured there would be some kind of peace treaty and she'd go home, maybe get a job at KFI. The word *treason* never crossed her mind.

The next day Plunkett was stunned when he was ordered to report to the Old Man. He had never, ever, been called before a general. He snapped smartly to attention when shown into Vandegrift's office in the Pagoda.

"At ease, sergeant."

"Sir," Plunkett shouted and went to the stiffest at-ease in the history of the Corps.

"I mean it, sergeant, relax," the general said kindly. Plunkett loosened just slightly. With blackout fabric lowered, the Pagoda's interior was dark as a tomb.

"I've just gone over your record and see that you're a good Marine. Been with us quite a while, eh?"

"Thirteen years sir," Plunkett snapped, jumping back to attention. "Enlisted in '29 sir."

"Oh for heaven's sake, Plunkett. Rest. Fall out. That's an order. Sit yourself down in this chair. Why I called you in was your suggestion about the ridge south of here. Colonel Twining and I went out and took a look for ourselves. You might be right."

"Beg pardon, sir, the lieutenant--"

"Yes, Lieutenant Gates told Captain Brush it was your idea, sergeant, and Colonel Hunt got the word to me. Perhaps I should be impressed that the lieutenant didn't take the credit himself, but then maybe he was afraid I might disagree with you." Vandegrift laughed. "We'll have to run the south portion of our perimeter right over that ridge and secure it with as many men and guns as we can spare. Otherwise, it might be an inviting highway for the Japanese leading straight back to their airfield, should they choose to attack from the jungle. I still think our main threat is along the beach, but I could be wrong. I want to wire that ridge as much as possible--we're short of barbed wire, like everything else. I'm going to move the Raiders there, as soon as they've had some rest, but there aren't enough of them to cover that whole sector. There's a ravine on the right flank leading down into the jungle."

"I 'member that little holler, sir." Plunkett thought there was something funny about the way Vandegrift looked in his direction. The Old Man seemed to be looking toward his voice more than at his face.

"You conducted a good night recon, sergeant, and you have a fine eye for ground. I wanted to thank you personally for your initiative. One of these days I'll find a decoration around here and pin it on you. By the way, your outfit will plug that gap on the ridge."

"An honor, sir." Plunkett stood and saluted crisply. After Vandegrift returned it, he extended his hand. Startled, it took Plunkett a second or two to grasp the hand and shake it.

"Wait'll the boys hear about this." Plunkett thought he'd said it to himself but it must have been out loud, for the general laughed again.

"We also need to know what the enemy has west of us, over at the Matanikau. Get an estimate of his numbers, find his strong points. Your platoon will make our next patrol out there, Plunkett. I've already given Captain Brush the orders."

Just then the air-raid siren wailed, a Japanese siren, among the equipment left behind when the Marines took the field. Enemy planes were approaching.

"Follow me, sergeant." That's what Vandegrift said, but in reality he didn't lead anybody. A staff officer took him by the elbow and helped him to a slit trench just outside the Pagoda, where Vandegrift, Plunkett and three officers took cover. The Old Man can't see a thing in the dark, Plunkett realized.

Crouching there, Vandegrift said the grading was finished and although the steel-mesh Marston mats hadn't arrived yet, the historic first landing on Henderson Field would occur in a day or two.

Marine antiaircraft gunners opened up at that moment.

Screaming down from 11,000 feet, Kimi Otomo put a crater in the center of the runway. Another bomber hit a supply dump and blew up several tons of precious food and ammunition. Zeros strafed the field and surrounding encampments and one was hit, trailed smoke, and crashed a mile away in the jungle. In ten minutes the attack was over and every enemy plane except the one Zero began the long run back to base.

Otomo thought fondly of his wife and home as the tedious hours droned by. Again his Type 99 was nearly out of gas when he touched down at Rabaul.

After Plunkett trudged off, Vandegrift reflected that since the abrupt pullout of the American carriers, the Japanese had regained complete control of the seas. He was convinced that the enemy was being reinforced west of the Matanikau, beyond his perimeter. That the almost-nightly shelling of the airfield by Japanese destroyers followed the unloading of men and supplies. His patrols had to find out about that.

■

CHAPTER 12

KENNY SLOGGED WEST for what felt like hours. The patrol, made up of two squads, mostly followed sodden jungle trails, now and then finding some easy going at the edge of a clearing. They lugged two inflatable rubber boats, and were always followed by a swarm of mosquitoes. A Melanesian guide from Kukum Village walked up front with Plunkett and the platoon commander, Lieutenant Gates, whom Kenny had labeled "Rusty."

"Me fella no likee Japanee," the guide said when Plunkett asked why he was helping the Marines. His skin was jet black, his hair wild and kinky, and he wore only a lavalava cloth wrap that looked to Kenny like a plain woman's skirt. His bare feet had calluses as thick as good American tires.

"Japanee fella him treat us bad. Him come, rob village, takee food, beat man fella, takee young girl for lie down, go bang-bang."

"Wouldn't mind some poontang for lie down, go bang-bang myself," Plunkett said.

"Cost you t'ree dollah 'Melican."

Plunkett laughed. "Oh, I get it. The Japs are bad 'cause they wouldn't pay for it. So you're a pimp, too, hey?"

"What means pimp, sawjen fella?"

"Tell you later. But, how come some of you natives are helpin' the Japs?"

"Some Japanee fella, him treat other village okey-dokey. Talk nice, no steal. Sojer fella him alla same, some good, some bad. No matter him Japanee or 'Melican fella." The islander shrugged, turned his palms up, and kept on walking.

Kenny had never been so thirsty, but he forced himself to take only a small gulp. The water in this canteen would have to last the whole day. As usual on these patrols, he focused on something to help him escape the realities of heat, bugs, sore feet and the constant gnawing fear that this day could be his last.

What would he like more than anything else in the world right now? Ah yes, a Pabst Blue Ribbon at the Blue Goose Tavern in Oquawka, after a morning of fishing. For a moment, Kenny was back there on the banks of the Mississippi, under age but guzzling a cold beer because he knew the saloonkeeper's son. He could hear the clatters and shouts from the pool room. Then an unearthly shriek from a huge red-maned bird unlike anything ever seen in Illinois shattered the picture and brought him back to the rainforest of the Canal.

The wide, muddy Matanikau lay west of Henderson Field, the direction in which most of the enemy had fled on the day of the American invasion. As they neared the east bank of the river, Plunkett said, "Keep your mouths shut and move slow. Japs could be anywhere."

Crouching, stepping lightly, the patrol reached the Matanikau. It looked to Kenny like a river of creamed coffee. "Where can we cross?" Rusty Gates whispered. Plunkett frowned at that.

"You wait, Japanee fella, him maybe other side," the guide murmured. Plunkett motioned the men to stay close to the vegetation.

The sharp clap of a rifle shot broke the calm, muggy air. The guide's eyes crossed, his nose split open in a mass of crimson goo, and he fell. Kenny hit the deck. Cold, ancient fear slithered over him. His heart hammered. A primeval signal to the brain said, "Go! Get out of here." Instead, he stayed glued to the spongy earth.

Plunkett hit the ground, too. "Now I'll never know what three bucks woulda bought me," the big sergeant said. "Japs were smart to get our guide."

More shots crackled. The Arisaka .25 sounded higher-pitched than the Marines' Springfields.

A private took a hit in the arm. He cried out, and belly-crawled back into the jungle, trailing blood.

Kenny heard Gates stammer, "God damn, what the hell. I

didn't expect . . . What are we . . ."

"It's okay Loot," said Plunkett. "Let's just lie low for a spell, figure out what we're facin', where that fire's comin' from."

Still more shots. Kenny and the others clung for their lives to the tangle of grass and roots and mud, eyes wide and white in grim faces.

He was stunned and pissed that these complete strangers wanted him dead. He felt a terrible naked aloneness, even though surrounded by a score of buddies. Every gun seemed to be trained on him and if he so much as blinked, enemy marksmen would see it and nail him. Was he this much a coward? But maybe the others were reacting the same. He realized his left leg was twitching and he couldn't stop it.

Over the next ten minutes, he gradually discovered he could move his head a little, talk to somebody and look about cautiously without losing his life.

Bit by bit, Plunkett and Gates, his poise regained, defined the situation. "Takin' small arms fire from both across the river," Plunkett said, pointing, "and over yonder, on this side. Them across the way got better concealment and also one of them nasty Nambu machine guns."

He began to move complaining, frightened men here and there. "You want me to go where? You're fuckin' crazy, Sarge." But they obeyed with great wariness, crawling or in exaggerated crouches. Plunkett told them, "Save your ammo. Don't be givin' away your positions. Nobody fire till I say."

"Let's hit the nest on this side," he told the lieutenant, "take some prisoners if we can, and then beat it." This was sneak and peek, not an attack. It would be suicide to cross the river.

"Okay. Good. We'll try the end-run," Gates said.

"I'll lead 'em," Plunkett said.

"No, I need you here." Gates chose Sergeant Moon Whitely, Kenny's squad leader, instead. Kenny, Scupper Harris, John the Baptist, and Augie Collins would be the others. They were ordered to creep to the east, then circle around to the south and hit the Japanese from the rear. When their shooting began, the rest of the unit would attack from the front.

Minutes later, carrying their Springfield rifles and moving carefully, they got into position, ninety meters from the enemy gun nest. Kenny saw them. His heart pounded. A thin, ragtag lot. Two wore steel helmets covered with netting, the others, cloth forage caps. They were crouched behind a coconut log in a tiny clearing surrounded by kunai grass cut in narrow swaths to create fields of fire, facing the other way, toward Gates and Plunkett.

Whitely assigned their targets, using hand signals. Kenny's was the man on the left. Jesus, he thought, I've really got to do this. Can't look chickenshit in front of the others.

His target was visible from the head to the middle of the back. Kenny took the prone firing position, steadying the gun barrel with his left hand while his right circled the trigger guard. He tried to convince himself this wasn't much different than October rabbit-hunting in the scraped-off cornfields around Galesburg. His stomach tensed. Blood drained from his face. If he hadn't been lying down, his knees would have buckled. He pressed his cheek against the walnut gunstock.

Figuring the back was a bigger target than the head, he put his sights squarely in the center of that fawn-colored shirt. His vision had never been so sharp and clear. Time stopped. They were in a tunnel now, Kenny and this Japanese stranger. No noise, no jungle, no buddies from the patrol. Just the two of them. Exhale. Fire as you exhale, his instructor at New River always said. Otherwise your breath will throw off your shot.

He began to squeeze the trigger. Time started again, and it moved fast. A fly buzzed into his right eye just as he fired. Still, the man jerked and fell, hit in the shoulder, it looked like. Okay, not a great shot but damn it he hadn't missed.

It looked as if all but one of them were hit in the first volley. Kenny and the others charged. Their battle blood was up. They fired on the run, emptying their magazines at the disrupted little band. The ground they had to cover was mostly flat, with a small dip just behind the enemy.

Augie Collins got it. Right in the chest. Must have been the one unhurt Jap. Augie fell like a bag of cement. Didn't move. But then that Jap went down and the Marines were on them. Frightened, seething with anger, almost choking on adrenalin, they wanted to punish these bastards, and did with all the fury and firepower they had.

They swarmed over the fallen Japs and finished them off with head shots. Kenny saw that men don't die neatly as in the movies. Bullets make a hell of a mess--skulls burst and chests explode. He also noticed a hard-on swelling from Scupper Harris' crotch.

He looked down on the body of the young man he'd just killed, sprawled there in a patched but clean uniform. Except for the blood. "I hope you died fast," Kenny said silently. He was just a kid, a lot like the Marines, only smaller and with an Asian face.

Scupper Harris knelt beside one of the corpses and pulled out his Kabar knife. What he did next sickened Kenny.

Plunkett's envelopment had worked. All six Japanese on the east side of the Matanikau had been wiped out. Kenny had killed his first man and it had given him a shockingly erotic tingle.

As the patrol limped back to Henderson Field carrying its wounded and the bodies of Augie Collins and their guide, Kenny felt guilty at the primal rush he'd got. He'd never been so alive as in those few jagged moments. It was better than pocketing candy at Mr. Tiboni's little grocery at North Seminary and Fifer without getting caught. He wondered if Mr. Tiboni was catching a hard time in Galesburg about Italy being in the war on Hitler's side.

He remembered the morning after he'd beaten the sixth grader bloody. "We just can't have fighting," the principal had said. "It just won't do. But I won't admonish you for defending a help-less young pupil. Next time, run fast and tell me, don't get into a fight." That night he'd asked his mother what admonish meant.

Kenny had just killed a man, paid the enemy back for scaring the hell out of him beside the river, and had somehow enjoyed it. He'd never experienced anything remotely like that. He worried, as they hiked back, although he'd done nothing like Harris had, that he must be some kind of crazy pervert.

Reliving the firefight, Kenny recalled that one of his fire team, John the Baptist McKenna, hadn't fired a shot that he knew of. Of course, he hadn't watched the Baptist every second--he'd been pretty busy himself. At the start, though, when they picked out their targets, the Baptist took careful aim but didn't pull the trigger, Kenny was sure of that. This may have been why one Jap survived the first volley and why Collins got killed. Troubling thought. He decided not to bother Whitely or Plunkett with this, but to keep it to himself.

He also came to the shocking realization that while he'd been afraid to fight, he was more afraid not to. Couldn't bear to disgrace himself in front of the other guys.

The patrol created much less noise on the return trek. They'd learned that silence is a friend. The survivors, some of them now killers, were not the same men they'd been in the morning. They'd aged years in an hour.

■

CHAPTER 13

BACK AT THE BIVOUAC, the chatter began, the men excitedly swapping stories of their experiences. Even Scupper Harris joined in for awhile, before going off by himself. Kenny wished he had a girlfriend he could describe all this to in a letter.

A curious thing happened. The two squads, especially those who'd done the killing, became the objects of admiration and envy from the rest of the company. The sudden attention made Kenny uneasy. He hadn't done anything wonderful, quite the contrary, and he somehow felt ashamed.

Plunkett and Rusty Gates rehashed the patrol at length with Sergeant Whitely and made notes. In the packs of the dead Japanese, they'd found maps of Guadalcanal far superior to the inaccurate ones the Marines had been furnished. "We can sure use these," Gates said.

Meanwhile, the wounded man was in the new open-sided hospital. He'd taken a bullet through a biceps muscle.

Later Plunkett called Kenny aside and said, "You did a good job out there. How was it, Nielsen?"

"I made a discovery today, Sarge. Being scared is nothing to be ashamed of."

"It's natural. Fear's your birthright. How did Harris do? He's been actin' weird tonight. I mean more'n usual. What are those shiny marble things he's been playin' with?"

"Sarge, do I have to answer that?"

"Fuckin' A, Mister, I gotta know."

"He was incredible. He's good. I don't think fear is *his* birthright. He got two of the six himself, but when it was all over, Sarge, he, he . . ."

"What? Kept emptyin' clips into 'em after they was good an'

dead? That's natural, too, liberatin' all the fear."

"No, it wasn't that, Plunk, he . . . he cut the eyeballs out of one of 'em. Those things you called marbles are the eyes of a Jap soldier. He calls 'em a down payment for Pearl Harbor."

Plunkett swallowed hard. He thought he'd seen it all in Nicaragua and Panama.

"That boy," he said at last, "has got some wires seriously crossed. Maybe I'll talk to Gates about surveyin' him down to Santo an' see one of them head doctors."

"No, Sarge, don't. Not yet. I think he'll be okay."

Late that day a young chaplain said some nice words and they buried Augie Collins. The small Marine cemetery near the mouth of the Lunga now bore eight wooden crosses.

As dusk fell, Kenny crawled into his net-covered hole. Beautiful ribbons of vermilion, maroon and gray layered the sky. God seemed to be saying the hell with your war, I'll do what I've always done. Kenny heard the eerie sound of Taps, rendered by a bugler at the Lunga cemetery. The melancholy music drifted across the ridge and his consciousness. He silently recited the words:

> Day is done, gone the sun,
>   From the lake, from the hills, from the sky;
>   All is well, safely rest; God is nigh.

Around midnight, as they had for almost a week, ships began blasting the field. When the first shells hit, Kenny shouted, "Here's the latest Tokyo Express," and of course it caught on. The nightly run of enemy ships down the Slot from then on was the Tokyo Express.

Every fifteen or twenty seconds, a shell rumbled in like a freight train, an explosion sprouted somewhere in the perimeter and the concussion hammered their eardrums. Occasionally a big fire broke out when the Japanese hit something vital.

* * *

"*I'm afraid I have a piece of bad news,*" General Vandegrift wrote to his wife Mildred. "*Frank Goettge was killed the other day on a mission behind enemy lines. Remember what a great fullback he was on the team at Quantico? As you know, he was my intelligence officer.*

"*It was a trick we should have seen through. A captured Japanese officer told us there were hundreds of hungry troops to the west of us seeking surrender. They showed a white flag in view of one of our patrols. Against my better judgment I let Frank talk me into letting him lead a patrol over there. I'm sorry to say they were ambushed with heavy loss. Some say it wasn't a trick at all, that it was simply the enemy flag and that our men hadn't seen the red circle in the center, but I don't buy that.*

"*In spite of such heartbreaking losses, our boys are hanging on here bravely, all pulling together to help us succeed in our task. I pray that you're well and not worrying about me.*"

The day after the little graveside service for Augie Collins, Kenny sat on a coconut log with Billy Ninetrees, discussing the peculiarities of the English language. Ninetrees wanted to know why Fight was pronounced Fite and not Figut. And for that matter, why was Corps pronounced Core and not Corpse?

When Kenny had begun teaching Ninetrees to read two years earlier, Billy had proved to be a good student. He'd mastered the alphabet quickly, and now was reading quite well, had even borrowed one of his and Skinny Wade's books.

"If this fight goes on much longer, Corps *will* be pronounced Corpse," Kenny said.

Ninetrees cupped a hand to his ear. "Plane coming."

Kenny was amazed. Man, what hearing, he thought, but a moment later he heard it, too. Sounded like two planes. They both searched the skies, poised to dive for cover.

It was late afternoon and they'd already had their ritual noontime air raid. Japanese bombers left Rabaul every morning, usually got spotted by coastwatchers along the Slot, and arrived over Guadalcanal about noon. The routine seldom varied, even though the Marine gunners were usually alerted and ready, thanks to the brave Australian planters hiding in the bush with their binoculars and radios.

It turned out to be one plane, but with two engines. Ninetrees saw it before Kenny did. "Look there," he said, pointing at a speck in the southern sky. "PBY Catalina."

Lieutenant William Sampson, the personal pilot of Rear Admiral John S. McCain, saw that the airstrip still didn't have its Marston mat. The runway looked muddy--must have been a heavy morning rain--but he was pretty sure he could set his amphibian down okay.

And he did, completing the first landing on Henderson Field. When the patrol plane wobbled to a halt he pushed back the canopy and, to his surprise, heard Marines cheering.

Sampson was soon telling General Vandegrift he'd had a pontoon problem that prevented him from touching down in the water. It was a fib. He'd wanted the honor of being the first man to land on Guadalcanal. He also wanted to score points by inspecting the runway for McCain, who commanded land-based air forces in the South Pacific.

Sampson pronounced the field acceptable.

Two days later he returned with McCain, a grizzled little Walter Brennan look-alike who was a welcome sight to Vandegrift's eyes.

The general, who rarely took more than one drink, poured bourbon for himself and McCain.

On folding camp stools under a tree, the admiral said, "Well, Archie, you don't have taxiways and other refinements, but my young pilot declares this field ready for fighter operations and by God I'm going to get you a little air force in here." He raised his glass to the general to seal the promise.

"That's mighty courageous and optimistic, Slew, in view of the continuous attacks we're taking here, from air by day and surface ship by night."

"All the more reason for you to get some air help. How you

making out, Archie? Level with me."

"We're hanging on. One of our patrols met the Japanese again the other day and we lost another man as well as a native guide, but we eliminated more of theirs. We're on two-thirds rations, supplemented by captured rice. I like my Marines lean and mean, but some of the boys here are getting too darn skinny. Malaria is starting to break out. I won't allow a man in sick bay unless his temperature reaches 103. We're that thin in the line. We don't know how many Japanese are on this island but they're being reinforced regularly and they're all around my perimeter. They run a convoy down from Rabaul almost every night and plaster us good before they leave."

"We're on a shoestring out here," Slew McCain said. "The Atlantic gets first priority on everything. That prima donna MacArthur, who can't get it through his head that he doesn't command the entire Pacific, is hollering much louder than Bob Ghormley, I'm sorry to say." Based in New Caledonia, Vice Admiral Ghormley was commander-in-chief, South Pacific.

"MacArthur? Is that publicity hound still sending out inflated press dispatches a mile a minute from Australia?"

"Oh yes, Archie. You know, there's the greatest story making the rounds. It seems this major general who's such hot stuff, this Eisenhower, says he studied dramatics under MacArthur in the Philippines. Isn't that a wonderful line? Anyway, old Doug Mac-Arthur is screaming loudest about the Atlantic getting more than its share."

"What's happening over there?"

"Top secret, but we're going to invade North Africa in a month or two, us and the British. Eisenhower will command. Keep it to yourself."

"No wonder we're short of ships out here. I'd rather we saved time and landed in France," said Vandegrift. "I'm sure my old Virginia friend George Marshall feels the same."

"Churchill's scared to death of facing the Germans in France, Archie. The Brits remember all too well the blood they spilled there last time."

"Nevertheless, Slew, it's bad strategy to piddle around with a big op so far removed from the enemy's center."

"North Africa notwithstanding, we've got to get you some land-based air so you can hold. This is a strategic piece of rock. You've got to hold it. Let the enemy wear himself out trying to take it back. He'll use up irreplaceable ships, planes and men in the effort. It'll help to turn the tide out here."

"That's as I see it, too," Vandegrift said.

"The *Long Island*, a small carrier," McCain said, "will be in Vila in a few days. I'll put some Wildcats and SBDs on her with trained pilots and sail her up to fly-away position. You'll have a small air force by the 18th or 19th. The steel mats will take longer, but Turner will make another blockade run with some supply ships, and that too is a promise."

Although spoken by McCain's scratchy voice, these words sounded so good in Vandegrift's ears he imagined he was hearing beautiful flute music. When McCain stopped speaking, the sensation lingered. The heat, the bourbon and the sudden good news must be giving him a buzz. Then McCain said, "Where the hell's that whistling coming from?"

Somewhere out in the jungle one of the Marines was whistling Rossini's overture to *La Gazza Ladra*. "Say, that young man is good. You ought to put him on Major Bowes' talent show," McCain said.

On that afternoon's raid, the Betty medium bombers came in hot and low, barely over the wavetops, in an attempt to foil American gunners and radar, unaware the Marines had no radar.

The Americans gave Japanese bombers female code names, hence "Val" and "Betty." The fighters got male names, the famous Zero being dubbed "Zeke."

The attack was coordinated with a dive-bombing by Commander Kimi Otomo's squadron, making its third raid over Guadalcanal.

When he pulled out of his dive, Otomo's Val dive bomber

took several .50-caliber machine gun slugs. The controls felt all right, though.

As he headed back up the Slot, his squadron smaller than before, as usual, he didn't think there was any serious damage. But before long it became clear that his fuel line had sprung a leak. The gas needle was dropping much too fast. He would never make Rabaul. Maybe he'd have to use his parachute for the first time, except for training. Half the men in the 11th Air Fleet didn't carry chutes, preferring death to the humiliation of losing one of the Emperor's planes. Otomo didn't see it that way. He would rather come back and fight again in another plane.

Now he began to think that maybe the Americans had the right idea. Their planes were slower, less maneuverable and had less range than their Japanese counterparts, but they could take more punishment. He and rear gunner Asakawa had shot several Wildcats and Dauntlesses full of holes but they'd kept flying--and their pilots, protected by armor plate, usually seemed unhurt. "Our planes often turn into fireballs after just a few hits. We've sacrificed a lot for speed and range," he said.

Tough foes, these Americans. Such immense dangers he faced attacking Guadalcanal. He wasn't going up against the Dutch colonial air force any more. Fuel continued to bleed away from his wounded plane.

A little over an hour after the raid, he coasted to an emergency landing on a beach at Shortland Island, next to the small naval facility there. Just below Bougainville, Shortland was where the Japanese ships from Rabaul laid over in daylight before making their nightly runs down the Slot.

Otomo gauged his landing perfectly, hitting the moist, firm sand near the water, but not so close that the surf would wreck him. Asakawa told him he was impressed by the landing, which ended their 42nd and last mission in this dive bomber.

Otomo knew how much he owed to the dedicated mechanics of his ground crew. "I hate to part with this plane that has served us so well," he said. "The crew chief will take this very hard. He is so very conscientious. When one of his planes does not return, it is as if he has lost a child."

Otomo returned to Rabaul by destroyer. His damaged plane was loaded on the transport *Daifuku*.

Able Company moved to a new encampment on the ridge 1,000 yards south of Henderson Field. There were still no tents. The men again dug holes. The more enterprising built elaborate dugouts and roofed them over with liberated Japanese lumber or rough-cut coconut logs. When covered with earth and leaves for camouflage they made good shelters from enemy attack if not from the tropical rain. In no time at all a gooey layer of muddy water appeared in the bottoms of the holes.

Plunkett and three privates engineered the largest and most intricate dugout for Lieutenant Gates. Three sheets of corrugated steel, liberated from the enemy stockpile, were lashed together to form a roof. Instead of covering it flatly, the roof was angled, lean-to style, supported by a beam and two palm-log uprights. The command post's opening faced south, the reasoning being that storms--either Mother Nature's or the enemy's--would come from Sealark Channel to the north.

That night after a feast of fried Spam and rice, the men took atabrine tablets to combat malaria. "Some damned dessert the gov'mint gives us," Plunkett muttered. The bitter pills tended to turn the skin yellow. Some of the men threw them away--they'd be among the first to come down with malaria.

In his dreams that night, Kenny was patching paper targets with masking tape at the New River rifle range, covering the bullet holes so the targets could be used again. But the target became a face, a Japanese face, and the bullet holes were in flesh, not paper. They oozed blood. He kept on trying to tape over the holes. He woke up in a sweat and stared at a half moon that made him sad. He was afraid to go back to sleep.

■

CHAPTER 14

.

AS HE SIPPED from a glass of Sapporo beer at Rabaul, one thing nagged at General Kawaguchi: Colonel Kiyono Ichiki.

Kawaguchi had formed his plan and it was a good one. He would strike the Americans from three sides at once, while the navy blasted away from the fourth. Kawaguchi's own force would land east of the airfield and swing southwest through the jungle. Colonel Ichiki's detachment, half of which had just reached the island, would remain east of the Tenaru River, and Colonel Akinosuke Oka would be positioned west of the Matanikau. Thus the airfield would be surrounded. The three forces would attack by night, all together, from the west, south and east, supported by artillery and offshore shelling from the navy. They would crush the Americans and retake the airfield.

In total, there would be 6,100 men--Ichiki's 2,000, Oka's 1,100, and Kawaguchi's brigade of 3,000. More than enough to do the job. His superiors on Rabaul believed the Americans now had 4,000 men on the island, but Kawaguchi felt the number could be double that. Both estimates were too low.

Kawaguchi and his men would board fast destroyers for their Rat Patrol journey to Guadalcanal. After a night's steaming, they were to lay over at Shortland Island before the run down the Slot the following night. Oka's force would go with them to Shortland, but the stubborn colonel insisted on going by Ant Patrol from there. The argument had yet to be settled.

Just now, Kawaguchi was more concerned about his other colonel, the one already on Guadalcanal. "What bothers me," he told his chief of staff, "is Ichiki's brashness and overconfidence. Those are not bad qualities, but discipline and timing are essential in this coordinated operation. Ichiki must contain his impatience. He must follow orders."

Ichiki at that moment was making a night landing at Taivu Point, twenty-five miles east of Henderson Field, with 900 men, the first half of his detachment. Dispatched from six destroyers, they splashed ashore through tiny phosphorescent sea animals that clung to their battle pants and leggings. This luminous glow on 900 pairs of legs trudging up the black beach made a ghostly sight.

The landing, like that of their enemy eleven days before, was entirely unopposed, adding to Ichiki's optimism. It would be five days before the rest of his detail arrived. He hated the thought of waiting.

"We have succeeded in invasion," he radioed Rabaul smugly.

The next day, Kenny's stomach started growling and it made him laugh. He hoped Skinny Wade hadn't heard it. Kenny had been fantasizing about food for days, ever since the Old Man put them on two-thirds rations. He'd often heard Wade's stomach rumble and had teased him, calling him things like Old Thunder Gut.

Then another damned noontime air raid came over. They'd become as monotonous to Kenny and his buddies as Washing Machine Charlie at midnight.

As usual the men of Able Company bounded into their slit trenches and foxholes. Twin-engine Betty bombers droned over at high altitude and their bombs fluttered down in a kind of whisper-rattle. Kenny knew that when he counted six explosions and was still alive, the stick of bombs from that particular plane wouldn't kill him. In a week and a half, he'd learned to distinguish the variations in the whistling sounds of the falling missiles and the concussions as the bombs walked across the terrain. He could tell when one was dangerously close. That day only one was, blasting a crater in the ridge not fifty yards from his hole, showering him with dirt, redhot shrapnel, and fear.

The conventional bombs were bad enough but the anti-personnel jobs were worse. These "daisy-cutters" were designed to fling jagged fragments into men's bodies, much like hand grenades. A daisy-cutter found one of the unit's cooks, a hot metal splinter cutting all the way through his arm. He screamed out in pain and was led to an aid station.

When someone mentioned a near-miss, Kenny scoffed and said, "You mean a near-hit. They all miss, except the one that gets you. Think about it."

Another stick began bursting and Kenny started his count. The third sounded close, the fourth closer and--he stopped counting. Peering out from his hole he saw Scupper Harris standing upright, firing at the sky, uselessly emptying a clip at the attackers.

"You crazy stupid Section Eight case." Kenny regretted urging Plunkett not to ship Harris off to see a psychiatrist. He'd forgotten his count, but the bombs missed.

As the high-level boys pulled away, Zeros and Vals swept in to do their work just above the tops of the cocopalms. Everybody dived back into their holes.

It wasn't only the planes. Something new had been added to the daily terror. The Japanese had put an artillery piece in action. The all-clear sirens had scarcely died out when the new gun began belching its rounds of torment. A shell rumbled in, sounding just like the Super Chief, and exploded 500 yards from Able Company's bivouac.

"There goes Pistol Pete again," said Plunkett. "Sounds like 155-millimeter. Hey, Nielsen, how's come you didn't name that Jap howitzer?"

"Pistol Pete? Criminy sakes, I've got more imagination than that."

The shelling stopped and they hunkered down in their muddy holes, accompanied by the omnipresent mosquitoes and flies. Some turned to their rations, trying to eat with one hand and shoo the flies with the other.

"Hey," Desmond Sweeney shouted. "Somebody stole my hash and left me these goddamn lima beans. Whichever horse's ass did this--you know who you are and I'm talkin' to *you*--God's gonna send a Jap into your hole tonight and slit your thievin' throat. God, I hate these crappy limas."

"I notice you ain't tossing 'em in the mud, Sweeney."

"I'm hungry, buttlick."

"Sarge," said Del Cranker, "how come you never peel your shirt off? 'Fraid them bulging muscles will scare us to death?"

"Naw, it's 'cuz I'm smarter'n you," Plunkett answered. "Your shirt gets soaked but it holds in your body moisture, keeps you from gettin' faint in the heat. And when the breeze comes up and hits that wet shirt it cools you. Learned it in Panama."

John the Baptist McKenna, observing the horseplay as the tropical twilight faded, smiled a faraway smile, not really hearing, lost in his own thoughts. He hadn't liked the nickname John the Baptist at first but it grew on him. Now he wore it proudly. It singled him out, gave him an identity.

A rugged youngster from the Shenandoah Valley, John was anything but a coward. A strong sense of honor had been passed down through the men of his family. His great grandfather had ridden with Hampton Wade's Confederate cavalry in the Civil War. John was devoutly religious and had been a star pupil in Sunday School at the Baptist Church. Nevertheless, he had never backed down from a schoolyard bully. His courage had never been questioned when growing up, nor in the Corps--he just hated the idea of taking a man's life.

He knew the Sixth Commandment, "*Thou shalt not kill*," didn't apply in wartime, the chaplain said so himself, but that didn't help much. John the Baptist tried to find comfort in Chapter 20 of Deuteronomy: "*When you go forth to war against your enemies, and see horses and chariots and an army larger than your own, you shall not be afraid of them . . . do not fear or tremble, for the Lord your God goes with you, to fight for you against your enemies, to give you the victory . . . .*"

He sometimes wondered why he volunteered for the Corps in the first place but he always came up with the answer that he'd really had no choice. It would have crushed his grandfather, a veteran of the Spanish-American War, and his father, who'd fought with the Marines at Belleau Wood in France. He worked on these thoughts, paying little attention to the horseplay. He knew he should have shot at the Japs on that patrol and was tormented by the possibility that he'd let down his buddies by upholding God's law.

■

CHAPTER 15

A CREAMY VOICE washed through the night air from the loud-speaker at the improvised news center at Kukum Village.

"Marines of the 5th Regiment on Guadalcanal, why do you try to hold onto a little airfield you have renamed for your Colonel Henderson? Don't you know it's in vain? You are outnumbered and will be vanquished by superior Japanese forces."

"Hey, guys, listen up, Tokyo Rose just said something about us. Swear to God, she said 5th Regiment."

"Don't you boys know you have been deceived by your misguided officers? You have no chance on Guadalcanal. You are destined to either die like your Colonel Henderson who perished in a futile attack on the superior Imperial Navy, or to become prisoners if you are lucky. This will be another Bataan for you. Wouldn't you rather be at home with your wives and sweethearts? How long do you think your women will remember you, so far away from home in a hostile jungle? Soon they will start looking at the young men around them at home. Smarter men, because they had the sense to stay where it is safe and warm and there is plenty of good food and women--your women."

"Wish they'd turn that bitch off. She makes me sick."

"Hell no, leave her on. She plays good music."

"And now, just for you poor men of the 5th Marines, since you won't be sleeping tonight anyway, here is the Tommy Dorsey band playing, *Begin the Beguine*."

Kenny sat beneath a cocopalm for awhile and talked with Plunkett. He felt privileged by these chats with the platoon sergeant, who'd become like a big brother.

"That Tokyo Rose bother you, Kenny?"

"Only the dope she gets on us. Otherwise, she's kinda funny, and the music's great."

"Yeah, it's smart propaganda," Plunkett said. "World's changin' awful fast, Kenny. Example: you know they're lettin' nigras into the Corps now?"

"Yeah, I heard. Down at Montford Point."

"Don't that beat all? Nigras in the Corps. Won't let 'em train with white boys, of course. Montford's a separate little camp, next door to Lejeune. I've known some colored folks who could sure as hell cook, but I don't know about fightin'."

"Fighting? What about Joe Louis, Plunk? I'll bet you wouldn't step into a ring with him. The way I look at it, a black man can shoot as straight as a white one."

"Some of those big pickaninnies might scare the Japs to death at that."

Plunkett gazed at the jungle for awhile in silence. "That was a good thing you done," he said at last, "teaching Ninetrees to read 'n' write."

"He learned fast," Kenny said. "Billy's a smart guy."

Plunkett recalled the lessons that had begun shortly after the Indian had joined up, about two years ago. Plunkett himself could read pretty well, but wished he could spell better.

Later, Kenny and the platoon settled in for the night. He slapped a mosquito. Too late. Hell, dozens had bit him. Rubbing only made the bites worse. Kenny hated that.

Finally getting the netting in place, he curled up. Instead of the usual dirty jokes and lewd comments about women, a chorus of *My Bonnie Lies Over the Ocean* greeted his ears.

At first only a few Marines sang, but more joined in. It was eerie, these young men lying in the dark, giving voice to their homesickness in melancholy harmony.

My Bonnie lies over the ocean, my Bonnie lies over the sea, my Bonnie lies over the ocean . . . .

"We will capture the airfield ourselves and present it as a gift to General Kawaguchi upon his arrival," Colonel Ichiki told his adjutant. "We will march to the west tonight, make camp east of the Ilu River, then tomorrow night we will sweep across the Ilu"--with their bad maps, the Marines still thought it was the Tenaru--"and take the field."

The landing of his troops had gone perfectly and he had absolute confidence in their toughness and fighting ability. Ichiki was aroused, being where he was, so close to the enemy. Cold military logic had abandoned him. General Kawaguchi had pegged his man correctly. Ichiki was dangerous.

"What difference does it make if the enemy has twice as many men? Americans"--it said so in the manual--"cannot fight at night. One Japanese soldier is worth ten Americans." His eyes glowed like the furnaces at Mitsubishi. "I see no problem at all."

"But *Taisa* (colonel), what of the coordinated attack General Kawaguchi has ordered?" the aide said.

"He will pin all the more medals on us when we have saved him the trouble."

The well-read young adjutant thought, There's a difference between being a skillful military gambler like Hideyoshi or Napoleon and taking foolhardy risks.

General Vandegrift already knew they were there. The pilot of a PBY Catalina search plane had seen the phosphorescent wake of the retiring destroyers and drawn the proper conclusion. Colonel Ichiki was lucky the flier hadn't spotted the ghostly legs running up the beach. By bombing and strafing, the Goony Bird could have done a lot of damage.

"They've been reinforced on each side of us, we know that for certain," Vandegrift told Colonel Twining, his operations officer. "They have us encircled."

"But we have no idea how many troops they put ashore there tonight, sir."

The general's Vandegut told him he'd better act quickly. "Nevertheless, Bill, we'll have to beef up the eastern perimeter.

Somehow, get some more troops over there."

"Aye aye, sir."

Kimi Otomo loved baseball and he was thinking about Eiji Sawamura, the pitcher who won 33 games in 1937 and threw three no-hitters in his legendary career. Sawamura had been called into the army and was serving the Son of Heaven somewhere in this vast ocean empire. Sawamura once struck out Babe Ruth, Lou Gehrig and Jimmie Foxx in an exhibition game. Otomo wondered if the man was keeping his arm in shape and could make a comeback some day, if he survived the war.

Otomo's reflections turned to his wife Kaneko and he wrote to her, telling of the forced landing at Shortland.

When I returned to Rabaul by destroyer I knew that attrition—both from the tremendous length of our missions and the surprisingly good American gunners—was decimating the 11th Air Fleet. But I was astonished to learn there were only eight operable Type 99 dive bombers on the entire base. At first there was talk of making me a Zero pilot, but then Asakawa and I were given one of the remaining helldivers, grounding a less experienced crew. They were terribly humiliated, poor fellows.

"We are being given a day of rest, then another to test-fly the new plane before going out on our next long mission back to the island I mustn't name. The news isn't all bad, however. Our air fleet has been reassured that fresh planes are on the way from Singapore and that a new air base is being prepared for us on Bougainville. That is much closer to our target.

"I miss you and our dear children greatly and long for the day that we all can again embrace. Be brave my love."

The censors approved only the last paragraph.

■

CHAPTER 16

"IT'S A BEAUTIFUL sight," General Vandegrift said. On a hillock overlooking Henderson Field, he stood watching with Bill Twining and war correspondent Richard Tregaskis of the International News Service. Nineteen Wildcat fighters and a dozen Dauntless dive bombers were swooping over the jungle in a loose pattern, and landing one by one. "Precious little birds," Vandegrift said.

Some of the planes touched down smoothly on the unfamiliar crushed-coral runway and others bounced badly, but all reached their new home safely. Kenny and his pals cheered and chucked their helmets in the air. "With an air umbrella, no matter how meager, the Japanese will no longer have complete control of the sea around this island," Vandegrift told the gaunt, bespectacled Tregaskis. "They're from the *Long Island*, a jeep carrier that sailed to within 200 miles of here. You can't use that, the ship's name I mean."

"We don't have many mechanics," he added, "and darn little equipment to service these birds with. No oxygen bottles for flying at altitude, not even any pumping gear. For the time being we'll have to use funnels and pour the fuel into these planes straight from the cans. We may not be a proper base yet, but by God we've got a little air force. Maybe we can hold out, at that."

"You know," Tregaskis said, "you've probably got a lot of boys on this island who know plenty about engines." The correspondent's uniform hung slackly on his long frame. Vandegrift thought him an Ichabod Crane type. "Kids who love cars, who've torn down their jalopies and put them back together. Maybe even a few who've overhauled a Flying Jennie. American boys really know how to tinker and improvise and scrounge. I think you'll find a way to keep these things flying."

"Good thinking. Let's get the names of some experienced young mechanics, Bill," Vandegrift said to Twining.

On patrol again, Kenny saw sudden movement in the jungle, then heard a wild thrashing sound. His spine tightened. A Jap rushing them? He wheeled toward the sound, saw something running, very low. Just a glimpse. Brown or maybe gray. Sure as hell didn't look like a Marine. All that took place in the space of a second. Kenny fired. Once, twice. The target cartwheeled and hurtled to a stop against a tangled liana vine.

Kenny agonized. Had he shot a lost straggler from another outfit? Or maybe one of the natives?

He and Plunkett approached at a crouch. "Rest of you, keep back," Plunkett called. "Keep a sharp lookout."

Then Kenny relaxed. He saw he'd killed some kind of animal.

Plunkett probed with the muzzle of his rifle. "I'll be damned. Wild boar. Look at them tusks. Good shooting, Kenny. We're gonna have us a real fine supper."

Plunkett used his poncho as a sling and told Skinny Wade and Connie Keugeman to carry the prize. "Keep it to yourselves," he said. "This'll feed the platoon, but not the whole durn company."

Kenny was a hero that night as they feasted on thick slabs of pork cooked over an open fire. "Nielsen for president," Del Cranker said. "Hell, Nielsen for chief buffalo hunter," Des Sweeney answered. John the Baptist bowed his head and gave silent grace before slicing into a juicy pork loin.

"Want these hog's eyes for your collection?" Skinny Wade asked Scupper Harris.

"Fuck you, Wade."

Toting his mess tin, Plunkett sat next to Kenny. "Another sea battle last night," he said. "I hear tell both sides lost some ships."

"That strip of water between here and Savo Island, better call it Ironbottom Sound," Kenny said. "Lots of busted-up steel lying out there."

"And more to come, prob'ly." Plunkett slapped him on the back. "Ironbottom Sound, yeah."

On Rabaul, General Kawaguchi, preparing to embark for Guadalcanal, read and re-read his latest wireless from Colonel Ichiki: "Have met no enemy at all. Like marching through a no man's land."

"Marching! Marching to where? I don't like that man's affinity for terse messages," Kawaguchi told an aide. "What else does it mean? Send a message to Ichiki; remind him that I have ordered him only to patrol and wait for the rest of us."

But Ichiki was receiving no more messages. He'd marched 800 of his men to within a mile of Red Beach, where the Marines had landed two weeks before. The force assembled just beyond the Ilu River. He'd left 100 others behind to guard his supplies at the base camp.

"We have learned some valuable lessons in this war," Ichiki told his adjutant. "The frontal assault, so ridiculed in the military schools, has proved effective when made at night by the Japanese Army. Directly confronting the enemy in a *banzai* charge, shouting and showing no fear, turns their testicles to jelly. This is especially true of white men. This was proved in Malaya and Java against the British and Dutch. The Europeans are afraid to fight at night and so are their American brothers. We will be heroes in Japan after we cut down these Yanks and take back our airplane field."

His men sheltered under the umbrella of jungle trees and tried to get some sleep. Ichiki planned to attack later that night. He was sure they'd reached this jumping-off point undetected.

"General, general, sir," gasped Colonel Twining, approaching at a trot. "There's someone down here in the intelligence hut you've got to meet."

After a short jeep ride, Vandegrift met an extraordinary man, Jacob Vouza, a retired police chief from a native village to the east.

A strong-looking fellow with a barrel chest, Vouza was bandaged around the neck and several other places, and caked with dirt and blood. Purple bruises blotched his face. He looked as if he would pass out any minute but Vouza snapped to attention in the general's presence.

"This man was observing the enemy for us, sir, one of Clemens' scouts," Twining said, referring to colonial district officer Martin Clemens. "Vouza was captured, tied to a tree, tortured, bayoneted across the neck and left for dead. He says he chewed through the ropes and made it here unseen through enemy lines."

"I tell nothing," Vouza said in an accent that was hard to understand. "They want know where you are, how many man you got. I tell nothing. I do it for the king."

Vandegrift saw that Vouza's bare chest had been badly gashed and his lavalava skirt was in bloody tatters. "Sit, please sit." Vouza did with embarrassed reluctance.

"They got many man other side of River Ilu, close by to here."

"This man is one of our native volunteers working for us through Clemens, who's become a military coastwatcher," Twining interjected. "We've heard the same thing from a Catholic missionary to the east of here, and our listening posts and patrols in that direction have reported many enemy contacts."

"How many men?" the general asked Vouza.

"Many. T'ree hundred, maybe fi' hundred."

"We've got Al Pollock's 2nd Battalion over there, right?" Vandegrift asked Twining.

"Correct, sir, and I suggest we release the reserve, Creswell's battalion, and move them south and east of the 2nd, to envelop this fellow from the rear and his left flank."

"Good idea, Bill, draw up the plans. And have some engineers lay mines on that sand spit at the mouth of the river as soon as they can."

"Aye, aye, sir."

"Ask Pollock to wire up tight and be ready for a scrap."

"Will do, sir."

Looking again at Vouza: "See that this man has food, water, medical attention and some of my bourbon."

Vouza somehow jumped to attention and gave an open-palm, British-style salute. "You velly good, sir. Better me die plenty than give Solomon Islands to Japan. I do it for the king," he repeated.

When Vandegrift said he had no king, Vouza was confused. The English and the Australians had a king and this was a British island. "All white man not have king?" After the general tried to explain about elections and President Roosevelt, Vouza was led to an aid station.

Vandegrift turned to Twining. "This will leave the rest of the perimeter very thin in spots. Let's fill the gap left by Creswell with some cooks and engineers, but not Stinky Davis. I need old Stinky working on the airfield." Tech Sergeant Davis, a twenty-year-man, was the most gifted improviser he had. Vandegrift thought it was a good thing that all Marines were trained to fight before being allowed to specialize.

"How much of this can I use?" asked correspondent Tregaskis, who had come along in the jeep.

"As usual, Dick, I haven't the time or inclination to play censor. Write what you wish. Just use good sense and don't say anything that will jeopardize my mission."

Turning back to Twining, Vandegrift said, "Do you think it's within my power to make that man Vouza an honorary Marine?"

"I'll look through the regs and let you know, sir."

"Do that, Bill. I want to make him a sergeant major."

An hour later Vandegrift met Lieutenant Colonel Dick Mangrum, the skipper of his new dive-bomber force. His Vandegut immediately liked him. Mangrum was tall, with a trim Errol Flynn moustache.

"Colonel, I'm going to move into a new CP and turn this Pagoda over to you and Charlie Fike. You think you could get a couple of planes in the air and do some scouting for us?"

"Does Gene Autry ride a horse?" The aviator remembered to add, "Sir." Yes, Vandegrift definitely liked Mangrum.

There was going to be a big fight, no doubt about it, but the general wasn't getting any messages of impending doom from the Vandegut. A good sign.

Kenny had walked to the news center at Kukum to check the baseball scores on a blackboard conveniently left by the Japanese. Above it, a cork board was labeled:

LATEST NEWS - SOLOMON ISLANDS DOPE
(GUADALCANAL GAZETTE)

Several Marines stood around, reading wire service teletypes of the world news, including some outrageously exaggerated accounts of their own exploits. Ball scores were chalked every day on the blackboard.

"Hot damn, the Cubs beat the Reds, 5 to 2," Kenny said. "Wonder if Claude Passeau pitched." He hoped they'd post college football scores when fall came, if he was still here and still alive. He was much more interested in college ball, especially the Fighting Illini, than the pros.

After hiking back to A Company's billet, Kenny learned there was a much longer walk in his future.

"Children, we're goin' on a little hike back where we came from," Plunkett was saying. "Lieutenant says we're in a hurry. Pack light. Bust your asses. Off and on," he added, referring to respective asses and feet.

"Where we came from? The Tenaru?" Kenny said. "I thought this was the strategic ground. This ridge was where the big fight would come." It was one of the few times he'd ever needled Plunkett.

"Never knew you for a wise-ass, Nielsen. This campaign ain't fuckin' over with. This is the most strategic ground we got."

Most of the men clipped two canteens of water to their belts. Their dungarees were worn and shabby. They cursed and bitched as they checked their packs and weapons--all but Scupper Harris, who slipped a Mason jar in his field pack. His eyes blazed with that demented gleam again.

"Strike the tents," Plunkett shouted, laughing at his own joke. What tents?

Sorry he'd mouthed off, Kenny checked the action on his Springfield rifle and stuffed extra clips of ammo in his pack.

It turned out to be easier going this time, even though they had to walk all the way. There were several trucks on the island, most of them still running, but no passable roads south of the coast yet, only a trail that had been upgraded in the past week from nonexistent to terrible, so there was no chance to hitch a lift. And that was where the regiment was heading, south of the coconut groves at Red Beach in an effort to get behind the Japanese who were supposed to be there.

Before long that old thirst struck again, but water was like gold to Kenny on these marches and he took only one swallow.

Crossing a stream, a private screamed, "Leeches. Goddamn leeches stickin' to my legs."

"Shut up," Plunkett said. "We'll burn 'em off next time we stop."

The tramping continued. Next a python the size of Ohio slithered across the trail. Shooting was out--Japs could be any-where--so the snake was stabbed and sliced by bayonets and Kabar knives. Its wild, corkscrewing death dance made it even more frightening.

Eventually, they made a rest stop and Kenny broke out his tasteless K rations. "These cracker things must be made of sawdust. They may sustain life but that's about it."

"Sustain life?" Plunkett snorted. "Where you get four-bit words like that, Nielsen? From them books o' yours? Sometimes you sound like a friggin' officer. Why'n't you shoot us another boar?"

The hike resumed. When the K rations formed a hostile knot in his stomach, Kenny tried to remember his last really good meal. Had it had been on the *Wacky Mac*, no, probably in Wellington. Yes, it had been in Wellington. To get his mind off the heat and the monotony of the march, he visualized some of his favorite meals. He kept coming back to a summer Sunday in a farmhouse dining room in Illinois, his plate stacked with fried chicken and mashed potatoes and biscuits and gravy and corn on the cob slavered in butter. And a red and white checked table cloth, definitely. Looking up at a swollen cumulus cloud changing its shape in a cerulean sky, he could almost smell the food and touch that Midwestern summer's day. It made him melancholy.

Sometime in the afternoon, he said, "We're the foot cavalry, that's what we are. Always on the go, gotta get somewhere fast."

"Foot cavalry, that ain't bad," Plunkett said.

"I can't take credit. Foot cavalry is what Stonewall Jackson's outfit called themselves eighty years ago."

"I don't think old Stonewall 'ud mind," Plunkett said. "Good Southern soldier like him."

Before dark the hike ended and the foot cavalry made camp along the Ilu, about three miles south of Red Beach. Not knowing the stream's name, Marines began calling it Alligator Creek. They didn't realize its menacing occupants were *crocodiles*.

Kenny sat against a wild banana tree and began wiping down his rifle. Then he rubbed insect repellant on his face and curled up under the tree, hoping to get some sleep. He regretted goading Plunkett. The gruff son of a bitch was always helping him out. He thought of his pervading loneliness and realized with alarm that he was probably closer to Plunkett than anyone on earth, including his father and brother. His grip on his rifle never slackened as he fell asleep.

His subconscious heard Plunkett say, "Rest up, children, it's liable to get rough tomorrow."

North of them, a Lieutenant Sakakibara, who knew more about it than Plunkett, told himself, "It is likely to be rough *tonight*."

∎

CHAPTER 17

AT 1:30 A.M. ON AUGUST 21 a flare split open the night. A Japanese mortar coughed. Nambu and Hotchkiss machine guns spat tongues of flame.

A sand bar blocked almost the entire mouth of the lethargic Ilu, which was more tidal lagoon than creek, providing a bridge most of the way across. Confident that he'd achieved surprise, Colonel Ichiki sent his men dashing across, toting their Arisaka rifles and screaming "banzai." Junior officers led the way, flourishing swords and urging their troops forward, certain they would rout the few surprised Marines they would encounter on the other side.

The Marines were scared but not surprised. Colonel Al Pollock's 2nd Battalion was there, dug in and waiting. When the attackers were two-thirds of the way across the sand spit, their machine guns and rifles smothered them with sudden concentrated fire. Japanese fell like wheat in a hailstorm.

Two miles away, Kenny's eyes popped open. He was awake in a second. He heard the gunfire, saw the ghostly green flares in the sky.

"Mercy, them polecats really do like to fight at night," Plunkett said.

In his command post, General Vandegrift also heard the din and knew the fight was on. "All I can do," he told chief of staff Jerry Thomas, "is sit here by these two slim wires that connect me to the front. I feel helpless."

At the sand bar, Marines began firing canister shots from 37-millimeter guns. They ripped up a dozen men at a time. The banzai charge became a Japanese disaster. The few survivors who reached the far side of the stream could only crouch and hide. Most of them fled back across the Ilu to their jumping-off point. Some sought safety on the beach.

Able Company got orders to counterattack. When Plunkett told the platoon to advance, Skinny Wade said, "Once more unto the breach, dear friends, once more."

Kenny and his buddies moved out, carrying their Springfield rifles at port arms, bayonets attached. He was just as scared as before, on that first patrol to the Matanikau, but somehow he was better able to cope with the fear. Was it because he'd been through this before? Because he knew what it was to kill a man?

It was morning by the time they reached the coconut grove after circling around from the southeast. Charlie Company was on the right, closing the trap on Ichiki's battered command, now cornered against the sea.

Word was passed along that Pollock's battalion had repulsed a second night assault, then counterattacked at first light, crossing "Alligator Creek" from the west and drenching the Japanese in a steady fire all morning.

The sun was up and hot when Able Company came under fire from two palm-thatched huts. That old fear seized Kenny by the throat. Sergeant Whitely, his squad leader, formed a loose skirmish line and the Marines blazed away. Kenny shot off nine or ten rounds. Chunks flew from the shanties like startled birds.

An enemy soldier burst from a hut and ran--away. Kenny took aim. Exhale. Fire as you exhale. And fired. The man was sixty or seventy yards off, but a tiny red blob materialized on his back. His head jerked upward. Momentum carried him three or four more steps before he crumpled. Kenny trembled. *Jesus.* His heart boomed.

He jammed the rifle butt against his shoulder and pressed the stock against his cheek, ready to fire if another target presented itself. It didn't.

One of the shot-up huts caught fire. Flames soon devoured the bullet-scarred slats and flared through the thatched roof. A Viking funeral for the enemy corpses within.

Plunkett shouted for the platoon to move forward. That's when Moon Whitely got it, hit by a Nambu. Whitely was no more than thirty yards from the concealed gun. He whirled sideways, clutched at his chest, then fell on his back. Everybody hit the deck. Kenny hugged the earth like he wanted to become part of it.

Whitely didn't move. Kenny slowly slid his rifle around in front of him, propped himself on his elbows and began to take aim at where he thought the shots had come from. Then he heard Whitely murmur, "Corpsman," the voice sounding as if from the bottom of a well. Jesus, he was alive. "Corpsman."

Whitely was maybe twenty yards away. Somebody had to go get him. Kenny swivelled his head. Damn, he was closest. The other guys were all behind him. "Help me." Whitely's voice even weaker now.

Kenny slithered forward, snake-crawling. He hadn't even thought about it, probably wouldn't have done this crazy thing if he had.

"No, Nielsen, no." Plunkett's voice. Kenny kept going. A bullet spiked the ground just in front of him.

"Well, shit, cover that fool, boys." Plunkett again. Shots zipped overhead now, the platoon pouring fire at the Japs. Kenny saw a bright splash of blood on Whitely's shirt. The sergeant was on his back, his boondockers sticking up like two fat chimneys.

Kenny reached out, took hold of those boots, and started squirming backwards. Whitely was dead weight. It was like dragging a couple of hundred-pound sacks of cement.

A bullet whanged off Kenny's helmet. His head shuddered like he'd been beaned by a Lefty Grove fastball. First Christian's big bell seemed to be bonging inside the chambers of his skull.

Keep moving. God, this was taking forever. Drag Whitely.

Slither back a few feet. Drag some more. Slither back. Drag.

Suddenly Plunkett was beside him, up on his knees, pulling the pin from a grenade, leaning back, hurling it. Seconds later, Kenny heard the blast from somewhere out in front.

Then Desmond Sweeney charged the gun position, firing on the run. Others followed.

"We got 'em," Plunkett said. "Baptist, Harris, get Whitely to an aid station. Real careful with him now. Use your poncho for a litter. Move!"

His ears ringing, Kenny was still lying on his belly. Plunkett grinned. "Will ya look at that dent on your helmet. Good thing that shot ricocheted off. You're one lucky Marine. Brave peckerwood, too."

Out in front, his clip empty, Sweeney stood there quivering like a poplar leaf, his finger still tight on the trigger. "That's enough, Sweeney," Plunkett said. "Get your ass over here."

"My hand's cramped." Sweeney shook all over. "Can't get my finger off the damn trigger."

Skinny Wade pried on Sweeney's fingers and massaged his hand for several minutes before he could uncramp and let go. Clint Carmichael--everyone called him Hoagy--laughed hysterically.

Suddenly Kenny stopped caring about all of this. He'd had too much of this degrading business. Whitely hit, maybe dying. Christ, he'd probably be next. It wouldn't even matter, he was so tired. Tired of every bit of this, the shooting, the Japs, the responsibility, the heat, the orders, most of all the killing. Tired in his gut and in his soul. Death would be okay, a way out, a way to just be left alone. Maybe he'd see his mother. And Augie Collins, who bought it at the Matanikau. Maybe even Lou Gehrig. Wouldn't that be something?

What snapped him out of it was something stupefyingly unexpected. If death was near, he never thought his friend Plunkett would be its instrument. But suddenly Plunkett snapped his rifle up in quick, deliberate aim--seemingly at Kenny. He couldn't believe it. His heart froze. Plunkett had gone mad. Plunkett fired. Kenny felt the bullet's pneumatic puff zip past his head. He jerked around and saw a Japanese face explode twenty yards behind him and sink back into the spider trap from which it had emerged. A sniper, his obligations to the Emperor very definitely concluded.

Saved my life! Holy smoke, Plunkett just saved my life.

Plunkett grinned. "You gotta stay awake, boy. I'm 'spectin' lots more bright ideas outta you 'fore you buy the farm."

Two minutes passed before Kenny stopped quivering.

Colonel Ichiki, badly hurt with a shrapnel gouge in his left leg and a bullet through his shoulder, told his adjutant, "There will be no surrender. Fight on. How in the world did the enemy get so many men here? And even in our rear?"

In the afternoon, informed of the suicidal resistance, Vandegrift sent in five light tanks. Kenny was too far to the southeast to see them but he heard the stories later. How the tanks clanked over the bodies of dead and dying Japanese and ground them like hamburger, all the time firing canister shots into the grove. They pursued cornered soldiers. Knocked snipers from trees by ramming them.

There were no tanks in the southeast, where Kenny's outfit still pressed the attack on the enemy rear. It was all small arms and mortars, even some hand-to-hand.

Kenny was out of ammo. He was reaching for a fresh clip on his webbed belt when a Jap suddenly popped out of the bushes in front of him. The Jap looked surprised as hell. Kenny knew *he* was. He thrust his bayonet into the soldier's chest before the guy could swing his rifle up to fire. Adrenalin and animal anger pulsing, he tugged his rifle free and stabbed him again through the neck. The Jap passed gas, a big smelly fart, and folded up, as if his bones had liquified.

Kenny wiped his bloody bayonet on the corpse's pants and

muttered, "Sweet Jesus, I'm glad Mom can't see me now."

His stomach was getting stronger. When he'd first seen corpses on this damned island--Augie Collins and that first Jap he'd killed--it was all he could do to keep from vomiting. Now the guy before him was just another dead man. His body butchered, not a shred of dignity to his death, just another dead man.

Kenny took a clip from his belt and reloaded his rifle.

When a blessed lull fell over the battlefield and his blood rush slowed, Kenny learned that Whitely was still alive. He'd be red-tagged off Guadalcanal, flown down to the hospital at Espiritu Santo. Guess I might've saved his life, he thought. I save lives, I take lives. What madness.

He marveled at his luck. He'd been shot at plenty in two scraps with the enemy and had only a dent on his helmet to show for it. It seemed like half his buddies had been grazed by a bullet, sliced by a knife or bayonet, or gashed by some spiky jungle plant. He almost felt ashamed that he didn't have a mark on him, but his detachment about his own death was gone. He was damn glad to be alive.

As the sun dropped low over Ironbottom Sound, he and hundreds of other Marines trod cautiously through the ruins of the Japanese position, weeding out snipers, searching for any sur-viving gun emplacements to eradicate, and collecting souvenirs. Scupper Harris got himself a sword with an intricate handle of lacquered wood, plus several small human items for his Mason jar. Trees were bent and mangled as if they'd been through a hurricane.

When a corpsman tried to help a wounded enemy, the Jap exploded a grenade, killing them both. That story spread fast. From then on, wounded Japanese were shot without mercy.

Lieutenant Sakakibara, the man who'd predicted a rough night, had evaded an approaching tank and saved his skin by darting into the surf, followed by his runner. They stayed under-water for hours, bobbing up for occasional gulps of air.

A few officers remained huddled around Colonel Ichiki. They

urged him to attempt escape east along the beach. This battle was at its end.

"No. Burn the colors," Ichiki ordered, the fire gone from his eyes. He unsheathed his sword and grasped the pommel with both hands. Beneath a twilight sky glowing blood red, he plunged it into his belly and jerked the blade right and left. Aides rushed up too late.

After dark, Lieutenant Sakakibara and his runner waded out of the surf, their skin wrinkled like prunes, and took their sad tale to the 100 men who'd been left behind to guard the supplies. They were nearly the only survivors from the entire attack force.

Able Company posted sentries and camped at the edge of the ghoulish battlefield that night. Lying on that terrible ground, Kenny faced the black fact that now he was a killer three times over. He also recalled that John the Baptist again had failed to fire his rifle. The Baptist had faked it, taking aim and pretending to shoot. Kenny couldn't overlook this much longer, but he was too tired and much too edgy to think about it now.

He'd never known darkness so suffocating. He seemed to be surrounded by ghosts who could float right out of their torn bodies and come after him. The man he'd killed with sharp steel would surely be back. Every tree, every shape, every shadow seemed to know him, to haunt him, to creep inside his bedroll, inside his dungarees, inside his mind. The shadows whispered his name. It was a long time before he fell into a troubled sleep.

■

CHAPTER 18

NEXY DAY, as the grimy, stubble-chinned Leathernecks humped back to Henderson Field, Kenny looked out from ancient, knowing eyes, eyes that had seen how thin the veneer called civilization can be. He thought about the fear that had clenched him again. He decided it was a good thing. Sharpens your senses, makes you more alert. The man who's not afraid out here will get himself killed.

Vandegrift, wearing a very un-Marine pith helmet--the standard steel chamberpot gave him a headache--toured the killing ground, now called Hell's Point. He could hardly take a step without treading on the remains of a Japanese soldier. Despite all he'd experienced in Haiti and Nicaragua, it sickened him. Bodies were strewn all over Hell's Point, half buried in the sand, dangling from trees, sprawled over coconut logs, trampled in the mud, almost none intact. The sight and the growing stench was over-whelming. If they've got this many men to waste so foolishly, how many thousands more, he wondered, do they have on this island?

Preparing individual graves was impossible, even if the Marines had been so inclined, so work details used captured Japanese bulldozers to bury the dead. The biting irony touched Vandegrift.

The general received reports of incredible courage by his troops. A blinded corporal named Schmid who continued to fire his machine gun; a sergeant who threw aside his jammed rifle and killed three Japanese with a machete; a Lieutenant McLanahan, so badly wounded he couldn't fire, who remained hunched in his hole unjamming automatic rifles for others. Vandegrift also got the casualty report: forty-three Marines killed. It could have been worse, he told himself.

He knew the consensus viewpoint among the staff officers was, "The bastards got what they deserved," but Vandegrift said, "Brave men, such brave enemy men." He too had observed the thinness of the veneer called civilization. Under the dappled shade of the lacerated trees, he felt an eerie anxiety. For those who believed in an afterlife, the place was afloat in Japanese spirits.

Vandegrift accepted a captured and bloodstained battle flag as a memento from Colonel Hunt, CO of the 5th Marines, then returned to his jeep.

Back at the Lunga, Vandegrift wrote out a message to be read to all the Marines on Guadalcanal.

"The commanding general desires that the entire division be informed of the results of the Battle of the Tenaru River." (It was the Ilu, not the Tenaru--those maps again.)

"The 1st Marines and supporting units, assaulted under cover of darkness by a well-trained, well-equipped enemy landing force whose mission was to seize the airport, defended their position with such zeal and determination that the enemy was unable to effect a penetration in spite of repeated efforts throughout the night. The 1st Marines, counterattacking at daybreak, and with the 5th Marines enveloping the enemy in the rear and on his flank, annihilated his force and achieved a victory fully commensurate with the traditions of our Corps. This command salutes the officers and men who carried through this outstanding operation."

Those words made even Plunkett feel good and he'd heard plenty of bullshit from Brass Country in his years in the Corps. In fact, since his summons to the Pagoda six days before, he was actually growing to like the Old Man. Was that possible? he asked himself.

After hearing Captain Brush read the general's statement, the men were dismissed. Scupper Harris sidled up to Plunkett and said, "I know everybody thinks my noggin's cracked, includin' you, Sarge, but it ain't. You know how my daddy was killed. I loved my daddy. He was 'bout the best man ever lived. He always told me you never hit nobody without first giving him fair notice. But that's 'zackly what them yellow bastards did to him and all the others who got it at Pearl. So I gotta kill all I can. It's a matter of honor. It's a matter of honor for all of us, are you hep?"

Plunkett laughed at the crude mixture of rhetoric and jazz slang. He put a hand on Harris' shoulder and said nothing for a long time.

"Harris," he said at last, "your daddy meant a lot to you. Put him up on a pedestal, didn't ya?"

"A pedal stool?"

"The killin's necessary," Plunkett said, "but I don't see how cuttin' off parts of their bodies honors your pap. I don't see that at all. Think on it."

But he doubted that Harris could. It was hard to reason with a mind so young, so unseasoned and so obsessed.

It fell to Lieutenant Sakakibara as one of the few survivors and the second-ranking officer left alive to send the dispatch to Rabaul. After fretting over the wording a long time, he sent this message: "Colonel Ichiki died with honor in attack on enemy airfield. Enemy forces and firepower overwhelming. Losses extremely heavy. Every Japanese soldier did his duty honorably. Reserve troops await instructions."

Fully half of Colonel Ichiki's outfit had not yet arrived on the island.

When General Kawaguchi received the message, he knew the significance of its having been sent by a lieutenant. He doubted the "reserve troops" would be many in number. He took it calmly. "It is done. He has joined his fathers. May his spirit find peace. Many more will die before we are through with that island."

Being a combat nurse was no stroll in the park. Claudia Chase learned that quickly enough. A big batch of casualties had arrived on Espiritu Santo Island, and Claudia and the others were hard at work beside the surgeons.

Espiritu Santo lay four hundred miles southeast of Guadalcanal in the French-controlled New Hebrides. When the impotent Vichy government let the Americans set up an advance base there, the U.S. Navy took over the colonial hospital.

The patients were veterans of the battle at the Ilu River. They suffered burns and wounds from bullet, shrapnel and mortar fire. One was blinded, another had lost his lower leg. The surgeon was cleaning up the man's stump below the knee when Claudia Chase first saw him. She wept at the sight. Hardened by a bleak adolescence, she hadn't thought she was still capable of crying.

She brushed away the tears and followed orders. Scissors. Scalpel. Clamp. Retractor. Two patients died on the operating table. It was a rough day for everyone.

After hours of assisting the surgeons and making their normal rounds, the women at last could shower and change. "We're going to the O Club and have a drink with a couple of the docs," Peggy Stratton said to Claudia. "Why don't you come along?"

Claudia hesitated. Maybe she should accept. Then she blurted, "No, no, you go on ahead. I've got a lot of things to do tonight."

Peggy pleaded. "C'mon, Claw, do you good. You don't have to sleep with any of 'em, if you don't want. Personally, I . . . ."

Claudia made her face a stone mask. Her only answer was turning away from the others.

"Gone internal again," Lucy Bates whispered.

Claudia heard, and didn't care. She felt immense fatigue. She knew a healthy 22-year-old woman shouldn't be this exhausted, even after a hard day's work in a hospital. She walked off toward her room. Always pestering me to join them and the male brass for drinks, she thought. What right do they have? They don't know what I've been through. She tried not to let an image of Lloyd, that bastard Lloyd, invade her mind. As always, it did.

Outside, from Espiritu Santo's new airstrip, a B-24 growled into the air, escaping to somewhere, as Claudia never could.

Otomo counted on an adrenalin boost as he crossed Florida Island and passed over Sealark Channel. He took one hand off the stick, pushed his goggles back and rubbed tired eyes. Weeks of combat and overlong flights were wearing him down. It was a few minutes past noon.

Son of Heaven! Here came four enemy Wildcat fighters, the first he'd seen since his initial flight down the Slot. The escorting Zeros would have their hands full. These planes must have come from the island itself. Enemy carriers had been gone for days. He snapped his goggles in place.

The Zeros and Wildcats tangled. One of the Zeros went down, but the others drove off the American planes. But when Otomo reached the field and began his dive, there were more.

He saw planes of both drab green and navy blue--his and theirs--dogfighting, spitting out tracer fire at lower altitudes. There was no doubt now: the Americans had fighters on the island.

The twin-engine Betty bombers had come over first and dropped their bombs from 19,000 feet so the American gunners hadn't had time to adjust for the fast-plunging dive bombers.

Otomo turned the plane on its back and plunged downward. He aimed at a clump of trees near one end of the airstrip, guessing that the leafy canopy sheltered either fuel or planes. Familiar G-forces pinched him, crushed against his nose and eyes like a giant fist. The knot of trees grew in his cross-hairs. The altimeter spun in its wild backwards dance. The ominous tracers made their deceptively soft, drifting climb. He hated that. Nine other killer shells were racing up for every tracer he could see.

This time they sailed past, their fuses set for higher altitudes.

He squeezed the bomb release at 900 feet and flattened out. In the rear seat, Takai Asakawa focused his Nikon for the picture. A sheet of yellow-white flame shot into the sky behind him. Otomo must have guessed right--hit some fuel drums.

As he climbed away to the north, tracer shells blurred past on both sides. Fifty-caliber fire. A Wildcat had latched onto him. Otomo jinked left, then right, but couldn't shake him off. With that damned immovable landing gear, the Type 99 was less maneuverable than the Wildcat. He didn't have enough altitude to effect a proper roll or a split-S. He saw a rain squall off toward Tulagi. Wished he could reach it, but it was too far off and the Wildcat was too fast. He'd never make it.

The American remained glued to his tail, his stream of fire hotter. *Ping ping ping.* Hitting him now. If only his back-seat gun mount faced the rear as on the Americans' Dauntless. If so, Asakawa could shoot right into that white-faced devil. As it was, he could only sit there, helpless.

Okay. One thing left to try. He pulled the nose up and snapped the plane to the left in a near vertical bank. The harness bit hard into his side. The plane almost stopped. He'd stall in another second or two.

Still at full throttle, the Wildcat slammed past, barely missing him. Now jerk the plane back to level. Good, the engine is racing again.

For an instant, he caught the American in his gunsight. He squeezed the fire button. Watched tracers slap through the Wildcat's left wing. A chunk of metal broke loose, flew right into Otomo's windshield. He ducked by instinct. A square foot of plexiglass starred like a spider web, but the glass held.

Looking to the right, he saw the enemy break off and head for base. There were no flames, but the plane was badly hit. He didn't know whether that misbegotten fiend would make it home and he didn't care. Then he was in the storm, snakes of rain slithering across the battered glass in front of his face. He climbed through the squall, buffeted hard all the way up. He had no idea where the rest of his squadron was. It had become every man for himself.

When he re-entered clear air, he found himself somewhere off the southern tip of Santa Isabel Island. There wasn't another plane in sight. He made a course adjustment toward the northwest, climbed to 16,000 feet, his best fuel-conserving altitude, and began the long cruise toward Rabaul. He pushed his goggles up and rubbed his eyes. Precious Buddha, help me to stay awake for three hours more.

Twenty minutes later he saw a small knot of Zeros several miles off his left wingtip, also headed home. The sight cheered him.

Reaching Rabaul, he learned that fourteen planes had been lost. Tears blurred his eyes. So many comrades dead. Yamada, Sakumoto, Kukura . . . .

Only nine operating dive bombers remained and Otomo was informed there would be no more. They would keep flying until by attrition there were none. All the dive bombers that could be scraped up were now going to the carriers.

While Otomo's devoted maintenance crew, who'd counted nine bullet holes, swarmed over the plane to make repairs, he fell onto his sleeping mat, sadness covering him like a blanket.

At the big forward naval base at Truk Island, 1,000 miles northwest of Guadalcanal, Fleet Admiral Isoruku Yamamoto, commander-in-chief of the Combined Fleet, pored over the latest digest of American news reports supplied by his intelligence officer.

"I see the Americans persist in referring to the Battle of the Coral Sea as the first great contest between aircraft carriers--the first sea battle in history in which the opposing fleets could not see each other." He pounded the table with a fist. "This offends me. What do they think our victory over the British in the Indian Ocean was, three months earlier? When Admiral Nagumo's carrier planes sank the British carrier *Hermes*. The insolent Americans apparently believe that does not signify since they were not involved."

Yamamoto, the architect of the attack on Pearl Harbor, had lived and worked in Washington years before as a naval attaché.

At the time of Pearl Harbor he had told Emperor Hirohito he could score many victories over the unprepared United States in the first year of war but could guarantee no success after that. Nothing had happened since then to change his mind. The loss of four vital carriers at Midway made his longed-for "decisive battle" all the more essential.

"Now then," Yamamoto told his chief of staff, "I reiterate that the army is taking this Guadalcanal business all too lightly. The struggle in the southern Solomons is of great importance to our war aims. If we fail there, it will not be possible to win in New Guinea and our entire southern flank will be threatened. We could even be driven back to the Philippines.

"I will protect the next shipment of troops and supplies to Guadalcanal with a large task force, including carriers. Send a message to that effect to General Hyakutake at Rabaul. Perhaps this will draw out the proud American Navy and we can have our decisive battle. If I can smash their fleet in one major stroke we may yet achieve our aims."

■

CHAPTER 19

KENNY STRODE SLOWLY toward the lieutenant's dugout. What's he want me for? he wondered. Did I foul up or something? Being summoned by Rusty Gates came as a surprise. If Kenny was in trouble, some sergeant would do the chewing-out, not the lieutenant.

He reached the dugout, eased back the mosquito flap, and entered.

Gates, who couldn't have been more than a couple of years older than Kenny, grinned boyishly under his light brown crewcut, returned the salute and said, "Stand easy. That was great work out there yesterday, bringing Whitely to safety. Now, Sergeant, I think you should sew these on your uniform." He handed Kenny a patch, a three-striped sergeant's chevron.

Me, he thought, a sergeant?

"Losing Whitely was a blow; he was a good man. Now you're getting his squad. I like the fine work you've been doing." Kenny thought Gates was trying to sound older than his years. For a moment, he wanted to object. He liked his own job. But then he also liked the idea of promotion. Better pay, too. Being responsible for nine men, hell, he could handle that.

"Aye, aye, sir, thank you, sir," was all he could say. "If you think I can do the job."

"Son, I *know* you can do the job." Son? Son? What a ridiculous thing for this boyish individual in--what, his mid-twenties?--to say. Kenny knew why most sergeants of his acquaintance thought they were better men than their lieutenants.

As if in salute to the new sergeant, Pistol Pete, hidden in the jungle hills west of Henderson Field, blasted away with its first 155-

millimeter round of the day.

The southeast trade winds played with General Kawaguchi's hair at the rail of the destroyer *Umikaze* as it pulled away from Shortland and into the Slot. The Rat Patrol was a beautiful sight as it got up to speed under a bright morning sun. The eight destroyers knifed through the water in two columns, two abreast. They would reach Guadalcanal an hour before midnight.

Ichiki's disaster hadn't shaken Kawaguchi's confidence that he could recapture the island, but he was convinced that it would be a tough struggle.

He felt sad to think that most of his men would perish in the effort. He found it difficult to look at them as the destroyers danced across the water at thirty knots. An hour ago, he'd heard them singing the haunting *War Song of Umi Yukaba*.

He gathered his officers around him and stepped onto a wooden box.

"Gentlemen, our faith is our strength. Men who fight bravely, never doubting victory, will be the victors in the long run. We have trained ourselves, haven't we? I swear to each of you that we will smash the enemy. On to *Gadarukanaru*."

"To *Gadarukanaru*," the officers shouted.

Before leaving Rabaul, Kawaguchi had learned that the Imperial Navy was covering his movement with a major force. Thus reassured, he had packed his gear, including his best dress uniform so he would look proper accepting the American surrender.

Colonel Oka, however, who was to land west of the airfield to complete the encirclement, took Ant Patrol. Oka had argued long and hard for motorboats and barges, convinced he could hide from enemy search planes in small lagoons by day and make good time at night. Now Kawaguchi was sorry he'd given in.

At the same time, a little to the east and within easy flying distance of both the Slot and Guadalcanal, Admiral Yamamoto positioned the most formidable aircraft carrier force since Midway: the fleet carriers *Shokaku* and *Zuikaku* and the smaller *Ryujo*. Along with them were three battleships, nine cruisers, thirteen destroyers and thirty-six submarines.

And as Yamamoto had hoped, the American Navy did come out to fight. Frank Jack Fletcher, the timid carrier commander who had abandoned the Guadalcanal landing three weeks before, sailed northeast from Nouméa with the carriers *Wasp, Enterprise* and *Saratoga*. Following Coral Sea and Midway, it would be the third slam-bang carrier brawl of the war between the Americans and Japanese.

Afterward, Colonel Thomas, Vandegrift's chief of staff, pieced together the Battle of the Eastern Solomons from radio dispatches and intercepts.

"I don't care to read it, Jerry," Vandegrift said. "My eyes are bothering me tonight. Just tell me."

"Aye, aye, sir. Well, Fletcher again showed what he was made of, and sent *Wasp* back for refueling on the eve of the fight."

"They're calling him 'Always Fueling' Fletcher," Vandegrift said.

"So I've heard. Apparently, he didn't believe his own patrol reports that the Japanese were as close as they were, so at this critical moment he had two carriers to the enemy's three. Next day, each side made several sightings and attacks, both by dive and torpedo bomber. The enemy lost the light carrier *Ryujo* and the battleship *Jintsu* was badly damaged. *Enterprise* took three bomb hits and lost about seventy-five men, but she stayed afloat and will be repaired. The final result was nearly a draw but tactically the enemy fared a little the better. *Saratoga* survived the battle intact only to be torpedoed afterward by an enemy sub. She'll be out of action for many months."

"*Saratoga*," Vandegrift lamented. "We had our pre-invasion conference with Fletcher on that old girl, remember?" He kneaded his temple with his right hand. "This 1942 has become a very trying year for American arms. If I calculate correctly, Jerry, that leaves

Wasp as our only operational carrier in the whole theater. We sent four enemy carriers to the bottom at Midway, but three months later here we are, down to our last flattop out here, while the enemy reinforces Guadalcanal and bombards us at will. Operation Watchtower has become Operation Shoestring."

"Yes sir," Thomas said, "but there's one more thing, and I think you'll like it. Fletcher got the Big Haircut."

"Say again?"

"Relieved, sir, sent to Washington. He'll be driving a desk for the duration."

"I've always made it a rule not to rejoice at another man's misfortune," Vandegrift said, "but I must admit I'm not displeased."

"Sir, why don't we listen to the 7 o'clock news from San Francisco? The USO Show comes on right afterward and tonight they're having Paulette Goddard."

"Who in the world is Paulette Goddard?"

Out in the darkness, beyond the new command post, a rough Marine voice exclaimed, "Hey, the Old Man doesn't know who the hell Paulette Goddard is."

Vandegrift heard. He blushed and turned his palms upward.

Less conspicuously, the voices in the night continued.

"Paulette Goddard? Is that the one Charlie Chaplin married?"

"Yeah, the lucky little fart. Bet she's a million bucks between the sheets. Who's in?"

"Couldn't be better'n Hedy Lamarr. That dame's got great gams. I'm in. Two cards."

"Not better'n Betty Gable. Dealer takes three."

"Grable."

"Huh?"

"Grable, stupid. Her name is Grable, not Gable. Who opened?"

"Whatever. She's a dream. Best stems in the world."

"Nope. Lamar. That Hedy Lamarr just drips sex. I'll bet it's 200 degrees 'tween her lovely legs."

"I opened. I bet a dime. Wonder how the Sox did today."

"The hell with baseball. Those guys oughta all be totin' rifles. I'll see your dime and raise you a dime. If this war goes another year, won't be nobody in the major leagues but 35-year-olds and teenagers."

And so it went in the muddy foxholes of Guadalcanal.

Sergeant Plunkett pounded Sergeant Nielsen on the back so hard he nearly broke his spine. Then they retired to Plunkett's dugout, where the platoon sergeant produced a bottle of moonshine he'd been hoarding.

"I fixed it up for you, Kenny."

"*You* fixed it up?"

"Natch. I'm Gates' right-hand boy. He does ninety percent of what I tell him. The other ten ain't worth worryin' about. Hell, when he got the platoon just as we was leavin' New River, I had to show him how to tie his shoelaces. I made him into a friggin' officer and I sure as hell can make a sergeant outta you. Fact is, it'll be a lot easier, on account of you're ten times smarter."

Kenny blushed. "Plunk, if you're gonna give me a drink, just pour, will ya?"

Lieutenant Gates' platoon contained four squads of ten to twelve men each, and in turn was one of four platoons in Able Company. Hadley Plunkett was Rusty Gates' platoon sergeant and now Kenny was one of four squad sergeants under him.

"You're part of an important club now, Kenny. It's good sergeants that run the Corps."

Kenny took a gulp of the clear liquid and a stream of fire plunged down his gullet. Eyes watering, mouth aflame, he gasped, "What *is* that?"

"Jungle juice. White lightning. Puts salt in your shaker, don't it? Get it from an old Carolina boy like me, over in 2nd Battalion. They got themselves a reg'lar still over there."

"Guy ought to get a Purple Heart for drinking this stuff. What do they distill? Some kind of berries?"

"Don't ask. Fella can't be choosy on this rock. Down home

we'd put some peaches in the jar, give it some flavor, but they ain't no peaches 'round here that I know of."

The second drink went down a little easier. Soon they were pretty mellow and even the stinking jungle and its terrible war didn't seem so bad. Kenny was beginning to feel more at home than ever before.

"Glad I could stay with the platoon."

"I ain't gonna lose you if I can help it, *Sarge*." Plunkett emphasized the word and it was a gratifying sound. It no longer frightened Kenny that he was responsible for nine other guys, ages 18 to 20, in a squad that was slightly understrength.

"I just hope you're tough enough. God knows you're smart enough. Gates got his eye on you, Kenny. Been over your records. Says you got high scores on all your tests when you joined up. Didn't surprise me none."

"Why is that?"

"Hell, I seen 'em, too. I'm his right-hand boy, like I told ya. I know everything he knows and then some." A lurid wink. "What a waste, Kenny, this war."

"What do you mean, Sarge?"

"When it's over, nothin'll really be changed, and we'll go back a-tradin' with the Japs. We'll sell 'em Frigidaires again and go back to buyin' their silk. Oh, we'll reduce the male population under 35 a bit first and break a lot of mothers' hearts, then we'll kiss an' make up and start in a-tradin'."

"You really believe that?"

"Sure. It's all about big money and governments not bein' able to understand each other."

"I thought it was about avenging Pearl Harbor and running the Japs out of China."

"Your Pearl Harbors is what happens when agreements fall apart between the governments. Wars have to start someplace--the Japs just kicked it off with more style than most countries do."

"How do you think the war will go, Plunk?"

"We'll turn the corner, maybe right here on the Canal. We'll knock 'em around for a year or two, then there'll be a peace settlement."

"What about Hitler and the Nazis?"

"Same thing. He can't beat us, the British Empire and the Russians all together. No chance. We'll kick his ass for awhile and then he'll give up, if he ain't already been thrown out by his own people. And we'll go buyin' their cameras and cuckoo clocks same as before."

"What'll you do after the war, Plunk?"

"I'll only be 38 when I get my twenty years in. Only six years off. Reckon I'd like to get me a little farm in the Piedmont. Beautiful country up there. Raise a few hogs and chickens and cows, maybe grow some corn or tobbacky. My wife makes the best fried chicken in the world. God, how I miss that fried chicken. My old lady, too, o' course. Miz Tillie's halfway 'round this planet from me. She's got a little somethin' in the oven, you know."

"A little something . . . you're pregnant? I mean, she's--"

"Yep." Plunkett grinned proudly. "Wish I could be there when we have that little feller, 'bout two months from now . . . Miss my radio shows, too. *Terry and the Pirates, The Thin Man, The Shadow*--"

"*The Shadow*, right. 'Who knows what evil lurks in the hearts of men? The Shadow knows'."

"Yeah, Lamont Cranston, The Shadow. Wouldn't it be bitchin' to make yourself invisible?"

"Sure, like when the Japs attack. You know, one of my favorite shows is *The Green Hornet*."

"Yeah," Plunkett said, "The Green Hornet and his faithful manservant Kato."

"You remember how Kato used to be Japanese? Right after Pearl Harbor he suddenly became Filipino. On Friday, December 5th he was Japanese and on Monday the 8th he was a Filipino. No explanation, they just did it."

"Didn't need no explanation. After Pearl, they couldn't have that guy be a Jap no more. Now what about you, Kenny? You gonna stay in the Corps?"

"Might. As good a home as I ever had, especially since Mom passed on."

"Ain't nothin' like a good woman."

Later, alone on his bedroll, when the new sergeant felt both feverish and chilled, he attributed it to the alcohol. He pulled his dark green Marine Corps blanket over him and realized it was the first time he'd done that on this island. When Washing Machine Charlie came over, Kenny was still lying awake in his hole, thinking.

■

CHAPTER 20

A PBY FROM ESPIRITU SANTO sighted the eight destroyers ferrying General Kawaguchi and his men down the Slot. Chilled by the thought of more enemy reinforcements, Vandegrift asked Colonel Mangrum if he would launch an attack with the Cactus Air Force.

Soon Vandegrift was watching Mangrum lead his dive bombers skyward, followed by Captain John Smith's fighters. "I wonder how many will come back," he said.

They all came back, and right away. They ran into a storm over Florida Island and had no chance of finding the ships.

Below the clouds, General Kawaguchi heard their engines. On the deck of the *Umikaze*, he watched the antiaircraft men scramble into their gun mounts, and was relieved when the heavy clouds kept the Americans away.

Thus spared an air attack, the Rat Patrol landed Kawaguchi safely that night at Taivu Point, twenty-five miles east of the airfield. The troops' legs shiny with the luminescent sea creatures, they were easily found by the remaining hundred men of the shattered Ichiki detachment. "See how ragged and hungry they are," Kawaguchi told his aide. "And emotionally shaken. They're hardly fit soldiers. What a fool Ichiki was to attack on his own with such a small force."

The next day, Vandegrift and Charlie Fike, the new commander of Marine Air Group 23, watched as reinforcements of a sort arrived at Henderson Field. A B-17 lumbered in and touched down, along with fourteen P-400 fighters comprising the 67th Army Air Force Fighter Squadron. The bomber could perform long-range scouting and the fighters could back up the overworked F4F Wildcats.

"These were all Admiral McCain could scrape up just now at Espiritu Santo," Colonel Fike said, "but he promises we'll get more."

"A sight for sore eyes," said Vandegrift, "but in my prayers tonight I'll ask for more fuel, spare parts, Marston matting and facilities." The mechanics had already taken to cannibalizing the damaged planes for spare parts to keep the others going--and doing it well, as correspondent Tregaskis predicted they would.

"That P-400 is an odd-looking bird," Vandegrift said.

"Sir, it's a modified version of the P-39 Airacobra, rear-engine-powered with a drive shaft running beneath the pilot to the propeller. Can't make half the Wildcat's altitude, so I doubt they'll be able to attack the Betty bombers. We can find a lot of useful work for them, though. Another PBY came in yesterday and McCain had it crammed full of oxygen bottles so the Wildcats can get above 15,000 and attack enemy bombers."

"I'm grateful, but that's no way to supply an air base. I need supply runs by ships. The planes are hungry and so are the men. We've barely got them on two meals a day."

But Vandegrift soon learned that some help was on its way. Admiral Kelly Turner, who'd brought him to Cactus in the first place, was running the blockade, sending a transport, escorted by destroyers. It carried aviation fuel, food, ammunition, the few airplane parts that could be spared at Nouméa, and a ground crew to service the fighters and bombers. Also aboard was a construction battalion--the famous Seabees. They were badly needed for airfield improvements and a lot of other jobs.

No matter that she had gone 7,000 miles from her home, nurse Claudia Chase's torment followed her like a shadow. Once again, the black memory invaded her thoughts.

She was barely 16 and just starting her junior year in high school when she got pregnant. Lloyd was 21 and an upperclassman at Ohio State. He was a letterman, an end on the football team, and an Alpha Gamma Rho. It was all so glamorous, her dates with a college man. The boys at Bexley High were just that, boys.

She only gave in to him that one time and that had been more out of rebellion against her peevish, intolerant mother than love for Lloyd. She thought it was safe, thought she'd carefully counted the days since her last period.

It happened in her bedroom. Mom was at a church meeting and Dad was on the road somewhere--wasn't he always? They'd had a couple of beers and Claudia was giddy; she'd seldom had a taste of alcohol before. Though her head was spinning, she knew what she was doing, wanted to unlock the mysteries of lovemaking that she and her girlfriends were always speculating about, giggling, blushing, fibbing.

But what she unlocked was no beautiful mystery. The act itself was painful, bloody, totally lacking any sense of sublime together-ness--and over so fast. And then came the look on Lloyd's face as he stood and buttoned his trousers. Not a look of love and compassion, but of conquest. That hurt as much as the fiery pain between her legs.

She told no one when she missed her period and started to feel frightening changes in her body. Her mother would go mad with anger. Dad, a traveling salesman, Claudia was about as close to him as the King of Siam. She didn't trust her girlfriends with the awful truth, either.

At last she told Lloyd and that's when any desperate hope that he harbored even a grain of decency vanished. She'd hoped that if he wouldn't offer to "do the right thing," he'd at least find and pay for a discreet doctor in someplace out of town like Zanesville or Dayton who could take care of the matter.

But no, Lloyd erupted. He hit her, knocked her around, punched her face and belly. "Trying to trap me, you little whore?" He threw her to the floor, swearing. Claudia lay there in torment, crushed in every possible way.

Bleeding from her vagina began immediately and continued for nearly a week. While she sank lower and lower into black hopelessness, she came to realize that she'd lost the baby, that Lloyd had killed it.

For awhile she was close to committing suicide, and only decided against it after talking with God. Then she thought about killing Lloyd, and even roughed out a plan for doing it. She didn't consult God on that one.

The inability to go to her mother, the preacher, anyone, about it, only took her lower.

An intense fear welled up every time a man smiled that certain smile that said he wanted her. The fear seemed to come from her private place, as if it had a mind of its own. Days and weeks of washing that private place did no good. Many times she doubted God and thought that, yes, killing herself would be best. Why had He punished her so? She was marked. A child of violence. Human wreckage.

Claudia's girlfriends couldn't understand her, and eventually they were no longer friends. So, the hell with them. Who needed them?

She became animal-like where men were concerned. They were the hunters, she their quarry. She would stay away from the enemy--men--stay away from them forever. She didn't know what was to become of her and the awful truth was that now, six years later, she still didn't know.

Kenny liked his squad. They were pros, hard bastards, all but John the Baptist. He was a problem. For one of his first tasks as a sergeant and squad leader, Kenny ordered himself to talk with him.

"Where you from, John? Virginia, isn't it?"

"Right, Kenny, I mean sir. Winchester, in the Shenandoah."

"You can still call me Kenny or anything you want except sir. I'm no officer. Good hunting around there? Winchester?"

"The best. Lotsa rabbit, deer, ducks in the fall."

"I used to hunt quite a bit back in Illinois. I know you're a fine shot, Bap, I've seen your scores from the rifle range, almost all fives and V's. And you're sure no coward. You're plenty cool when the planes come over or Pistol Pete cuts loose. So what's the problem? You know what I'm talkin' about. You come back from a firefight with too much ammo."

"Yeah, I know." John the Baptist was quiet for a minute, contemplating his trembling hands. "It's just that I can't make myself shoot a man in the back," he said at last. "Every time I've had a bead on a Jap he's been heading the other way."

"That was tough for me the first time, too. My conscience really yacked at me when I pulled the trigger on that patrol to the Matanikau. But--you know what?--it got easier. It's like the conscience is a square box and every time you do something like that, it takes a ninety-degree turn. And it hurts, 'cause the sharp corners of the box scrape when it makes that turn. But each time it turns, some of the corner is scraped off, so every time it hurts a little less. I haven't admitted this to anyone, not even Plunkett, but I don't dislike killing them any more. Keep that to yourself, Bap. Worries the hell outta me. Maybe the war is turning me into a pervert."

Kenny felt a sudden rush of fever and the realization struck him: it was a malaria attack. He struggled to keep his mind on the discussion at hand.

"Kenny, the other fellas say the same thing. A few of 'em talk about it. They're ashamed too, 'cause killing gives 'em a secret thrill. I don't know if I can explain myself. Look, I went to Sunday School when I was little and I believe most of that stuff, 'do unto others' and 'thou shalt not kill.' Gee whiz, I believe in fighting for my country but to me that means a fair fight, not shooting somebody in the back. If my conscience is a square box like yours, I guess I'm scared of the corners rubbing off."

"Bap, I don't think God sends people to hell for doing the killing that's demanded in a war. But have you thought about transferring out of a combat team? Become a company clerk or a mechanic or something?"

"No, please, no. I like the outfit. I wanta be in your squad. I'll try, honest I'll try. I know it's my duty."

"Okay, but if you don't, some of our guys may die because of it. Think about that. . . . We'll keep this between ourselves for now."

"Thanks, Sarge."

Kenny was glad Scupper Harris wasn't in his squad. One problem child was enough.

Sunday dawned and Kenny answered church call. While engineers worked on Fighter One, a new grassy landing strip just south of Henderson Field, ninety men gathered for services in a shady grove near the shore on the Lever Brothers plantation. Beneath cocopalms, they sang *Marching to Zion, Sweet Hour of Prayer* and other hymns. In his sermon, a Presbyterian chaplain told them God was on their side. Kenny thought the Holy Joe was wrong about God taking sides in mankind's wars, but the services and the camaraderie made him feel good anyway.

On the night of September 7th, General Kawaguchi heard firing near the shore. "*Oi*, my arm," a voice cried in the darkness. "I've been hit." What happened? Kawaguchi wondered. The distant voice sounded as if it had come from offshore.

Minutes later, an aide brought word of a bad mixup. Some of Kawaguchi's men had fired on a small boat that turned out to be on patrol from the Ichiki rear guard. Two soldiers on the boat had been killed and others wounded.

"A most serious error," Kawaguchi said. "Surely the shooting has alerted the Americans. I should like to change our position and move inland, but we must remain here until we get word that Colonel Oka has landed in the west. Then we can carry out our preparations for the attack."

Kawaguchi was right. It seemed only minutes before he heard airplane engines and saw flares lighting the forest. American Wildcats began bombing and strafing.

"Why did I ever agree to let Oka go by Ant Patrol?" he said. "We need him here now." A bomb exploded nearby, providing the exclamation point.

His troops dug in and toughed it out. They had been joined by the other half of the Ichiki detachment--the thousand who'd still been at sea when their reckless colonel had attacked.

The Americans bombed for several days and the raids steeled Kawaguchi's resolve to recapture the field. "I owe it to Japan and to my men, the gallant young men I brought to this accursed island." Afraid to make fires because the Americans would see the smoke, they lived on fruit and uncooked rice.

Six tortuous days later, the luckless Colonel Oka landed west of the airfield. Sighted by Australian coastwatchers, his motorboats and barges had been raided repeatedly by warplanes from Espiritu Santo and Guadalcanal. When the Americans weren't attacking, Oka was harassed by storms. When at last he made his landfall, fewer than half of his 1,100 men had survived and they had little food or ammunition. Weary and hungry, they were in no condition to attack. Not wanting to shame himself, Oka vaguely informed General Kawaguchi that he had "suffered some losses."

The new sergeant no longer marveled at his luck. Kenny still didn't have a scratch on him, but now he had malaria. He was shivering with a chill in the field hospital and listening to the doctor, Captain Brown. The sturdy structure had a corrugated-metal roof, rough-hewn ceiling joists and rafters, and a heavy log ridge beam. There were no bulkheads, the sides open so the wounded could be moved quickly to the nearby slit trenches during air raids.

"You're down to 140 pounds, son," Captain Brown said. "We need to fatten you up."

"On what, sir, K-rations?"

"Touché. We'd all like a few more good meals."

"Tell me about this malaria, doc."

"Malaria is spread by the Anopheles mosquito. When it bites

someone who has malaria, it sucks red blood cells infected with microscopic parasites into its own belly. There the malarial parasites multiply. Then when the mosquito bites you, it injects the bad blood cells into your bloodstream. Bingo, now you've got it."

"I understand, sir, but how long does it last? It's curable, isn't it?"

"We're not really sure if malaria is curable. We don't know yet if our modern drugs simply fight off the symptoms or actually kill the parasite. This is still a pretty new game for us. Quinine has always worked best, but our supply of quinine is critically low."

"The cinchona tree is found in South America, isn't it?"

"Aha, smart lad. Quinine comes from the bark of the cinchona, yes, but the South American trees haven't done well. Most of the world's quinine comes from Java, and we know who's got Java--our little yellow friends."

"Another good reason to beat the hell out of 'em."

"Right. Now, I want you to double your intake of atabrine tablets and go back to work; that's all the treatment I can prescribe. Your symptoms should abate rapidly."

At Kenny's downcast look, the doctor said, "Look on the bright side. You won't have to donate blood any more."

■

CHAPTER 21

KENNY SAT ON a coconut log beside his machine gunner, Del Cranker, who was scraping dried mud off his boondockers with his Kabar knife.

"Tell me about your farm," Kenny said.

"The farm? We've got 400 acres, my Dad and me, sectioned off in five fields, plus some pasture land. It's between Muscatine and Iowa City."

"Say, that's not far from Galesburg, maybe seventy, eighty miles west, across the big stream."

"Up till last year we had 'er all in corn, but this year I told Dad to put in some soy beans."

"How come?"

"Uncle Sam's paying good money for 'em. They process soy beans to make hard resins. Windshields and gun bubbles for planes and such. They call it plastic. Besides, I think it's good for the soil not to be growin' the same crop year after year. The ground needs a break ever' now and then. After the war, I'm gonna grow corn in two fields, beans in two, and leave one fallow, just plow in the stubble and let 'er rest. Rotate the fields ever' year. Grow a few oats to feed the horses."

"Makes sense, Del. Sounds to me like you're a darn good farmer."

"I'm tryin'. . . . You know, whenever you go to the store to get one little item it takes three hours even when you're in a rush 'cause you have to stop and talk to ever'body in town." Cranker's eyes grew wistful. "Corn harvest's a-comin' up, and the roof on the barn needs fixin'. God, I miss the place, Kenny. Can't wait to get home."

* * *

With Tulagi and Gavutu secured, Vandegrift summoned the Raiders over to Guadalcanal and called Red Mike Edson to the new command post at the jungle's edge. Little remained of the red hair that had earned the colonel his nickname.

"Job well done across the sound, Mike. You cleaned up a tough situation in good Marine fashion. Now our circumstances over here are this: We're surrounded and the enemy has been reinforced several times. We're thin all along the perimeter. I need to plug your Raiders into the line."

"At your service, sir."

"There's a ridge just south of here. Runs at a ninety-degree angle to the field. Mostly grass, very little jungle. The enemy just might use it as an avenue of attack."

"Sure, we'll go out and plug up that ridge for you, sir."

"Let a man finish, will you, Red? I want you and also the Parachutists on that ridge. You've just completed a hard mission and I wish I could let your men rest, but I can't. I've got kitchen units in the line out there now."

"Good idea, sir. Feed the Japs some of our chow, make 'em good and sick."

"Don't let Butch Morgan catch you saying that. Those eagles on your collar wouldn't cut any ice with him."

"Sorry. I know the cooks are doing the best they can."

"That they are. And I'd like them to put down their rifles and get back to their field kitchens. But first, Mike, before you set up on the ridge, I want you to take a few of your men and have them do what they do best."

"Raid, you mean."

"Right. We've still got a few Higgins boats and LCIs running-- left behind in Fletcher's haste to leave us." The general moved to a tattered map tacked to an easel. "We know the Japanese have landed a force east of here, near Taivu Point. We've been hitting them with our little air force. I want you to send a raiding party over there, insert by night, shoot them up a bit, and get the heck out."

"Tonight be okay, sir?"

"Red, you'll have your general's star in a matter of months."

"I figure you're right, sir."

Next on Vandegrift's agenda was a little ceremony to present a Purple Heart to the native hero Jacob Vouza.

Martin Clemens, the colonial official, was on hand for the rite. A former member of the rowing crew at Cambridge, the Scotsman Clemens had been commissioned an officer by the Australians. He'd organized sixty native constables into a scouting force. Vouza, one of its leaders, arrived in his lavalava skirt--and nothing else. He stood at stiff attention, his chest sticking out like a bantam rooster's as Vandegrift stepped up to him.

"Where the devil can I pin it?" the general said.

A short intermission took place while Clemens found a stately sash in his gear and draped it diagonally across Vouza's chest. As Vandegrift secured the medal to the sash, he saw tears form in Vouza's eyes. No wonder the man believed in kings. For him, this was a royal moment.

General Kawaguchi sent a four-man patrol to search for Colonel Oka, who was somewhere to the west. He had to be found. Had to attack on schedule.

As Kawaguchi prepared to move out, after giving the patrol a two-day head start, planes from the accursed American airfield continued to pound his position. He would march west along the coast from Taivu Point to the mouth of the Tenaru. There the artillery and what was left of the Ichiki detachment would move directly west toward the airfield. Kawaguchi would pivot south and west with most of his brigade and get behind the field. When Oka got in position, the coordinated attack would be carried out, Oka from the west, Kawaguchi the south, and the Ichiki detail from the east. At the same time, the navy would lay down a strong bombardment from the fourth side, the sea.

The soldiers tramped through the forest at the edge of the shore, dragging their artillery pieces. It was rough going. They couldn't actually walk on the beach; that would leave fatal tracks.

"I forbid fires," Kawaguchi told Major Suzuki. "This is hard on the men, but it cannot be helped. Those Yankee devil aviators would find us."

That night, he watched sadly as the exhausted soldiers ate wild berries and cold rice, sucked vines and savored the rare tin of crabmeat or sardines. The box lunches the navy had provided as a parting gift were but a memory.

The second night of the march he heard engines and saw enemy landing craft pass by close offshore. "If they are going to attack our base camp, as I presume," he said to Suzuki, "there is nothing we can do about it." He shrugged helplessly. "I cannot afford to send men back to help. The reserve party must deal with it as best they can."

Colonel Edson's raiding party headed for Taivu Point. Not all the Higgins boats were still running; two were towed by motorboats. The company stormed ashore near Tasimboko village and drove off the defenders in a violent firefight. The outnumbered Japanese fought hard. Even after escaping into the jungle they attacked the Marines with mortars.

The Raiders pillaged the bivouac, filching medical supplies and food, including cans of crabmeat. They destroyed what they couldn't carry and wrecked the radio transmitter.

"Looky here," said an excited sergeant. "A general's dress uniform. I guess their CO planned on going to the opera in Sydney." Thus the splendid uniform in which Kawaguchi had planned to accept the American surrender went missing in action, the proud souvenir of a Marine.

When the Raiders pulled out, they slashed open and urinated on the bags of rice they had to leave behind. They piled two captured 75-millimeter guns into the boats. Also, four dead buddies.

Kawaguchi and his main force reached the Tenaru, where he parted with the artillery and the Ichiki men, and led 2,100 members of his brigade into the jungle. They headed for the south side of the airfield, just beyond the ridge Sergeant Plunkett had identified as vital ground a month before.

It became a nightmare trek in the relentless rainforest. They climbed up and down gorges, forded streams and hacked their way through tangled liana vines. Kawaguchi dreamed of food and pure water and the comfortable hammocks he'd once known on board ship. Too weary to lug their sixty-pound field packs any farther, some of his soldiers abandoned pieces of equipment. Only a fierce loyalty to their Emperor and each other kept them going. Those who knew some English coached the others in taunts to yell at the Marines.

Each night, Kawaguchi gave them fatherly pep talks. He hoped that, through it all, they still believed in their invincibility.

General Vandegrift kept the Cactus Air Force busy, fighting off the lunchtime air raids and blitzing suspected Japanese strong-points on the island. Although his fliers weren't trained in night fighting, Charlie Fike had them line the strip with cut-down oil drums, set them alight, and actually make a night attack.

Before they took off, Vandegrift told Fike, "Tell your men to keep an eye out for white streaks in the water. There's something in the sea here with a phosphorescent quality and ships leave shimmering white wakes. It's a good way to spot the Tokyo Express at night."

"Will do, sir."

But Vandegrift knew that constant action and such exploits as rare night attacks were taking a toll. "What's your count today, colonel?"

"Five of the nineteen Wildcats flown in from the *Long Island* have been destroyed," Fike said. "Only eleven can still fly. Just nine of the twelve dive bombers are operable. We did pick up a few orphans from *Enterprise* after the carrier battle, but overall, it's not good."

Yet the picture soon brightened a little. After Fike left, Colonel

Thomas informed Vandegrift that a transport had arrived at Lunga Point, covered by two destroyers, and was unloading.

"Thank you, Jerry. The first new supplies since the invasion. Good news."

Thomas said, "Turner's a screwball but he's got more guts than Fletcher and Ghormley combined." Vice Admiral Ghormley, Commander, South Pacific, who believed Guadalcanal a lost cause, still hadn't visited the island, even though the entire operation was his responsibility.

■

CHAPTER 22

NEXT MORNING, the radio crackled and in came the usual report from an Australian coastwatcher farther up the Slot: the daily air raid was on its way. "We'll launch immediately," Colonel Fike said, and the shrinking Cactus Air Force scrambled once again.

Only Betty bombers and Zero fighters made up this attack force. Commander Kimi Otomo and his handful of remaining dive bombers had the day off.

Before the raid arrived, engineer Stinky Davis and six assistants tramped aboard the transport along with the unloading parties. Davis had been trying to bridge the Lunga west of the airfield but didn't have enough lumber.

The enemy planes arrived and the ship got underway, zig-zagging evasively. The crew raced to battle stations. During the commotion, Tech Sergeant Davis roamed below decks with his party of Marines and began stacking up the ship's emergency damage-control timbers. When one of his men said, "You really think we oughta be doin' this, Sarge?", Stinky told him not to worry.

The Americans met the attack and shot down three bombers and two Zeros. Despite their losses, the Japanese dropped their bombs precisely, crippling a destroyer in Lunga Roads, flaming a dump of priceless aviation fuel and damaging several planes. Thirty minutes later, the raid was over and the Marines were down to eleven fighters and nine dive bombers.

When the unscathed transport was back in position near the beach, Stinky Davis and his henchmen serenely loaded their contraband timbers, hidden beneath sacks of rice, onto a small barge. They waved their thanks to the ship's crew, and made for the shore.

The looted transport was at sea two days before Stinky Davis' pilferage was discovered. By that time, the precious lumber had reached its destination and was being transformed into a sturdy little bridge. "Much more valuable to the war effort thisaway than it woulda been on that rusty old steamer," Davis said.

Marine officers asked no questions when the needed span appeared. They simply praised Davis, an orphan from Appalachia, for doing the impossible once again.

Commenting on the loss of more planes, correspondent Dick Tregaskis asked General Vandegrift, "Can we hold?"

"We'll defend this airfield till we no longer can. If that happens, we'll take what's left to the hills and fight guerrilla warfare. But you can't write that."

When Tregaskis was out of earshot, Vandegrift said to Colonel Twining, "When we landed in China in 1927 old Colonel Miller had me draw up three plans. Two concerned the accomplishment of our mission, the third a withdrawal from Tientsin in case we got pushed out. Bill, draw up a plan for going guerrilla. In complete secrecy."

Twining would do that, of course, but the look on his face said he didn't like it. He probably thought Vandegrift shouldn't consider, even for a moment, the possibility of losing the airfield. Too bad, the general thought. If it comes to that, we have to be ready.

Kenny and his squad trudged along. Captain Brush had ordered Able Company to set up a new bivouac on the west side of the ridge, just above a ravine leading down into the jungle. He said they were filling one of the gaps in the ridge the Raiders and Paramarines couldn't cover.

Digging their new foxholes was a two-man job because half the men had small picks, the other half shovels, World War I issue. "I hear the Army's got those new multipurpose entrenching tools," said Connie Keugeman. "Wouldn't you think the War Department's poor cousins on Guadalcanal could get some?"

Kenny became aware of something. During the big fight at Alligator Creek, and out on patrol, too, his buddies had the eyes of wild animals: alert, intent and cruel. But in bivouac, they were flat and vacant, staring into infinity. Reflecting what? Maybe a sickness in the soul. Maybe they were gazing at their own deaths, or at the screwed-up heads they'd have when all this slaughter was over.

Only Plunkett seemed immune to the long-stare phenomenon. There he was now, pointing to a low spot off to their right. "Nielsen, we gotta be sure an' cover that ground there."

"Right," Kenny said. "The Japs might try to come through that swale."

"Swale? There you go again with them four-bit words."

Before the holes were finished, it started to rain.

"I hate this fucking place," Des Sweeney said. "I don't even know what the hell Guadalcanal means."

"Swampy channel," Skinny Wade said, looking up from the letter he was writing. "It was named by a 16th century Spanish explorer."

"Smelly-ass water," Sweeney said, "that's what he meant."

"Yeah, could be. This explorer was looking for King Solomon's mines. He never found them, but that's how these islands got their name."

Sweeney frowned. "Well, la de da, big college boy. I still hate the fucking place."

Hoagy Carmichael had been cutting on a coconut with his knife. "Ah, take away the rain, the mosquitoes, the heat and the disease," Carmichael said, "and it's not bad at all. South Carolina with Japs."

"Know what I like about the place?" It was Connie Keugeman. "You don't have to spit-shine any damn shoes."

Skinny Wade used his poncho to shelter the letter he was writing. Envy pinched at Kenny's heart as he watched Wade scribbling away to his fiancée back in Dearborn, a wistful smile on his face. Kenny longed to have someone to write to. Jacqueline

Nordquist, his old high school girlfriend, who'd moved to Chicago and right out of his life--what was she doing now? He wished he knew. Married, probably.

He didn't feel like writing to his brother or his father. Wouldn't be the same. Hell, not just write to a woman, he wanted to talk with one, confide in her about his hopes and fears, and about some of the incredible experiences he'd had out here. Wanted her arms wrapped around him. Some serious spooning and kissing. And even . . . well, better not think about *that*. He'd drive himself nuts.

Later that day, when the rain stopped, Kenny and Plunkett hiked down to the Lunga. "This is just like the swimming hole back home," Kenny said as they stripped bare and dived into the river. "Makes me forget about the war for awhile."

They'd reached a wide spot in the river where a fallen tree jutted forty yards into the stream, forming a deep lagoon. Someone had put up a diving board. Marines from various outfits were swimming, splashing about, even washing their clothes. Stinky Davis had built a crude purification station on the opposite bank to provide the division's drinking water.

Kenny dived in, went deep, and for a brief moment had the bizarre thought that maybe he could just rest on the bottom for awhile and be cleansed of all this horrible war-slaughter business. Weird. It passed in a flash and he popped back to the surface.

Now clean and refreshed for once, he perched himself beside Plunkett on a large boulder and let the sun do the work of towels. Plunkett sucked on a Chesterfield. "Look at that old Injun go. He's quite a sight."

"Yeah, 'Trees is a regular fish," Kenny said, looking at Billy Ninetrees. "Started swimming in the Arkansas River before he could walk. . . . Hey Plunk, I saw a tremendous sight over at Kukum this morning. The air raid showed up when I was checking the news board. I ducked into a slit trench and watched the fight. The Japs were trying to hit one of our transports. Our flyboys were giving 'em hell. Dogfights all over the place, right over Henderson, Kukum and the water, mostly the water. One of our Wildcats got hit and the pilot parachuted into the sea."

"They ever hit the transport?"

"Nope, some close splashes, but they never hit her. Two of our planes went down and maybe five of theirs. Anyway, this Navy pilot is floating around out there in his Mae West, enjoying the show, less than half a mile offshore. When the raid's over, the transport stops zigzagging in the sound and heads back to the pier. About the same time one of our small boats goes out to rescue the flier. The boat isn't a hundred ·yards offshore when a Jap sub surfaces."

"They got recon subs out there all the time," Plunkett said, "pickin' up Jap pilots and sendin' dope back to Rabaul."

Kenny took a sip of water from his aluminum canteen and made a face. "This sub's about as close to our flyboy as the small boat is. The topside hatch opens and out pop these sailors. One heads for the deck gun and the others are carrying rifles. Hell of a sight, Plunk. They start taking potshots at our flier. Well, small-arms fire opens up from the beach and the rescue boat both, plus some .50 caliber from the after deck of the transport. Stuff is poppin' all around this sub so they hustle back inside, button up and take her down. All this happens in two, three minutes, then the boat picks up the flier and brings him back to the beach. Didn't seem to be hurt a bit."

"Great little sideshow, Kenny. What I can't figure is why the sub didn't put a fish into the side of that transport instead of coming up for a surface shot. Stupid, if you ask me."

"Maybe he was out of torpedoes."

"Guy's gotta be crazy to sign up for submarines," Plunkett said. "A sub ain't nothin' but a large pipe. Go to sea in a sealed-up steel coffin? No thank you."

"At least they're not contending with mud, mosquitoes, snakes and three inches of rain a day. . . . You know, Plunk, I just thought of something. A lot of fliers are going down in the ocean in this war and a trained pilot is a hot commodity. How do we rescue 'em?

Small craft or subs or maybe a PBY. Slow. Every one of those methods is slow. I saw an autogiro one time at the Knox County Fair. Damndest flying machine you ever saw. It took off straight up, hovered stationary for awhile, then did all kinds of stunts a regular airplane couldn't do. And it doesn't need a runway. That autogiro's got real possibilities."

"Helicopter," Plunkett said.

"What?"

"The word is helicopter now, Kenny. They don't use autogiros no more." Plunkett put another cigarette in his mouth and offered the pack to Kenny, who waved him off.

"Okay, helicopter. Here's what I'm getting at: rescue at sea. We build those birds by the hundreds, put 'em on everything of destroyer size and larger, and on island bases like here. They could pluck flyboys out of the water pretty as you please. Just hover there and drop the guy a line or a rope ladder."

"Might have something there, Kenny, if those things get perfected."

"Sure, and they could do all kinds of other jobs, like flying recon and pulling wounded outta the jungle."

"Now there's an idea. If those things only need a small clearing to land, they could evac the wounded, get 'em to the field hospital fast, and we wouldn't have to lug the poor bastards. But them things is still experimental. Wonder how long till they're perfected."

"I like autogiro," Kenny said. "Got a better ring to it than helicopter." Then he trembled with a malaria chill. "Ah, damn."

Red Mike Edson had placed his Raiders on the ridge, too. Since they'd had a tough fight on Tulagi and were now positioned well south of the airfield, the Raiders assumed it was to rest. But when the Tokyo Express came down the Slot that night and began shelling, the ships hammered the ridge instead of Henderson Field. Colonel Edson figured that his movement to the ridge must have been reported by a Japanese recon man aboard one of the bombers in the noon air raid.

The barrage was heavier than usual. The Raiders, as well as the 5th Regiment's Able Company, hunkered in their dugouts, another night's sleep messed up.

"Some damn rest area," a sergeant griped to Edson. The Raiders did things like that. They didn't salute much or say "sir," either. "And hey, skipper, we're hungry."

"You want food?" The colonel grinned fiendishly. "There's plenty on this island. The Japs have it. All you have to do is take it." A five-inch shell streaked in and exploded in the vicinity but Edson, standing upright, didn't so much as crouch.

Writing to Mildred always put Vandegrift in an exalted mood. In fact, the first movement of Mendelssohn's Fourth Symphony had been running through his mind as he wrote. The expressive strings of the German composer's "Italian Symphony" always moved him. He supposed it wasn't unpatriotic to have an occasional kind thought about Germans and Italians.

"My Dearest Mildred,

"You wouldn't know the old man. After a month of climbing up and down cargo nets on the McCawley and another month of hiking around this island in the heat, not eating much, I look rather lean and tough. The football knee bothered me the first few days here, but it's been okay lately.

"Our men are enduring great hardships but doing so with much fortitude. A third of them have malaria and many have dysentery. This island is aswarm with noxious insects and parasites. While officially this is Operation Watchtower, several officers have rechristened it Operation Pestilence. I'll find it hard to forgive the Japanese for occupying it in the first place, thus forcing us to come. But you mustn't worry about the old boy, I dutifully sleep beneath my mosquito net every night and my aides make sure I swab on every insect repellent we have, not to mention some dubious native remedies, all over my face and arms.

"My engineers have completed new quarters for me, and I've

turned the Pagoda over to Air Group 23. It will make an ideal CP for them as it's near the airstrip. My new building is well hidden at the edge of the jungle, three feet up on stilts to keep out the bugs and snakes (we hope). The sides are covered with canvas which can be opened when it's hot (when is it not?). The rain sounds pleasant on the overhead (Japanese wood) and it rains at least twice a day. But it's quite comfortable, all in all, with plenty of wicker furniture kindly left for me by the enemy. Sometimes I feel like Robinson Crusoe.

"The boys hope to have a kerosene-operated Japanese icebox running by the end of the week, and they've even rigged up an outdoor shower of sorts. I pull a lanyard and water is released from a drum. The water temperature is about right at 0900. By afternoon, it's scalding.

"We are still very short of everything and the major crisis of the campaign is just ahead. My Vandegut tells me so. Our perimeter is as sturdy as we can make it, but our little friends have the rest of the island and are situated on all sides of us. They will come soon. A major battle is certain. But I don't mean to sound alarmist. I am fully convinced that your old fellow will get through this and return to you as the same cranky old Marine you know so well.

"Knowing you're with me in spirit, as you always have been through so much over the long years, is a great sustaining joy to me. Your letters mean so very much.

"With all my love,
Archie"

He screwed the cap on his fountain pen and put it down, but the music continued. It wasn't in his head after all, it was in his ears. Someone out in the jungle was whistling the first movement of that Mendelssohn symphony in perfect *allegro vivace*. Now who in the world could be doing that on this odious island?

∎

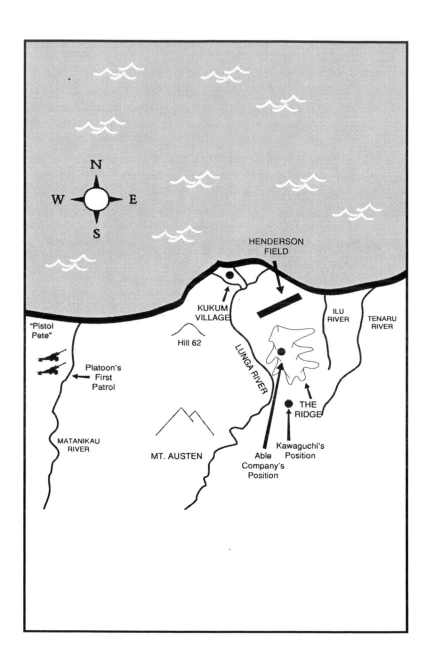

CHAPTER 23

BY LATE MORNING, General Kawaguchi and his outfit reached their destination, a wooded hillside hidden by a canopy of rainforest, three miles south of the Marines' airfield.

Orderlies set up folding camp stools in a clearing for Kawaguchi and his officers. Chief of Staff Suzuki approached.

"*Kakka-dono* (your excellency), one of our patrols has captured a document that shows the enemy is calling this campaign Operation Shoestring."

"I assume that means they are under-supplied," Kawaguchi said. "If this is Operation Shoestring for them, it is Operation Silk Thread for us. They have much more of everything than we do."

Nearby, a lieutenant said, "Marine, you die. Marine, you die," reciting the line he'd been taught. Suzuki posted sentries and the other officers dropped into welcome sleep.

Kenny's squad was responsible for the ground in front of it and the ravine to its right. Kenny explored the terrain for a spot to place a Browning medium machine gun and found the perfect spot for his fire team fifty yards down the gulch, sheltered by trees and rocks, and with a commanding field of fire. The position would be damned hard to see, plus it would have enfilade on anyone coming up that gulch. "Baptist, Keugeman, give me a hand with the gun here. Get some ammo belts. Be careful now." They quietly carried the gun down to the spot Kenny had picked.

On the ridge, the rest of the men were stringing barbed wire in front of their position. There was only enough for two strands but it was better than none. To the left of A Company, the Raider battalion also was putting up wire and beyond that, even farther left, so were the Parachutists.

Kenny heard a sunburned, half-naked Raider yell out, "Think you little old reg'lars can hold that line, or you gonna need some he'p from the Raiders?"

"You candy-asses take care of your sector if you can," Plunkett shouted back. "We'll cover ours. If *you* need some help, just holler and we'll bail *you* out."

"Come over here and say that, fatso." Kenny knew the massive Plunkett was not fat. With the heat and short rations, no Marine on the Canal was.

"Knock it off," said Rusty Gates. "Save it for the enemy."

"Yeah," said Scupper Harris, fondling his jar of morbid souvenirs.

In the midst of all this preparation for battle, Plunkett, a Carolinian who knew his tobacco, suddenly detected an unmistakable scent. His head swivelled. "Hey, that's a cigar, a good cigar. Who the hell's got a cee-gar?"

The blue cloud of smoke rising from Skinny Wade was his answer.

"Wade, where the hell'd you get that stogie?"

"Liberated it from the flyboys down at the Pagoda."

"Why the hell didn't you liberate two? Didn't I bring you up right?"

"A woman's just a woman, but a good cigar is a smoke," said Wade. Who was he quoting? Kenny wondered. Kipling?

A lieutenant named Nakayama led the patrol General Kawaguchi had sent in search of the western prong of the attack, Colonel Oka's detail. The patrol ran out of food, water, stamina, almost everything. Cutting across the tip of the ridge below the airfield, Nakayama and his three men actually penetrated the American lines before angling northwest in the direction of the Matanikau River. They almost drowned fording the Lunga, which flowed past the field only a few hundred yards downstream.

"Airplane engines," said Nakayama, and they dropped in tall

grass, wet and weary, realizing they must be very close to the field. To their right, American voices came from a V-shaped ravine that led up to the ridge. Nakayama heard, "Baptist, get some ammo belts. Be careful now," but he didn't understand English; it was just gibberish. He resisted the temptation to fire on these Yankees, and signaled his companions to lie low. Their mission was to find Oka. Besides, they were too tired to be effective. Thus Kenny Nielsen was spared a sniper attack.

When the voices disappeared and they felt a little rested, Nakayama led them on. On a small hill near the sea, partially stripped of trees by bomb blasts, he discovered a shell crater that had been used as a foxhole. He found empty ammunition boxes and, the Sun God be blessed, some unopened rations. What kind of soldiers could be so wasteful?

The four squatted in the hole and feasted on tinned ham and beef stew. "Even uncooked, this is splendid," Nakayama said.

One of his men passed gas and yelled, "Smell my fart, American." It was amazing how much better the purloined meal made them feel.

Alone in her room on Espiritu Santo, Claudia Chase examined her feelings. She wanted to be normal. Wanted to stop thinking of men as the enemy. To be able to talk with a man, comfortably, without the cold fist of fear cramping up her insides. She also wanted to be able to forget her mother, just forget her. But her thoughts went back to that weak woman who was always hiding in the Bible. Her mom never really worked at being a mother, and she never stood up to Claudia's father, the traveling salesman. Mom's lord was Jesus; Dad's was Jim Beam.

As a child, Claudia got good grades and had a great curiosity, but her mother couldn't be bothered with her questions. "Not now, dear, can't you see I'm busy with the pies?" Claudia couldn't talk about much of anything with her, except the Bible. An avid churchgoer, Mrs. Chase believed in an avenging God. If she fervently obeyed all His laws, she would get into heaven. That was more important than dealing with mere mortals, even her own daughter.

Just once Claudia had made an effort to talk with her mother about the terrible crushing episode with Lloyd.

"Mom, there's . . . there's something I need to . . . need to talk with you about."

"That Floyd fellow?"

"Lloyd, Mom, Lloyd." Tears built in Claudia's eyes. Mom didn't even know his name.

"Not now dear."

"Please, Mom."

Whack. Her mother slapped her. This was nothing new. Claudia cringed, her cheek burning.

"I said not *now.* I'm in the middle of my Bible study."

Claudia ran to her room.

Her mother often struck Claudia when she troubled her. Her attitude was that if she heard nothing bad, nothing bad had happened. A nice, neat, chickenshit way to avoid life's accountabilities.

The memories were still fresh and painful, here on this island half a world away from Ohio. Tears blurred her vision of the filigreed wallpaper of her room. But I needed you, Mom. I needed you so badly. I want to be normal. Please, God, I want to be like the other girls.

One of Colonel Twining's radio operators entered the command post that night and approached Vandegrift. "Sir, I've just decoded a radio message from Admiral Turner at Nouméa."

Vandegrift was glad for the interruption. Martin Clemens had been talking his ear off. He seized the message.

"Merry Christmas, Archie. Transport *William Ward Burroughs* at sea with supplies, provisions. Will arrive yours tomorrow A.M. Eat hearty."

"At least someone down there cares about our plight. Sergeant, send this reply: 'Many thanks from friend in need. Our air will keep enemy away. Entire force here grateful'."

He turned to the Cambridge man, who'd been obviously desperate for some Caucasian conversation. Clemens had kept the HQ staff up for hours, his glass never empty. Was there no end to the Scotsman's stories?

"I hate to be a poor host, Clemens," Vandegrift said, "but I've got to turn in. You've depleted my stock of bourbon considerably. I do appreciate all you've done for us out there in the bush, but now good night to you."

Clemens nodded dolefully. As Vandegrift left, he turned toward Twining and chief of staff Thomas. "Perhaps you chaps--"

"Sack time for me, too," Thomas said, getting up and capping a near-empty bottle. Twining was already out the door.

At Truk Island, Admiral Yamamoto's chief of staff said, "The task force has embarked for Guadalcanal, sir, and will arrive on schedule."

"Thank you, Ugaki."

From a shady ridge west of the field, through his binoculars, Lieutenant Nakayama sighted a party of soldiers a mile away, crossing a stream. Small men in fawn fatigues with World War I-style puttees swaddling their calves. He'd found Oka's detail at last.

Half an hour later he met Oka's advance patrol. "*Yama*," he said, and was answered with "*Kawa*." Mountain and River, the password and countersign.

When Nakayama appeared before Oka, it was impossible to say who was the worse for wear. Their uniforms were in rags and the puttees wouldn't stay wrapped on their thin legs. They were between the Matanikau and the airfield's western perimeter. Oka gave the four men water, heard the battle plan, and asked about the terrain ahead. "I will be in position in one more day," Oka said. "Let us die together for Japan."

* * *

Kimi Otomo was falling through space, surrounded by flames eating at his flesh with unbearable heat. The wings of his dive bomber were bent, broken, useless. The noise the plunging craft gave off as it sliced through the air was a shrill, whining, wild-animal scream, much worse than the whistling sound he knew diving planes to make.

Through the flames he saw the face of his wife Kaneko, serene at first, then laughing, mocking, seemingly saying he had made a terrible botch of things. Then another face, that of the stern intelligence officer at Rabaul. It was a cold, brittle mask of disapproval. "You have failed the Emperor. You have failed the Emperor. You have failed---." The fall continued and so did the terrible inferno, scorching his feeble flesh. The flames were not yellow, but purple and green. How could this go on so long? Was there no ocean below in which to plunge and end it all?

Then he awoke. Sweat soaked his sleeping mat. Heavy rain drummed on the barracks roof and it took Otomo a moment to realize he was at Rabaul, the nightmare had been so real. The part about his wife taunting him for his weakness, so unlike her, was especially troubling, even more so than failing the Emperor.

Otomo thanked the gods that it had only been a dream.

The *William Ward Burroughs* arrived at the mouth of the Lunga River the next morning, accompanied by a pair of destroyers, and began unloading. Vandegrift knew the mechanics and spare parts it carried would be a Godsend for his fliers, whose planes needed lots of attention. After two weeks of constant operation in the dust and mud it would be dangerous to go aloft in them even if there hadn't been a war on. Desperately cannibalizing parts from damaged planes, the Cactus Air Force was down to five working fighter planes.

Vandegrift was happy to learn the new supplies included a radar set, which would give extra warning of air raids, on top of what the Australian coastwatchers provided.

* * *

The plan had seemed so good to General Kawaguchi when he'd devised it in the comfort of an office at Rabaul, beneath a cooling overhead fan. But the awful reality of the sodden jungle was something altogether different.

"If Hyakutake and Yamamoto could only know what we've gone through to get here and the terrible challenge that lies ahead," Kawaguchi told operations officer Suzuki at the jumping-off point. "We have had such difficulty contacting both Oka and Yamamoto. It is essential that the attack be coordinated from all sides. The response from Oka was so vague. He sounded exhausted--no doubt he was--and was evasive about the number of men still available to him. He left Shortland with approximately a full regiment. I should not have allowed him to use Ant Patrol. I should have stood firm for destroyers. . . . Now, please tell me again what Yamamoto said."

"He said his ships would attack on schedule, your excellency, and give the enemy a murderous pounding."

"Then he will. Yamamoto's gunnery men are the best night marksmen in the world. Summon the company and platoon commanders. I wish to make patrol assignments to probe the enemy positions."

■

CHAPTER 24

FOR KENNY, September 12, 1942 dawned much like any other day on Guadalcanal. Instead of roosters as back home, screaming cockatoos woke the Marines, who fussed about their foxholes, making coffee, shaving, cussing. They never got more than three or four hours' sleep at a time, often less--interrupted by the Tokyo Express, Washing Machine Charlie, Pistol Pete, the air raids. It showed in their dirty, emaciated faces from which dull eyes peered expressionless from dark, sunken sockets, and in their lethargy when not on patrol or under fire. They still laughed, joked, gambled, smoked, lied about girls, but not with the enthusiasm of a month ago.

But in mid-morning they snapped to alertness when a series of firefights broke out on the southern edge of the ridge.

"Jap patrols, feelin' out our lines," Plunkett said. "Somewhere out in front of the Raiders. They can handle it. Just stay in this here sector, boys. The big push'll come later, prob'ly tonight. Them Japs love their night attacks."

One enemy unit broke through on the far left, too far over for Able Company to be called in. Later the scuttlebutt was fairly accurate: "They surrounded a couple of our squads and cut their communications, but we held. It was a bitch of a fight, but not the big attack."

The air raid came early that day. It wasn't shaping up to be a normal day on Guadalcanal at all.

Twin-engine Bettys and four Val dive bombers appeared over Henderson Field before 11 a.m. Kenny counted only five Marine fighters going up to contest them. He and his buddies watched the show from their holes, a steel helmet on every head because the sky began raining hot shell casings.

"They call themselves the Cactus Air Force," said Skinny Wade, "but it ought to be the Hiram Walker Air Force. I hear those flyboys have a lot of hooch down there."

"Look, we got one of the yellow bastards," cried Scupper Harris. A Betty trailed a comet of fire from one of its engines. "This is swell, better than the movies."

The plane lost altitude and three black specks tumbled into the sky, parachutes blossoming above them after a few seconds. The plane jerked sharply to the right and plunged into the jungle near Mount Austen. The spectators saw the explosion and the first greasy black smoke before hearing the rumble of the crash. The three fliers floated down to the green hills beyond the Marines' perimeter. "Hope the bastards hang themselves in the vines," said Harris.

"Hey, Sweeney," said Del Cranker, "why'n't we organize a little raid of our own and liberate some of that booze? Like durin' tomorrow's raid."

"Now you're talkin'."

"We'll get down there around eleven-hundred. When the attack comes an' our planes go up, we just walk in like we own the place an' fill up a seabag with hooch. Ever'body'll be in the trenches or else shootin' at the Japs."

"What if they post a guard, Cranker?"

"Create a diversion. Set off a grenade outside their hut."

"How about tradin'? Be a lot safer. Three bottles for a Samurai sword, two bottles for a battle flag. We got lots of doohickeys those flyboys would like."

"Nah, let's steal the stuff."

Kimi Otomo made his dive, the three other bombers trailing behind him. He picked out a shack near the east end of the runway, partially sheltered by trees. The tiny building grew rapidly in his cross-hairs as the plane shrieked earthward. G-forces hugged him. The flicking tongues of tracers sought the plane, but Otomo felt this was a good attack run. He pulled the release handle at the proper instant and the bomb began its short freefall. He tugged the stick back to level off. Camera at the ready, Takai Asakawa recorded the explosion.

Otomo pulled out across the beach and began climbing above Sealark Channel, hoping the building he'd bombed was the radio hut. It would be nice to knock Guadalcanal off the air. He looked back, pleased to see his three squadron mates had survived and were still in formation. Although he'd taken off from Rabaul, Otomo headed for a new airstrip just completed at Buin on the southern tip of Bougainville Island. Until the last Type 99 was inoperable, the remnant of his squadron would now operate from there, much closer to the enemy.

Not long after the raid, a C-47 Dakota landed and Vandegrift watched Admiral Turner climb down. Once inside the general's new command post, Kelly Turner produced a bottle of scotch and poured for the two of them and chief of staff Jerry Thomas.

Vandegrift had been sparring with Terrible Turner, nominally his superior, since before the invasion. He was tired of it. So what if Turner was one of the early advocates of amphibious warfare? He knew little about strategies and tactics on land, but that never stopped him from telling Vandegrift how to fight his campaign.

"Kelly, we just came through a heck of an air attack."

"That may have just been the preliminaries, Archie. You'll be taking fire again before you know it. Our code-breakers say Yamamoto is planning a major attack, and he'll use the Combined Fleet. He's pulling out all the stops to try and chase you off this rock."

"I didn't know about their navy, Kelly, but the rest of it jibes. Our aerial patrols have sighted enemy troops on all sides of us, but we're wired up tight and ready. Late yesterday our boys reported a larger than usual number of ships heading down from Rabaul so we're expecting a pretty good Tokyo Express tonight."

"There's worse." Turner handed Vandegrift a Navy communications form from ComSoPac Ghormley. The general read what he'd just been told about the enemy fleet. He continued on.

"Because of my shortage of ships and airplanes, and lack of supply, as well as enemy strength in the area, the Navy can no longer support the Guadalcanal operation."

The words stung. Vandegrift read it a second time. *"The Navy can no longer support the Guadalcanal operation."* The lines around his eyes looked like canyons.

"Ghormley's decision, not mine," Turner said, refilling Vandegrift's glass. "I'll get the 7th Marines here. I think I can still do that." The 7th Regiment of the 1st Marine Division was somewhere between the Panama Canal and Espiritu Santo, but it damn sure wasn't where it was needed: on Guadalcanal. It had become known as The Missing Regiment.

"But after that, well, we'll still get some items through their blockade by air and submarine but nothing in quantity. You'll have to hold with what you've got for--"

"For how long?"

"An indeterminate time, Archie."

Never one to criticize a fellow officer, Vandegrift remembered Ghormley's early doubts about this whole operation. "I don't see how we can land at all," gutless Ghormley had said before the invasion, "and I am going to take it up with General MacArthur." MacArthur? Why did Ghormley defer to that showboat? Guadalcanal was outside his Southwest Pacific Theater.

Jerry Thomas, who called 'em as he saw 'em, had often told Vandegrift that Ghormley was burned out. He said ComSoPac--who headquartered aboard the *Argonne* anchored off New Caledonia rather than ashore among the Free French--was "a broken reed."

America's first offensive of the war, and Vandegrift was being deserted. The general was sorely tempted to go over Ghormley's head straight to Admiral Nimitz, the Commander in Chief, Pacific.

After the best lunch Butch Morgan could produce, they toured the perimeter by jeep. All afternoon, Turner kept trying to sell Vandegrift on a scheme of landing the 7th Marines in small pockets all along the island's coastline, to obstruct further Japanese landings.

Depressed by the message from Ghormley, Vandegrift told himself he wouldn't take any more of Turner's meddling. "No!" he declared. "I won't scatter my forces piecemeal. I will concentrate them here. My mission is to check Japan's drive to the south. Air supremacy in the southern Solomons accomplishes that, preserves Australia, and positions us for counterattack. Strategically, this airfield *is* the island."

Terrible Turner's eyes flared beneath his bushy black brows, but he said nothing.

In late afternoon, another patrol flier came in and reported the central Solomons alive with enemy ships. He had counted a cruiser and four destroyers, plus many other vessels too far in the distance to be identified.

On hearing the scouting report, Vandegrift told his operations officer, "Disperse the planes as well as you can. Don't give them any easy targets." He shook his head. "My God, I wish we had some hangars or hard shelters of some kind for those birds."

From his concealed hillside camp beyond the ridge, Kawaguchi had been busy sending messages, meeting with officers, marking up his maps. He shared his last tin of sardines with chief of staff Suzuki, drank a little tea, then sat cross-legged and closed his eyes in meditation for ten minutes. The encampment was crowded but no one disturbed him. Kawaguchi dreamily thought of home and his wife, of his country and his duty, and then he actually fell into slumber for a short while. For a few seconds he dreamed of his garden, an immaculate combination of dwarf trees and shrubs, stone lanterns, carefully placed rocks, and a fish pond spanned by a tiny wooden footbridge. Afterward, he arose wistfully, yawned, stretched, and checked his wristwatch.

"No matter what the manual says," he told Suzuki, "it is extremely difficult to take an enemy position by night attack. There were a couple of such victories on a small scale in our war with Russia, but if we succeed here we will become a wonder in the annals of military history." Then Kawaguchi stopped and looked embarrassed. He'd said too much.

Nearby, the young lieutenants who would lead the night attack were taping white strips of cloth to each other's backs in large X's so the men following behind could see them.

"Summon the commanders," Kawaguchi said. "We will go over the maps and the plan of attack one final time. Suzuki-san, if we do not meet again afterward, I want you to know you have been a good and loyal officer."

"Thank you, excellency." Suzuki bowed, knowing those words translated to: "We are both likely to die."

Before nightfall, Kenny sent three men down to the .30-caliber machine gun he'd sited in the ravine, relieving the two who'd spent the afternoon there. He hadn't expected trouble by daylight but at night he wanted one man to fire, one to feed the belt, and one to serve as lookout. On paper, a fire team should be four men, but Kenny's squad was too understrength for that. He ordered a line for a sound-operated telephone laid so he could have direct communication with his gunners.

Upon becoming a squad leader, Kenny used his executive powers and made himself the BAR man. He'd always wanted something that fired faster than his model 1903 Springfield and the answer was taking over the squad's Browning Automatic Rifle. Some of these Marines' fathers had used the Springfield rifle at Belleau Wood and Haiti. Kenny soon learned how much heavier a BAR was than a Springfield.

He drank some foul-tasting black coffee from his aluminum cup and pried meat from a coconut bartered from an engineer in exchange for a Japanese forage cap. Then an old familiar sound ratcheted down from the darkening sky.

"Washing Machine Charlie's early tonight," he said. "It's only a little after dusk. Can't be much more than, what, nineteen-hundred? What's it mean?"

Again the eerie green flare. Kenny hated those flares. They

seemed to strip him naked, pinpointed before the whole enemy air force. Charlie dropped a lone bomb. Before long, Charlie's cousin, "Louie the Louse," showed up. At 10 o'clock another green flare lit up the terrain and the Tokyo Express played its first thunderous notes. Sounded like 8-inch cruiser guns and smaller stuff from destroyers. They played like cruel tympanies on the ridge. Like the daytime planes from Rabaul, they targeted the ridge instead of Henderson Field. The Japs must have acquired good dope on the Marines' positions and radioed it to Rabaul.

For half an hour the shells rained down as the ships sailed back and forth in Ironbottom Sound.

Kenny could tell by the whistling that this shell would be close. It was, exploding in the center of the ridge. A shower of rocks and mud clods cascaded on his steel helmet, proving its worth. A voice screamed in the darkness. "I'm hit, Jesus God, I'm hit. Can't feel my hand."

"Corpsman. Corpsman," Kenny called out.

The bombardment shifted to the airfield. The Japanese seamen were particularly accurate that night. The SBD squadron's bivouac was hit repeatedly, killing three fliers and wounding two others.

Then the shooting stopped and an abnormal silence fell over the ridge and airfield. The almost constant clamor of bombardment had become second nature. Its sudden absence was unsettling. Quiet as a graveyard. Hundreds of men looked inside themselves and knew they would soon learn what they were really made of.

". . . *Do not fear, or tremble, or be in dread of them,*" John the Baptist was whispering.

Silence crept out of the hills and trees and pressed against Kenny like a bad memory. He couldn't even hear birds or insects. Everything on the island seemed to be waiting for what would happen next.

Then he heard Plunkett say, "There's a shit-load of Japs out there, children."

■

CHAPTER 25

KENNY PEERED OUT from his hole. Somewhere out in the black jungle a voice with a bad accent cried out, "Eleanor Roosevelt eat shit." It came out like "Losa-felt."

"Hirohito eat shit," Del Cranker yelled back.

"Babe Ruth eat shit," answered a voice from the dark.

"Japs," someone shouted.

"No lie?" said Plunkett. "I thought they was friggin' Eye-talians."

Kenny heard Raiders, Parachutists and Marine regulars laugh uneasily. The tension broke, but not their anxiety. A combination of Raiders and the 5th Marines' 1st Battalion, Kenny's outfit, held the western side of the twisting ridge. The bulk of the Raiders covered the center, and the Chutes had the eastern sector.

Even though his eyes were fully acclimated to the dark, Kenny could see almost nothing. He picked up his telephone and spoke softly with Desmond Sweeney, who said, "This ravine's god-damned quiet. Not a fucking thing happening." Sweeney: profane, fearful, tense, alert. Situation normal.

As if waiting for Kenny to finish, a shell whistled in and crashed down on the ridge. More followed, many more. It had to be the Tokyo Express attacking from the north. From the east, beyond the Ilu River, artillery joined in.

From the jungle south of the ridge a red flare arced into the sky and a voice shouted "*Totsugeki*." Charge.

Kenny's new BAR was out in front of his face, its folding bipod supporting the barrel. On one side of him lay John the Baptist, on the other, Hoagy Carmichael. The barbed wire was sixty meters ahead, giving them a good field of fire if anyone reached it. Or worse, got through.

They heard gunfire and shouts off to the left but still saw nothing in their sector.

"Be patient, boys, they'll come to the picnic," Plunkett called out. "No jitterbugging." He meant firing without a target. "And the smoking lamp is out. Light a match now and you screw up your night vision." The big man's voice gave Kenny a little comfort but that old familiar fear still gnawed at his guts.

"Ah, gee, Sarge," Skinny Wade said, "you're no fun."

"War is hell, boys, ain't s'posed to be fun. Don't you go to the movies?"

"I wanna cut off one o' their peckers."

"You do, Harris," said Plunkett, "an' I'll castrate *you*, you fuckin' maniac."

"Will you guys shut your faces?" It was Lieutenant Gates. "Pipe the hell down or we'll never hear the enemy."

Rifle and machine gun fire began crackling. Kenny heard the "womp" of a mortar. The clamor seemed to come from everywhere, but more so on the left.

"Them safeties better be off," Plunkett shouted.

The attack began five hundred yards to the left, in the Raiders' sector.

Moments earlier, their CO, Red Mike Edson, had sent a message to the 11th Marines' artillerymen, giving them coordinates for the ground in front of his troops.

The sky turned bright with flares. Hundreds of Japanese swarmed out of the jungle, scaling the incline on the run.

"Yankee, you die," one of them yelled.

"Wait," a sergeant shouted. "Wait'll they get to the wire." Seconds passed. "Now. Open fire. Now, now."

A tempest of metal whipsawed the Japanese. Many fell but still they came. "Holy God, they're through the wire," someone shouted.

Red Mike ordered a smoke screen. Smoke pots were set off. Soon explosions began reflecting on the man-made fog, and a

Japanese voice yelled, "*Dokugasu! Gasu kougaki*." Gas attack.

Soon the Japs seemed to be swallowing up the whole southern end of the ridge. Edson called up the artillery and the 11th Marines began pounding the preregistered positions in the jungle. "Closer, closer," he cried and gave the gunners new coordinates.

He was speaking with one of his captains by phone when a third voice came on the line. "Our situation here is excellent, Colonel Edson. Thank you, sir." Edson never heard a Raider talk like that. The line must have been cut and tapped into somewhere on the right, meaning that F Company was in danger of being cut off over there and had to be pulled back. With that line out, Edson had a big-voiced sergeant yell at the top of his lungs, "Fox Company, pull back. Red Mike says pull back."

Back at Able Company, Kenny heard a cadenced slapping of gun butts in front of him. Voices chanted, "Marines be dead to-morrow." It was spine-numbing, ungodly. "Marines be dead to-morrow, Marines be dead tomorrow."

"That way lies madness," said Skinny Wade, quoting *King Lear*.

"Shrinks your gonads, don't it?" said Had Plunkett, quoting Had Plunkett.

Then the first of them were in front of Kenny's platoon. A lieutenant carrying a battle flag materialized in Kenny's gunsights. His Browning stitched three rounds into the man's torso. He jerked in a full circle. Spinning away, the enemy officer revealed a peculiar white criss-cross on his back as he went down. Looked like some supernatural message straight from the devil, meant just for Kenny.

Kenny knew he'd squeezed the trigger but it seemed to be someone else, as though he'd divided into two people and was watching from a safe distance as his other self performed. White flame spat from his Browning in staccato bursts. The fright that always gripped that other self beforehand seemed to have burned right out of him once the shooting started.

Other Japanese at the wire now, lots of them. Kneeling, firing, falling dead, cutting the wire, jumping over the wire, falling dead, coming on, coming on. Kenny was too busy firing to see if John the Baptist was doing the same. Bullets buzzed through the night like hornets. Getting hit or not became simply a matter of luck.

"Gimme a clip, gimme a clip. . . God, this barrel's gettin' hot. . . Anybody got a grenade? . . . Holy Mother, look at 'em out there . . . Gimme a clip, gimme a clip."

Kenny knew they'd have to be stopped soon or Henderson Field would be lost.

General Kawaguchi crouched and looked through his glasses. A spectacular sight, shellbursts and flares coloring the sky everywhere in front of him. Between bursts, he heard shouts from the distance, some in Japanese, some in English.

"How are the men doing, Suzuki?" He realized his chief of staff could know little more than he.

"Everyone is fully engaged on this front, excellency. We are getting few reports. The men are too occupied to call in."

"I can see that the attack has begun in the east and that the navy has done its part, but what of Oka? Is Colonel Oka attacking in the west?"

"I do not know, excellency. We've heard nothing from that sector."

Kawaguchi put his glasses down and lit a cigarette, cupping his hands to shield the match. "I heard the taunts. Some of our men believe that denigrating their baseball hero, *Bebi Rusu*, is the ultimate insult." He exhaled cigarette smoke. "We must have broken through by now."

"We're pulling back," Plunkett shouted over to Kenny. "Japs broke through in Edson's front. Gotta fall back or we'll get cut off."

"I knew those candy-ass Raiders couldn't do the job."

"Shut up, Harris. Kenny, you hear?"

"I hear you, Plunk."

"The squad on your left will pull back first. You cover 'em. Then haul butt behind 'em. Back a hunnerd an' fifty meters. Got it?"

They shouted back and forth under fire.

"Yeah, but I got a machine gun and two rifles down the slope. I gotta pull 'em out."

"Then move your ass, man. We gotta retrograde."

Kenny had finished a clip, reloaded, and got off four more BAR rounds while hollering with Plunkett. He picked up his phone. Nothing. "Sweeney, do you read me? Sweeney?" Still nothing.

"Dead. Line's been cut. Baptist, go down there and pull that fire team outta there. Bap?"

"Right now, Sarge," he said.

But the Baptist sat still as a rock for another five seconds while bullets whined through the air, as if thinking about it. Or praying. Then he was up and running in a zigzag course, bent at the waist. Kenny intermittently saw him in the flickering light of mortar and grenade bursts, framed each time in a different pose, giving him a comic, silent-movies look.

The Baptist's heart pounded as he bolted into the throat of the ravine. He heard the stutter of the machine gun and knew his buddies hadn't been overrun. Then he stumbled in a crater that hadn't been there in the afternoon. He lay stunned for a moment, then checked himself for injuries. Finding none, his hand grasped a shredded piece of telephone cord on the side of the hole. That explained the dead line.

The machine gun fell silent. "Skinny, Sweeney, Cranker, we're pulling out. Hear me?"

"Who the fuck is that?"

"McKenna, you clowns. Disengage. We're pulling back. Get the heck up here."

Machine gunner Del Cranker and the two riflemen crept up to the Baptist.

"Seen many Japs?" the Baptist asked.

"No, asshole, we been dancin' 'round the maypole," Cranker snapped. "Jesus, we been through hell. Musta knocked off twenty, thirty goons."

Skinny Wade said, "Used up forty belts of .30-caliber. Ran out of water to cool the barrel. Took turns pissing on it. Sure glad to get outta this godawful gully."

"Go on ahead," said the Baptist. "I'll cover you." As the three passed, he faced down the slope away from them, his bayoneted rifle held ready. A starshell burst overhead, bathing the gulch in a flash of light. The Baptist saw a pile of enemy soldiers beyond where the machine gun had been placed. They lay sprawled in all manner of awkward death. Must have been mowed down like wheat.

Empty shell casings crunching underfoot, the Baptist turned to go up the hill. He caught movement from the corner of his eye. He wheeled back around. Before his unbelieving eyes one of the enemy had risen up and was approaching. Fast.

All the Baptist had to do was pull the trigger. He didn't. Couldn't. That conscience-box of his was flexing its muscles again. Or did the ghostly enemy soldier have a spell over him? On he came. In the eerie light, the man's eyes were black holes. He wore a forage cap, no helmet. The Baptist's breath blew hard and frantic. The left side of the Jap was basted with blood but he gripped his rifle, also bayoneted, in his right hand and kept coming, coming, coming. The Baptist remained paralyzed.

Now the Jap was almost too close to be shot. He too seemed to be in a daze. Probably couldn't believe he'd gotten this close to the American without getting blasted. The Jap lunged, his bayonet aimed at the Baptist's chest. At last the Baptist moved. Jerked hard to his right. Because the Jap was shorter and downhill from him, the bayonet hit below its mark, grazing the Baptist's thigh as he dived to the side.

The enemy was beside him, the bayonet already beyond. The Baptist clubbed the top of his head with his rifle butt. It struck hard, sickeningly hard. Must have crushed the skull. The Jap fell on his face. Instinct took charge. The Baptist shot him in the back.

Once. Twice. Then pumped a third round into his head.

He stood there stupefied for two seconds that seemed to take an hour. The poor Jap must have been out of ammo. Then, his thigh dripping blood, the Baptist stumbled up the hill to his squad. What have I done? he thought. Oh, God forgive me, what have I done?

Cranker said, "What happened? What about those shots?"

"Nothing. I stumbled."

"C'mon, no time for talk," Kenny shouted. "We're pulling back."

The Baptist tied his green Marine Corps handkerchief around his thigh and joined the little parade. As they stumbled northward along the ridge, Kenny lifted John's left arm onto his shoulder and helped him walk.

"You got 'em out, Bap. Good work. How'd you get hurt? What happened down there?"

"Nothing, Kenny. I fell and cut my leg, that's all. Stupid mistake."

"What about those shots?"

"What shots? I didn't fire any shots. There's firing all around us. Shots everywhere, Sarge."

Kenny gave him a curious look.

On the extreme left of the ridge, Captain Harry Torgerson's Parachutists were in trouble. The terrain leading to the ridge was easier here. The enemy had pierced his lines in two places. Torgerson, who had been shot in the leg and ass while personally blowing up some Japanese caves on Gavutu, knew if his outfit folded here, the defense would be flanked. The airfield could fall.

The Chutes faced an onslaught. Bullets flew like raindrops in a windstorm. One in four Chutes was hit in the first few minutes.

Private Wendell Pitt had fought as well as any at Tulagi and here, but this was when he reached his limit. He saw the man on the left go down, then the one on the right. A ricochet sang off his helmet. That was it, he'd had his fill of terror, bullets, Japs and blood. Pitt leaped to his feet and ran for the rear.

Thirty yards back, Torgerson blocked his path. "Where the hell you going?"

"Back for more ammo," Pitt lied.

Torgerson grabbed him by the shoulders. Their eyes were inches apart. Pitt's were dull, unfocused in the flickering light.

"It's a pisser, ain't it, Pitt?" Pitt hadn't known that Torgerson even knew his name. "But you got plenty of ammo, man. Gonna let your country down, hey? Gonna let the Japs have the airfield, hey? You want us to lose the airfield, then the island, then New Guinea, then Australia? That what you want, Pitt?"

The staredown lasted another ten seconds that seemed much longer. Then a bullet whined through a tree beside them, amputating a small branch.

Pitt took a deep breath. "Okay sir," he said, and turned back toward his ravaged outfit.

Torgerson followed, calling other Chutes by name. He kicked, shoved, cussed and cajoled them back into the line. He dared them to fight. "You're Marines. You gonna let the Japs whip you?"

In the CP, Admiral Turner said, "Jesus, Archie, hell of a show you put on for a guest."

"It's a big attack, Kelly." Vandegrift and Turner huddled by the field telephone in the command post, following the battle like a football game.

"Can you hold?"

Vandegrift didn't know. "Seems I hear that question every day now. We'll give it the best we've got."

"Archie, I'm ashamed of having to bring that message from Ghormley. I'll do all I can to get you some help."

"The best thing you could do for me would be to expedite shipment of my 7th Marines." The Missing Regiment was still in the Samoas, not on Guadalcanal where he needed it. Needed it badly.

"That'll be tough, with Ghormley looking over my shoulder,

but I'll sure as hell try." A Japanese mortar round exploded close by. Turner ducked. When he sheepishly pulled himself upright, he said, "Just where would you like the 7th landed, Archie?"

Kenny's squad reached its new position. Counting noses, he found everyone there. The only wound was John the Baptist's leg cut. On this night of nights, he was certainly considered an "effective" and would stay with the squad.

The southern spur of the ridge had been lost to the enemy but that wasn't so bad. "The Japs have to cross more open ground to reach us," Kenny said, "and we've got better fields of fire."

Looking left, he saw two wounded members of the next squad being helped to the rear.

"Skinny, I want you on the machine gun this time. Cranker's kinda worn out." Kenny liked Cranker. The farmboy had something of the honesty of the soil in him.

"Hoagy, keep 'em supplied with ammo." It dawned on Kenny that he loved the idea of running a squad in combat. Later he would contemplate the fact that he had just killed three more men. Not now.

"You okay, Bap? Let me see that leg."

"I'm okay, Kenny, leave me alone."

"Goddamn it, let me see it. Hold still." Kenny removed the bloody handkerchief and examined the gash. It was deep but only through flesh, not bone. "Somebody give me a gauze wrap." Kenny bound the wound as tightly as he could. "This'll take some stitches, but not tonight. We need you tonight."

Kenny slapped the Baptist on the back and gave him a wink. In the bad light he doubted if the Baptist caught it.

Suddenly rifles began popping on their right. Three Japanese soldiers charged. "Where the hell did they come from?"

The squad blasted away. The infiltrators crumpled in crazy patterns, brave bodies no match for gunfire.

"Damn fools coulda done a lot more damage by taking cover and sniping," Hoagy Carmichael said. "They got guts but no brains."

Kenny noticed that the Baptist had fired right along with the others. Must have put two or three rounds into the attackers. Kenny thought of winking at him again, but in a flicker of light he caught the torment in his eyes and thought better of it.

Then he saw that Desmond Sweeney wasn't moving. He lay face down behind his rifle in such a way that Kenny knew he would never move again. He crawled over for a closer look and rolled Sweeney over. A bullet had gone straight into his right eye. His face sat frozen in the surprise of death. Kenny felt a surge of nausea, sadness and anger. Sort of like seasickness.

"Aw, son of a bitch," said Connie Keugeman, looking over Kenny's shoulder. "He owed me five bucks."

"Nice epitaph, numbskull."

Then, remembering something from Skinny Wade's *Complete Works of William Shakespeare*, Kenny said, "The valiant never taste of death but once." From *Julius Caesar*, he thought. Seemed right for Sweeney.

He posted lookouts and told the others to dig in. Kenny knew that behind him was a thin line of reserves, and behind them the artillery, then the CP and the airfield. Sweeney would just have to lie here till morning.

And then it *was* morning. John the Baptist lifted his head off his rifle. First light was creeping over the jungle from the east.

"How long've I been out, Sarge?"

"'Bout two hours, Bap."

"You should've woke me."

"No need. We had sentries posted and nobody attacked. You needed some shuteye."

"What happened while I was out?"

"Few sniper attacks. Small pockets of Japs here and there."

"My God, we held, Kenny, we held. We held the airfield."

"Edson says they were just testing. Raiders think the big attack'll come tonight."

The Baptist's shoulders slumped. He seemed to shrink. He and the others were at the end of their endurance. How could they possibly cope with a bigger attack tonight?

■

CHAPTER 26

AS MONDAY DAWNED, General Vandegrift thought his Marines looked like anything but winners. The dirty, exhausted automatons suffered from dysentery, malaria, malnutrition, too much killing and too little sleep. His field hospital was overflowing, and he could expect no more help. He had that in writing.

A few isolated Japanese remained trapped on the ridge where they'd broken through in small spearheads. They sniped awhile during the morning and caused some casualties before being rooted out. But mostly the hideous battlefield belonged to the insects, now swarming over corpses moldering under a sun that had come up like a white blaze, amplifying the smell of butchered flesh.

Seven hundred yards away, Kenny was wishing he had a surgeon's mask; the penetrating smell was that bad. He laughed out loud at the thought that came next. What if they all had them? Might scare the Japs to death, facing hundreds of Marines in face masks.

He sent John the Baptist to the field hospital. The main part of the hospital was intact, but the annex, a canvas shelter, had been hit by the Tokyo Express and ripped into a bloody mess. It was three hours before a surgeon could sew up John the Baptist's leg and his rush job wasn't very neat. He would have a scar but he would live. If he didn't die of infection or disease or gunshot.

After squaring away his squad, Kenny sank against a tree. The horror of the night rushed back. The gunfire, the ghoulish flickers of light from flares and shells. The ghostly enemy running, firing, twisting, falling, ripping apart.

The sounds. My God, the sounds. The noise of small arms fire, grenades and artillery had mixed with human commands and screams of terror to form one loud cacophonous hum, a steady drone of desperation. You soon forgot about this cauldron of sound, but it never drowned out the stark fear that was your constant companion.

The smells. The acrid stench of gunpowder and cordite. The sharp biting smell from hand grenades. What was in those deadly pineapples? TNT, if he remembered right from boot camp. Worst of all, the stench of rotting bodies. He hadn't become aware of that till morning, when the sun started broiling that human debris.

His own performance. He'd led the squad well. He hoped Moon Whitely, wherever he was, would be proud of his replacement. And he hadn't turned coward. Fought as well as anybody. Did his share of killing. Why? To serve the Corps, his country, his flag? Yeah, sure, but mainly not to let down his buddies. Most of all, to save his own skin. Was he ashamed of that? Hell no. He was a killer, a professional killer, and he wanted to stay alive.

The ghastly landscape shimmered. Mirage lakes rippled along the ridge. The forest itself seemed to be in agony, quivering, out of focus, in waves of heat that hurried the process of decay. The vile odor from the bodies was inescapable. Kenny couldn't bear to look at them. Their blood, so vital and red yesterday when they were living, breathing, loyal young men, now was hard, black, used-up stuff like old motor oil. A squadron of vultures circled overhead.

A mile away, General Kawaguchi saw the vultures. Tears moistened his cheeks. He was sickened by the thought that they and the flies and the ants would feast on the remains of Nippon's finest young men. His young men.

Kawaguchi reckoned that he had about 900 effective soldiers left after the survivors of the ridge crawled back to the foothills of Mount Austen. More than 1,200 were dead or badly wounded.

It was apparent that Colonel Oka had never attacked in the

west. Why? What had gone wrong? Kawaguchi knew that his grand plan had failed, that night attack on this scale was impossible, that he would be seriously disgraced within the army.

"Perhaps we cannot win here, but we must die with honor," he told Kai Suzuki. "We must put courage in our stomachs. I will personally lead the men tonight. Instead of attacking the southern end of the ridge we will work our way around to the side. We may yet break through to the airfield, but if not we will punish the enemy before we die."

Colonel Hunt called his gunnery sergeant over and said, "This battle report must get to General Vandegrift right away. It's my assessment of our sector's situation and our head count. Don't send one of the usual runners, Gunny. Use one of our best men." He handed the sergeant a canvas pouch. "Get it to the CP fast."

"Aye, sir." The gunny turned and bellowed, "Plunkett, send me Sergeant Nielsen."

Vandegrift sat in a rattan chair outside the new CP drinking coffee from a delicate Japanese cup, going over the early battle reports. Admiral Turner was nearby, finishing up his reconstituted eggs. Sergeant Major Sheffield Banta, an old hand from the First World War, sat between them typing a report.

Kenny, forty yards away and approaching at triple time, suddenly heard shouts of "banzai" and saw two Japanese soldiers and an officer rush out of the jungle toward the CP, the officer wielding a sword.

Shef Banta calmly drew a bead with his .45 and shot the officer down just as he hurled his sword toward the unarmed Vandegrift.

Kenny whipped his rifle off his shoulder, snapped the safety off, and drilled one of the infiltrators. Then his rifle jammed. He leaped at the last of the Japs. As he made his flying tackle, Banta fired a .45 round that caught the Jap in the head, spraying blood, flecks of bone and brain tissue over Kenny.

Jesus, Kenny thought, pulling himself to his feet, that damn sergeant major could've killed me. He looked down at the fresh corpse, then wiped at the goo on his shirt. He flashed Banta a quick mean look.

"Nice shot, Banta," Vandegrift said. "What's your name, young man?"

Kenny straightened himself and saluted. "Sergeant Nielsen, 1st Battalion, 5th Marines. I have Colonel Hunt's report, sir."

"Thank you, Nielsen, thank you very much. Timely arrival. Write that name down, Banta."

He took the satchel and stared kindly into Kenny's eyes for a moment. Then he calmly raised his cup, took a sip, and returned to his reports.

Kenny knew he was dismissed. He wanted to tell Banta off; he was handling that Jap just fine without the sergeant major taking that stupid potshot. But no, Banta was on the commanding general's staff. He'd have to let it go.

As Kenny picked up his rifle and walked off, Vandegrift continued to scan the reports. He realized that he had won a victory. His weary troops might be too spent to square themselves away with any speed, but it was clear that they'd dealt the enemy some appalling losses. If the Japanese could mount another attack tonight they were supermen indeed.

Besides keeping the ridge, another good thing soon happened, almost unnoticed amid the aftermath of the tempest. Twenty-four Wildcats from *Saratoga* streamed in and landed. Vandegrift knew their big carrier would be out of action for months after being torpedoed, so they were on loan to Cactus.

"A beautiful bonus for our little air fleet," he said.

On his way back, Kenny detoured over to the Lunga and scrubbed some of the blood and gore off his ragged dungarees.

Later, in his bivouac, he shivered with a malaria chill. The attacks seemed to come every three days. He tried to eat something at the field kitchen. Thank God for these cooks, he thought, though he had little appetite. He felt a mixture of satisfaction over leading his squad through the horrendous night and guilt that Desmond Sweeney had been killed. He knew he couldn't have prevented it, that other units had taken heavier losses.

But, holy smoke, maybe he'd just helped to save the general's life. That was something.

Driving over by jeep, Vandegrift showed Kelly Turner the wreckage a cruiser's shell made of the hospital annex. Then the admiral went to the airfield and took his leave on a PBY, more convinced than ever that Guadalcanal needed help.

Vandegrift was glad to see Terrible Turner go. As it turned out, his exit came none too soon. The air raid came in early again, only ten minutes after the PBY took off.

Kimi Otomo knew this one would be a little different. At the raw new airstrip on Bougainville, Otomo was ordered to rendez-vous with the long-range Bettys and Zeros coming down from Rabaul and to land at Guadalcanal if the airfield was in friendly hands. It was supposed to be.

It had rained hard during the night. Otomo's plane splashed and skidded as it struggled to free itself from the muddy strip at Buin. The fourth and last pilot in line couldn't get up enough speed and had to abort. Trying desperately to brake in the slime, he groundlooped. Another dive bomber wrecked!

Otomo led his pitiful group of three planes away from the lumpy green island, beautifully silhouetted against gray-white clouds that towered to nearly 40,000 feet. It took several minutes to locate the formation from Rabaul, but for once fuel wasn't a serious problem. They joined up and completed the run to Guadalcanal.

Otomo's excitement mounted. At last he would land on that cursed field, the American intruders driven into the jungle.

But as he passed over the mouth of the Lunga River

downstream from the airstrip, his heart sank. Familiar black puffs blotched the sky above the field. Marine antiaircraft fire. "No Japanese aviators will land by choice on this island today," he told his gunner. "The Great Master did not will our night attack to succeed."

A flight of P-400s marked with white stars approached. With hand signals, Otomo told the others to climb away from them, up to attack altitude.

On the ground, inertia ruled, despite Red Mike Edson's insistence that the major attack was coming that night. The Marines sluggishly buried their dead, bulldozed dirt on some of the fallen enemy, sought cover when the air raid came over and did so again later when Pistol Pete unlimbered. Walking zombies now, they also repaired the wire where they could and dug in for the night.

Edson knew the lines were pulled considerably back and made tighter. The southern part of the ridge had been forfeited to the enemy and his Marines were uncomfortably close to the airfield, but they had good fields of fire and better internal communications. The artillery's 105-millimeter howitzers were preregistered on the approaches to the line of defense.

Kenny's squad dug in and placed coconut logs in front of the holes. "I'd kill for an orange," Del Cranker said. "A nice, juicy orange."

"We have killed for less," said the Pawnee, Billy Ninetrees, and it stopped conversation dead in its tracks.

When the digging was done and there was time to think, Kenny couldn't conjure a vision of Galesburg or the Blue Goose Tavern in Oquawka, nor could he recite the Cubs' lineup. He scarcely knew his own name. But he did find the strength to welcome John the Baptist back to the squad in late afternoon. His leg, now bandaged and wrapped with tape, had taken twenty stitches.

"Nice going last night, Bap. You were a good Marine. Now grab some sack time."

Kenny was trying to fall asleep in his hole, eyes covered by his helmet liner, mind wrestling with troubling thoughts, when artillery rumbled across the hills from the west. Whatever it was, it came from a sector at least a mile away. Neither Rusty Gates nor Plunkett was barking orders, so Kenny continued to lie immobile, at war with his conscience. Sweeney dead. That big lug who'd once told Plunkett to go shit in his hat. Goddamn it.

In the foothills to the south, General Kawaguchi also heard the firing. Marine howitzers and the chatter of machine gun fire answered it. It could only be one thing: the hapless Oka, attacking at last. Within twenty minutes the gunfire died away. Kawaguchi knew what that meant. The pitiful, uncoordinated attack, nearly a day late, had failed. He was not angry, just sorrowful.

Three hours later, when darkness was complete, Kawaguchi told Suzuki, "Let us go then." Orders were called out and the grimy Japanese soldiers gathered their packs and weapons and formed up.

They crept off the hill and into the jungle valley leading to the ridge. For many, it was like a repeat of a bad dream, only they noticed that the jungle was considerably thinned out from the night before. A few, like Kawaguchi, who hiked along with his men, felt sanctified, believing they were about to martyr themselves in a noble cause. In the darkness, Kawaguchi stumbled against one of his staff officers, who blurted, "Watch where you walk, you clumsy fool," having no idea who he was talking to. Kawaguchi chuckled and tried to obey.

They reached the outer spurs of the ridge after forty minutes of trudging through the blackness. The captains and lieutenants huddled, synchronized their watches, and led the remnants of their companies and platoons to their appointed attack routes, various dark ravines and gulches.

There were no reserves. All the survivors would rush in except the command staff, which would stay at the base of the ridge to get reports and give orders. The radio was positioned there and Suzuki unfolded a canvas stool for his general.

Kawaguchi heard none of his men shouting slurs about the First Lady's eating habits. He knew their confidence was battered by the results of the previous night.

Less than a mile away, Kenny clutched his BAR and watched intently, aware of his own heavy breathing. Time dragged.

■

CHAPTER 27

AS USUAL FOR KENNY, the waiting was worse than the fighting.

His squad crouched in "Kenny's Craters," two foxholes about a hundred feet apart, behind logs notched to create gun rests. They were on the platoon's right flank, Plunkett and the others off to their left. The position seemed secure and defensible. To reach the platoon, the enemy had to get through the wire and cross about a hundred yards of open ground. Brownings, resting on their bipods, poked out from eighteen-inch gaps between logs.

Kenny saw a red flare. They were coming. Why did the Japs announce their attacks with flares? Pretty stupid. Just shows us where to aim.

He gripped his BAR and heard a Japanese voice shout "*Totsu-geki!*" In a minute he saw them reach the wire, little men in brown fatigues, ghostly in the flickering light.

"Fire, fire," Plunkett shouted. Kenny squeezed the trigger. His BAR chattered.

A torrent of gunfire rained over the Japanese. The boom of artillery explosions convulsing in the center of the enemy positions joined the small-arms din ringing in Kenny's ears. Shell casings clinked to the bottoms of the holes. Many fell, but the damned Japs kept coming. Some began to use bodies of their fallen comrades for shelter, firing their rifles from behind wretched human walls.

Several didn't lie prone and fire. They sprinted straight ahead, shouting and shooting from the hip until they were cut down. They lay frozen in their grotesque death poses. The still-living crawled for cover, fired where they fell, or tried to hurl grenades.

This chaos went on for five minutes that seemed like forever.

Then came a comparative lull breached by the occasional single crack of a rifle shot. It seemed as if the attack had broken. Kenny checked around him in his hole. Everyone was all right.

At that moment a downed Jap lifted himself on one elbow and lobbed a grenade at the other hole. It fell short but skipped on a rock and skidded close to the frontal logs before detonating. Kenny saw the flash, heard a scream. Then nothing.

"Baptist, Cranker, you guys okay?" he shouted.

Nothing for a moment. Then someone gurgled, "We're hit bad." It was John the Baptist, in something very different from his normally high-pitched voice.

Oh, Jesus. Kenny put a hand over his eyes.

After a long silence, John called again, feebly, "Corpsman."

"We've got no corpsman right here," Kenny said to Clint Carmichael at his side. The volume of small-arms fire around them picked up again. What to do? Kenny was closer to the Baptist's position than anyone else in the squad.

"How bad is it, Bap?"

"Think I'm . . . only one . . . alive." The Baptist still sounded nothing like himself.

"Can you crawl over here?"

"Can't move, Sarge."

"Then hold on, Baptist. I'm coming."

"Don't go out there, Kenny," said Carmichael.

"Give me that aid kit."

"No, Sarge, I'll go. I can outrun anybody in the platoon."

Kenny knew he had to go out there if it killed him. He stuck a .45 under his belt.

"Corporal Carmichael, stay here. You're in charge till I get back. Cover me."

Kenny was up and running, weaving from side to side in quick, darting turns, propelled by cold fear. The forty yards or so seemed as long as three football fields. A bullet whipped up dust at his foot. He stumbled on a rock but managed to keep his balance. For an instant, he thought he'd better turn back. Who would know? Maybe there was no one left to save anyway. But he sprinted on. At last he reached the hole, his heart rattling like a machine gun.

" . . . *He leadeth me beside still waters,*" John the Baptist was saying. "*He restoreth my soul . . . .*"

Kenny saw four or five bloody punctures on the left side of the Baptist's blouse where grenade frags had hit. The rest of him had been protected by Del Cranker, whose head was sheared off at mid-nose. The others were dead, too. He stared at Cranker. Poor old Cranker, sprawled there with only the lower half of a face, his mouth agape, white teeth prominent as if laughing at the cruel joke the war had played on him. How he'd bought the farm--when he already had a farm.

". . . *Yea though I walk through the valley of the shadow of death.*" The Baptist again.

Kenny slumped, closed his eyes and held back tears. His squad, his men, his friends, his *responsibility*--four of them dead, another badly hurt.

". . . *For thou art with me; thy rod and thy staff, they comfort me . . .*

Kenny reached into the medical kit, took out a styrette of morphine and plunged it into the biceps muscle of the Baptist's left arm. "You'll be okay, Bap, I promise you. I promise you."

". . . *And I shall dwell in the house of the Lord forever.*"

Kenny pulled the Baptist's good right arm around his neck and started to get him to his feet. Suddenly Kenny, who'd grown as alert as a leopard, saw movement from the corner of his eye. A Japanese soldier bolted from a depression off one of the ridge's spines and charged them.

Drop the Baptist, Kenny's instinct screamed, but he just couldn't do that. He untangled himself from the Baptist's arm and took precious seconds to put him down like a newborn baby. Had he just committed suicide? He pulled out his .45 and snapped off the safety. The Jap was within ten feet now. Why didn't he fire? Was his rifle jammed? The Jap lunged forward with his bayonet. Kenny dodged, firing his pistol as he jumped aside. One round caught the enemy's head. It burst like a ripe tomato.

For a moment, Kenny looked dumbly at the remains of the

man. He hadn't had a rifle at all--it was a bamboo spear. A bamboo spear! No bayonet.

Kenny shook his head like a dog shedding water. Then he tucked the .45 into his pants and again lifted the Baptist to his feet. He was almost dead weight, the morphine kicking in. "Hoagy, cover us."

In the split-second flicker of a shellburst, he glimpsed a naked leg. Young, muscular, bent at the knee, the leg looked as if it would move at any moment and take its owner somewhere. But of course it wouldn't. Wouldn't ever.

The two began staggering back, ever so slowly, Kenny propping the Baptist as bullets streaked around them. It was impossible to run, to zigzag, to crouch, to do anything but plod on toward that hole. Through the valley of the shadow of death.

As Claudia filled the woman's cup, she wished she could be more open, maybe even a little like Nicole.

The French staff at Espiritu Santo had little to do but tend the occasional need of a planter or one of the natives, and Nicole was one of the French nurses who sometimes helped the Americans. She and Claudia were drinking coffee in the old colonial hospital's lounge. Heavy rectangular pillars, high ceiling, gaudy glass chandelier, threadbare carpet, brocaded armchairs, tired Louis XV coffee tables.

Nicole offered Claudia a cigarette.

"Thanks, I don't smoke."

"Ah, that is good, it is a filthy habit, *oui*? What after the war do you wish to do, Claudia?"

"I don't know, maybe start some kind of all-woman business. Not something common like a dress shop or a dry-cleaners, maybe home nursing care, something like that."

"Why only women? This I do not understand." Nicole drove twin plumes of smoke from her nose.

"I don't want to have to deal with men."

"How you can say that?"

"It's personal, Nicole." Claudia's hands clenched so tightly they were turning white.

"Ah, men can be very good as well as very bad, is it not so? This is not a proper--what is the word, attitude?--if I may say so."

"It's a proper attitude for me," Claudia snapped too brusquely. "I'm sorry. Look, I'm afraid I've never met any very good men and don't figure I will. They're only after one thing."

"That has not been my experience." Nicole snuffed out her cigarette in an ornate brass ashtray. "Oh yes, men are interested in that one thing, as you say, and some of them--*merde*!--only that. But also there are men who are obliging and sensitive."

Claudia felt disbelief shadow her face.

"*Mais oui*, it is true."

"Not in my experience."

"Oh, but you, what experience you have had? You are young, you are from the small town, no?"

What experience have I had? Claudia thought. You wouldn't want to know sister! You wouldn't want to know.

"It is because, perhaps, you prefer the love of women?"

"Prefer the love--?" Claudia flinched. "No, God no, it's nothing like that."

"Then one day surely you will marry."

"No. I don't ever want to get married." After a long silence, Claudia's eyes narrowed. "You've, ah, had sex with men?"

"But of course, often. That is what God intended, no?" At Claudia's look of protest, Nicole said, "Sometimes it is not so good, but most times it is quite satisfactory. Not to have known the pleasure of good love is not to have lived."

Claudia's arms crossed tighter and she said nothing, frost seeming to form in her eyes.

"I am sure you will meet kind men. Surely you will make room in your life for one."

"Maybe." Why did I say that? I meant to say no. Definitely no.

"Why does it seem so difficult, *ma amie*? You have had trouble with men, yes? Or with one man, perhaps? It would help to talk about it?"

"I have to go now." And Claudia abruptly vanished.

"The poor woman," the French nurse said to herself. "*Extrément* troubled. God help her."

Exhausted, Kenny reached the hole at last. He helped John the Baptist down into it. He refused to congratulate himself on surviving that terrible walk, knowing he'd left four dead squad members behind.

"Sergeant Plunkett, we need a corpsman over here," Hoagy Carmichael shouted. "And stretcher bearers."

Kenny heard random, scattered firing in the distance. Either the attack was smashed or the big one was still to come.

"Thanks, Kenny," the Baptist said weakly. "You kept your promise." He squeezed Kenny's wrist momentarily as litter bearers lifted him. Then he cupped his hands in front of his face. "*Our Father who art in heaven . . .*"

"You'll make it, buddy," Kenny said.

It was quiet now on the ridge. Half an hour passed without an enemy probe. Kenny sent Ninetrees and Keugeman to the other hole to drag back their dead. One of the bodies, Kenny realized, would be Del Cranker, a good man and his best machine gunner. He wondered if he'd ever be able to shake the image of Cranker's bisected head grinning at him.

He gazed around in the feeble light and saw a grim field littered with lifeless men--many Americans and even more Japanese.

The poor guy he'd killed must've run out of ammo and improvised. But I didn't know it wasn't a rifle. How could I have known? He was just a boy. Why hadn't he just gone to the rear, the stupid ass? Kenny knew this memory would stick with him forever, like that naked leg and Cranker's half-face.

Then an old familiar clatter approached from the north.

What now? Washing Machine Charlie? Hadn't A Company earned some rest?

Again the flare and a moment later the whistling of the one

harmless bomb. After all he'd been through on this hellish ridge, Washing Machine Charlie's hundred-pounder was nothing. Just a nuisance.

The whistling came closer. Reluctantly, sluggishly, the remains of Kenny's squad crawled into their holes.

The explosion was surprisingly loud. Rocks and dirt clods showered on them and--what the hell?

A sudden stinging sensation hit Kenny's chest, just below the left shoulder. It didn't hurt much at first. Felt like he'd been jabbed with a needle, like the smallpox shot he'd had at Cottage Hospital. He grew a little dizzy, though. "Sarge, Sarge," came a voice sounding far away.

Now came the hurt. A scorching tunnel of fire began eating into his chest. Then he drifted into a murky twilight.

Images floated. His mother, six years dead. His father, home from work carrying his tin lunchpail. The Burlington tracks threading through Galesburg. The gray facade of First Christian Church on Broad Street. Dearborn Station in Chicago. His drill sergeant at Parris Island. Broadway Pier in San Diego. The *Wacky Mac* out at sea. Officers in the ship's radio room. Tokyo Rose. "This song is for all you brave Marines. Enjoy your beer while you still can." As if out of a long gray tunnel, Hadley Plunkett's face.

Plunkett?

This wasn't a dream. Not any longer. He really saw Plunkett's face. And grew aware of stretcher bearers lifting him.

Plunkett took his hand, said, "You'll be okay, kid, you'll be okay. Prob'ly get red-tagged outta here, lucky SOB, get some great chow and some o' them clean sheets to sleep on."

Kenny lifted his head and peered numbly down at his shirt, wet with blood. "You were right about this ridge, Plunk," he murmured.

"Yeah, but it ain't got a name. So what's it gonna be, Nielsen?"

"Bloody Ridge I guess."

■

CHAPTER 28

FROM A NEARBY slope, Kawaguchi stared in tears at the forlorn ridge. His brigade was decimated. "My worst fears about this malevolent island have been realized. I pray for the souls of the fallen men."

Only about a fourth of the 2,100 soldiers who had tramped with him to the ridge remained alive. All he could do was get them to the coast as soon as possible, so he ordered a retreat to the northwest, behind Mount Austen. It would take days.

Kawaguchi felt deep anguish as the pathetic column groped--marched was not the word--toward the Matanikau. "It is no use attempting to keep units together," he told his officers. "Let the soldiers move along at whatever pace they can manage."

There was no food. Supply was nonexistent. His thin, emaciated men wore rags. They ate roots and betel nuts, but usually nothing, and drank only the tiny amounts of rainwater they could catch in their forage caps. Stretcher bearers were so weak they soon had to leave the badly wounded behind. To die alone. One man limping with a leg wound was killed by a crocodile while trying to ford a stream. His screams haunted Kawaguchi.

Ga, the first syllable in *Gadarukanaru*, has several meanings in Japanese, one of them being hunger, and soon the black humorists in the retreat coined the name "Starvation Island."

One soldier turned his head and said to the man behind, "We were told the Americans didn't have *seishin* (fighting spirit). We were lied to, weren't we?"

A hero eight months ago for taking Borneo, Kawaguchi now thought bitterly of the dress uniform and the surrender he had planned. "It was an heroic effort," he told Suzuki. "Every one of the men performed with great honor." I, however, have failed the Emperor, he thought.

Kenny's mother stood before him in a white gown, the kind she wore in Cottage Hospital the last few weeks of her life. But now she was standing, gazing straight at him, a slight smile on her face. She'd worn the same look back when Kenny had done something good, like repairing the cranky old lawnmower. She'd never wanted to overpraise him, let him get a big head. She would just give him that brief little smile.

Suddenly she was gone.

Now he was tackling that Jap infiltrator outside the Old Man's CP. That sergeant major's big .45 came out of nowhere and fired, scattering blood and gore over him. Then that vision faded and vanished.

Kenny grew vaguely aware of a jouncing, cold, illusory voyage. The sky or whatever was above him was a murky, gridlike substance that wouldn't hold still. It drifted in small, slow circles. Whenever he tried to lock in on one of its features it devilishly drifted away from his focal point. Nothing made sense, except that this had to be some kind of dream.

Once he saw Galesburg floating in the distance, as he had on the *McCawley* five weeks before. Just five weeks? Surely a year. Galesburg was distant this time, just a fuzzy, snapshot-town in the sky of his mind. Nothing else. Nothing else.

He briefly slipped out of his morphine stupor, and the gridlike vision turned out to be the interior fuselage ribbing of a plane. A foggy memory of being loaded onto an evac plane emerged. He dozed off again.

Somehow he knew that more time had passed. Surely he'd been killed and was now in heaven for next, the image of an angel took shape. He squinted to see better. Jagged light stabbed, painful to pupils long accustomed to nothing but darkness. But it was definitely the face of an angel.

"Good morning, Marine. You're back with us, I see."

What was that she said? At last he got the face in focus. Not an angel after all--angels didn't wear funny little cut-in-half sailor's caps. Hazel eyes, a compassionate mouth ringed by a dimple on each side, short, honey-blonde hair. And no halo.

"I guess this isn't heaven," he told the apparition, slurring his words. He hadn't spoken in a long time.

"Some of the nurses think it is. The weather and the beaches are nice and we get a new motion picture every week or so."

The face looked down on him from a distance of maybe three feet with a warm if cautious smile. Kenny's soul trembled. It was about the nicest face he'd ever seen.

"What happened, ma'am?"

"You've been in surgery, Sergeant. Had quite a chest wound, apparently from a bomb fragment. You were lucky. It missed your heart and only nicked your left lung. You've been under for a long time, but you came through quite well. The surgeon did a fine job."

Kenny tried to feel something, anything, in his left side. He couldn't. "Where am I? Is this Santo?"

"No, it's the Empire State Building."

Kenny liked that. A sense of humor.

"Actually, yes," the nurse said, "Fleet Hospital, Espiritu Santo, the New Hebrides. Or 'Somewhere in the Pacific' as the war correspondents would say."

"You're an officer, aren't you, ma'am?"

"I'm a nurse, Marine. Just a nurse." Her simple white dress, buttoned up the front, was starchy stiff. Checking her clipboard, she said, "May I call you Kenneth?"

"No, ma'am, everybody calls me Kenny. You can too if you want."

"Then I will, Kenny. I'm Claudia."

"Claudia? But I'm supposed to call you sir or ma'am or something. I can't call an officer by her first name."

"You'll call this one by her first name. Claudia. Got it?"

"I'll try, sir, I mean . . . Claudia."

She laughed then, a quick, infectious laugh. Drugged though he was, Kenny smiled. She stuck a thermometer in his mouth and strapped a blood-pressure cuff around his good right arm and pumped it up.

She made a notation on her clipboard and their gazes met again as she retrieved the thermometer. Ensign Claudia's eyes seemed to--what, plead? They weren't smiling along with the mouth and yet they weren't hostile either. Kenny thought they were distant or pained or something. He was too woozy to reflect on it more. She read the thermometer, shook it, and wrote something else on the clipboard.

"I suppose it was rough out there, Kenny."

He said nothing. He didn't want to talk about the things he'd seen and done. She seemed to understand.

"Yes, I know what you mean," she said slowly, surprising him. "I'll see you later, Kenny."

"I hope so." He watched her leave. She moved regally.

After the Battle of Bloody Ridge--all the Marines were calling it that--the 1st Battalion moved to a new bivouac northwest of the ridge, half a mile from the sea, a scrawny knoll between the Matanikau and the Lunga. Plunkett told Hoagy Carmichael this was where General Vandegrift expected the next enemy attack. Carmichael had been named acting sergeant and given what was left of Kenny's squad. Five men, less than half its original strength.

It just isn't the same without Nielsen here, Plunkett thought. He'd grown to like and respect the imaginative Midwesterner and he'd enjoyed their conversations.

Plunkett wished he could do a postmortem with Kenny on the battle and Scupper Harris' performance. The two had real empathy on the problem of Harris. The crazed teenager had fought well the last two nights, had probably killed a dozen Japanese, and had collected only two bayonets as souvenirs. This was because Plunkett had actually tackled him the first morning when Harris started toward the enemy bodies littering the field with that scary look in his eye. "You leave the platoon for any reason, dickhead, and I'll beat the living shit out of you," he'd said.

So instead of talking *with* Kenny Nielsen, Plunkett went to Lieutenant Gates and talked *about* him.

"Sir, savin' John the Baptist like he did under fire was one of the greatest moments in the history of this here regiment. I think Nielsen deserves somethin' besides the Purple Heart."

"I agree, sergeant. I've heard three or four reports identical to yours. I've already spoken with Captain Brush about Nielsen, and he promised to see the major. You know, there are going to be a lot of field commissions on this island if this thing goes on much longer, which it looks like it will. I wouldn't be surprised to see Nielsen made a second lieutenant. If we get him back, that is."

Plunkett heard those words with great delight. "Hell, he'll get back to this rock, even if he's gotta take French leave from the hospital."

Rusty Gates smiled.

Knows he's got one hell of a good platoon sergeant, Plunkett thought.

Their ridge rose only a small distance above the surrounding jungle and was designated Hill 62 on the situation map. With Nielsen gone, somebody had to make nicknames, so Hoagy Carmichael dubbed it Turner's Tit. His reference was to actress Lana, the Sweater Girl, not the admiral.

The usual grumbling took place as the men collected their gear, trudged to their new position and dug their holes. The men weighed an average of fifteen pounds less than when they'd first reached the island. A third of them had malaria, several had dysentery. Plunkett doubted they could put up another fight for quite awhile.

Colonel Hunt gathered the battalion around and read the men General Vandegrift's report. The commanding general had nominated the Raiders' Colonel Edson for the Medal of Honor. The enemy had launched a series of ferocious attacks, each ending in furious hand-to-hand combat. A courageous counterattack by the Parachute Battalion, despite suffering forty percent casualties, had defeated a flanking movement that threatened the entire U.S. position. The Raiders, Parachutists and regular Marines, greatly assisted by the 11th Marines' artillery, had gallantly fought off repeated attacks and added another superb chapter to the proud history of the Corps. It was an honor and a privilege to lead such men, the message concluded.

An hour after Plunkett heard the report, the author himself showed up. As usual, the Old Man wore a pith helmet. A private sprang to his feet and cheered. Plunkett and others joined in, and soon the whole battalion was up, helmets raised aloft, shouting, "Hooray, hooray."

Vandegrift was moved. He found them looking tough, lean and exhausted, their uniforms almost rags. He gave them a pep talk. "You men were magnificent on the Ridge." He ended with, "I apologize for keeping those with low-grade fevers in the line, but we're just too thin. I know you'll all do your duty."

Instead of telling them to take their atabrine tablets, he set an example by simply swallowing one himself.

Despite the funny headgear, which they thought looked silly, they liked the Old Man. His personal attention bucked up their morale.

After his departure, the jokes began.

"I say, old top, nice chapeau on the field marshal, what?"

"Righto, old chap, righto."

"What's he gonna do, stay here and run the plantation when this war's over?"

To his driver, Vandegrift said, "I don't think American troops have cheered a commanding general since the Civil War. I can't tell you how touched I am."

"Hi, Kenny."

Kenny hadn't been thinking about French leave. He was gazing around the high, pillared room and hoping the beautiful nurse would return. Suddenly he was rewarded.

"Hello, ma'am, er, Claudia."

"How are you feeling?"

He was beginning to ache on the left side--the morphine was wearing off--but he wouldn't say so.

"Just fine. I'd forgotten how comfortable a real bed could feel." He noticed a sudden slight but definite change in Claudia. Was it that the dimples flattened out, meaning her facial muscles had tightened? Yes, that was it. And the eyes had pulled back. What had he said? Only that the bed was comfortable. Nothing improper there. Surely she didn't think--no!

"I see you also have malaria." Claudia was checking her clipboard, not looking at Kenny.

"Yes, ma'am. Doc up at the Canal says it's not likely to kill me."

"Not likely. We'll do what we can for that. We've some quinine here and sulfa drugs, too. Has it been bothering you?"

"Tell you the truth, since I got hit I have no idea what's bothering me. I don't remember much of anything, till your face, ma'am, and that looked, well, real nice." Unaccustomed to complimenting women, Kenny felt himself blush. How stupid, but it seemed to relax the nurse. The dimple was back and the eyes regained some sparkle.

"Claudia, not ma'am. Got it?"

"Yes, ma--, Claudia."

Her quick laugh seemed to brighten the room and cover the smell of ether.

"I was always a little slow to learn."

"I don't believe that for a minute." Her eyes smiled again as she pulled a thermometer from a pocket. "You had a little temperature before, just a notch over a hundred, nothing to worry about. What? What is it?"

"I'm just uncomfortable, I guess. Never talked much with a nice woman, except for one schoolteacher, since my mom died."

"You're uneasy with me?" Claudia was silent for a moment, but the chill that had briefly masked her face didn't return. "Interesting," she said.

Kenny sensed the wheels turning in her head but had no idea

what was going on there. Her left hand touched his forehead, checking for warmth. He felt that wonderful touch even in the tips of his toes.

Claudia noticed the blushing and smiled inwardly.

He's uneasy with me? she thought. A man? As this remarkable fact struck home it seemed to give her strength. I'm surprised I feel so comfortable with this guy. Is it because he's so weak and helpless lying there? But most of my patients are that way.

"I see you don't have a tattoo. So many of the Marines in here do. The globe and anchor, or some such."

"Not the type, I guess. I don't care for tattoos."

"I don't either. . . . Well, let's see what we have this time," she said, putting the thermometer in his mouth.

When she removed it a minute later, Kenny said, "Did you have a Sergeant Whitely in here a few weeks ago?"

"Whitely? Yes, he died, I'm afraid."

"Died? Whitely?" Kenny's face clouded over.

"I'm sorry. He had a very bad abdominal wound. We did all we could for him. He was a friend of yours?"

"My squad leader."

Claudia saw Kenny's face scrunch up in grief. He turned his head away and let it sink sideways onto the pillow.

"I'm so sorry." She reached out with her free hand as if to touch him, but stopped inches short. She walked off. Poor kid; he's a sensitive guy. She looked at the thermometer. Ninety-nine-four. Not bad.

Back at the nurses' station, she checked the birthdate on Kenny's chart. Hmm, she was three months older than he was. Now, why ever had she looked that up?

■

CHAPTER 29

IT TOOK KAWAGUCHI'S pitiful column six days to reach the coast of Starvation Island west of the American perimeter. At last they made contact with the handful of survivors from Colonel Oka's detachment and the naval troops who operated Pistol Pete. Kawaguchi watched sadly as some of his delirious men staggered into the surf and tried to drink the seawater. Others sucked the salt from beach pebbles. The wiser ones simply lay in the shade of a grove and then drank and ate coconut milk and meat when they felt a little stronger.

At Rabaul, General Hyakutake read Kawaguchi's report and hurled it aside. "I will take charge of Guadalcanal myself," snarled the commander of the 17th Army. "I and the mighty Sendai Division will clean up that island once and for all. I will move the entire Sendai Division there along with all of the 17th's Army's artillery. Those boys from Sendai are the army's finest.

"Since Kawaguchi knows the island and has had useful experience, I might keep him on in some capacity."

Kenny was having a troubled dream, a confused amalgam of many things. Claudia's face was there and so was the leg he'd seen in that foxhole just before he'd saved John the Baptist, and there was a bamboo spear in there somewhere. Then he was trying to drag Moon Whitely off the battlefield but something sticky kept pulling against him. He'd gain a few inches, then Whitely would get yanked back just as far. It was a tug of war.

He awoke and lay in his bed staring at cracks in the ceiling-- one looked like his Aunt Gertrude in profile. Whitely dead? He hadn't saved him after all. Not for long anyway. A red haze of anger washed over him. His hands became fists. Why the hell were Marines and Japs killing each other on that damned, disease-ridden island? That was rhetorical. He knew why. Tears welled in his eyes. What a bizarre species the human animal was.

Then nurse Peggy Stratton came by and said he had a visitor. A ruddy-faced man in an Army uniform with a war correspondent patch on the shoulder pulled up a chair and introduced himself.

"Sergeant, I'm Jake Weaver of the *Los Angeles Herald-Express*. Just arrived from stateside. Been a reporter a long time but I'm just startin' out in this here war correspondent business. I'll be here a coupla days, then I'm goin' up to Guadalcanal."

"You're going to the Canal?"

"Yep, end of the week. Me and Bill Stoneman of the *Chicago Daily News*. Like to ask you a few questions."

This red-haired man had a winning smile and honest eyes.

"Hear you were quite a hero on Guadalcanal."

"No I wasn't, sir."

"Tell me what it was like."

"Nothing to tell. We fought hard, they fought hard, and a lot of people didn't make it."

"Fellow down the aisle here," Weaver said, nodding toward a nearby bed, "tells me you saved his life."

That's how Kenny learned that John the Baptist was here in the same ward. He'd been evacked on the same plane.

"How is he?"

"Not too good. Got a buncha holes in him, but he'll make it."

Weaver probed on for fifteen minutes but Kenny clammed up about the fighting. When Weaver asked what combat was like, he merely said, "We kill people."

On the other hand, Kenny was forthcoming about his back-ground, hometown or any other subject. "I was editor of the school paper, *The Streak*, my senior year," he said.

"Hot damn, another newspaperman. That's good."

"You're from L.A.," Kenny said, "but your accent sounds Southern."

"Originally from Loozy-anna."

Peggy Stratton came and said time was up. Weaver said, "Well, thank you kindly, young man. I'll write something that'll make the folks in Galesburg proud. I'll be here another day or two, so I'll catch you again."

The next day, September 18, was a big one for General Vandegrift. First, the Missing Regiment arrived from Samoa. Even though the Navy was temporarily down to one aircraft carrier and one battleship in the Pacific, transports reached Lunga Roads that morning and began unloading. Off came the 7th Marines, 4,000 more troops. They carried eight-shot, semi-automatic M-1 Garand rifles, the first up-to-date weapons to reach the island. With them came trucks, jeeps, light tanks, ammunition, barbed wire, aviation fuel--and food! The Marines had been on two meals a day, abetted by enemy rice, for weeks.

"We now have more than 20,000 troops on the island, sir," Colonel Twining told Vandegrift.

"Good. Now I'd like to double the wire all along the perimeter, plug up any weak spots you know of, and add more machine gun emplacements. I'd also like to conduct some reconnaissance in force in the west, do some damage to that enemy stronghold beyond the Matanikau."

An hour later, Vandegrift had a visitor, Roy Geiger, who'd just arrived to be CO of the 1st Marine Aircraft Wing. General Geiger had been a classmate of Vandegrift's at Parris Island in 1909 and a member of the Wide Water Gang. Their paths had crossed many times in the three decades since those bull sessions on the Virginia plantation, as each worked his way upward in the Corps.

"Archer, I just heard you were almost killed the other day. I've just seen the bloodstains outside the CP here."

"No, no, Roy, just a little incident. A few of our friends came for breakfast without invitation but my men quickly reasoned with them."

"You sound as unruffled as ever."

"I try. It's a strange fight here, Roy. Control of the sea changes every twelve hours. By day, with our little air umbrella, we can manage to get a few supply ships in, and small craft shuttle back and forth between here and Tulagi. At nightfall, our small boats run for cover and soon the enemy arrives with his Tokyo Express. Cruisers and destroyers, sometimes battlewagons. He shells us every night, then leaves before dawn or else our aircraft will smack him good. I'm mighty glad you're here to take charge of those planes."

"I know it's been tough, Archer. Say, I've got a bag of fan mail here for you from Admiral Turner."

"Fan mail from Kelly Turner? Is that a joke, Roy?"

"Nope. Better see for yourself." Clinking sounds came from the obviously heavy mailbag as Geiger swung it onto a bamboo tabletop. Vandegrift examined it. The fan mail turned out to be a case of whisky.

Vandegrift checked each bottle. All twelve were fifths of scotch. His smile faded. He was a bourbon man.

"Tell you what, Archer," the aviator said. "I've got a case of bourbon and I'll swap you level even, although mine are quarts."

"Done," said Vandegrift.

After they jeeped the priceless scotch to his new hut, Geiger searched the place, first slowly, then in a panic. Finally, he said, "Hell, Archer, it's been stolen. What have you got here, old friend, an island full of thieves?"

Vandegrift gave him two bottles of scotch. When Geiger's mood remained bad he invited him for dinner. "Someone caught some good-looking bass for old Butch to cook up."

■

CHAPTER 30

KENNY FINISHED OFF a generous plateful of scrambled eggs, the most delicious meal he'd eaten in about a light-year.

He was itching beneath his bandages, a good sign, the docs told him. Tissue healing.

After the dish was taken away, he lay there mesmerized--for how long, he didn't know--by the slow turning of the ceiling fan. He thought about his platoon on the Canal. Wondered how those bastards were doing, and who'd taken over his squad. Wade or Carmichael, probably. He missed those guys, those who were alive. He thought about Desmond Sweeney and Del Cranker, surely resting now under fresh crosses in the cemetery at Kukum. Augie Collins, who'd bought it on that first patrol to the Matanikau. And Moon Whitely, who'd died after all, right here in this hospital.

He even missed crazy little Scupper Harris. Hoped Harris was getting a better grip, was growing up some. Most of all he missed Had Plunkett. Plunk had become his big brother. Hell, they were all his brothers. His family. The most family he'd ever had. Would he ever see them again? The thought that he might not brought pain.

Minutes later he was wishing that Claudia would stop by. And she did.

"I have a surprise for you," she said, pushing a wheelchair. "Doctor says you can get out of bed for a few minutes at a time so I'm taking you for a stroll." Kenny had never liked the way nurses said "doctor" instead of "the doctor." Made them sound like gods. But coming from Claudia he didn't mind. Her presence always gave him such a lift, how could he complain about anything she said?

Claudia pulled back the covers, put an arm around his back--at her touch, warmth washed over him--and helped him into the chair. When he was settled in, she patted him on top of the head, playfully but also affectionately, he thought.

She pushed the chair partway down the aisle, the wheels going *wup-wup-wup* on the tiled floor. She turned the wheelchair and stopped beside a bed, where Kenny looked into the sleeping face of John the Baptist McKenna.

"Bap, Bap," he said. His comrade from the Canal opened his eyes and smiled. "I heard you were here," the Baptist said weakly. The two young men, whose experiences together on the island had created a strong bond, talked for two or three minutes.

Then Claudia said, "That's it. Mr. McKenna is still pretty weak. I'm taking you out for some sunshine, Kenny."

The landscaped grounds behind the hospital, bathed in trade winds, featured palm, kauri and banyan trees, a riot of bougain-villea, frangipani and birds of paradise, plus a central fountain approached symmetrically by four shell paths.

"How is he?" Kenny said.

"McKenna? Fine, considering. Doctor thinks he got all the steel splinters. Fragments punctured a lung, though. He's probably going all the way home."

Claudia turned the chair and Kenny got his first good look at the building. And gasped.

"What?" she asked. "What is it?"

Kenny stared at the creamy white stucco and the ornate arched doorways. The rows of classical ornaments above the leaded, green-trimmed windows. "I saw this place in a dream the night before we landed on the Canal," he said.

"Really?"

"Absolutely."

"It must have been some other old building of this type you saw a picture of, some time or other."

"No, it was this very building. The dream was very distinct. That flagpole was positioned exactly as we see it now."

Claudia shook her head. "I've heard about precognition. You must have had a dose of that in your subconscious. Fascinating."

No, *you're* fascinating, Kenny thought. The rubber wheels crunched softly on the pathway's shells as she pushed him on through the garden. She chattered about precognition and lots of other things. Being entertained by this woman was heaven.

When she asked about his experiences in school, he said, "There's not much to tell. I played some basketball at Galesburg High and was editor of the school paper."

"You like to write then?"

"Yeah, I really do. I wrote a short story once that got an honorable mention in a contest the *Chicago Daily News* ran."

"Bravo. Tell me about it."

And he did. This was the happiest and most carefree he'd seen Claudia since his arrival at Espiritu Santo.

"How do you feel, Kenny? Is this tiring you?"

"I feel fine. You people are taking great care of me. What a luxury it is to have clean pajamas, to eat with real silverware."

"It must be terrible up there."

Kenny lowered his head and pursed his lips. "We live like animals," he said softly.

"You have an awful knowledge, Kenny, something that people like me will never be able to comprehend."

What a prescient woman. Good-looking, too. "May I say something, Claudia?"

"Sure, why not?"

"This is kind of embarrassing, but my feeling great's really got nothing to do with creature comforts. What I meant to say is I feel great when I'm with you."

Their eyes met. Claudia said nothing. He wondered what was going on in her mind, how she was reacting to those words. Maybe he'd said too much. Then her right hand mussed his hair. Affectionately, he was sure of it this time. It was all the answer he got but it was enough.

The grounds, facing the Coral Sea to the north, offered a stunning view. Kenny drank in the palm-lined beach, the blue-green sea, the huge white clouds tossed here and there, giving the sky great depth.

A PBY droned across his sightline, ruining the moment. He realized he was looking north, toward Guadalcanal.

From his headquarters aboard the superbattleship *Yamato* in Truk Lagoon, Admiral Yamamoto sent a message to General Hyakutake at Rabaul. Yamamoto was fully aware of Guadalcanal's importance and was growing anxious over the army's failure to recapture it.

"I will transport you and your troops to the island safely with all your supplies. I will support your attack on the airplane field with the most punishing naval bombardment yet."

The battleships *Kongo* and *Haruna* with their 14-inch guns would join the cruisers and destroyers to give the Marines a shellacking the likes of which they had never known.

"I have designated the day of our coordinated attack, X-Day, and scheduled it for October 12."

On Bougainville Island, Kimi Otomo received orders transferring him to an air group at Wewak on the northern coast of New Guinea after two more missions to Guadalcanal. Otomo didn't have anything like a full squadron anyway and he could be more useful on the world's second largest island fighting General MacArthur's Americans and Australians.

He bowed in the tropical twilight and prayed in thanks that he could serve his country and the Emperor, that he had been granted a fine family, and that he had been allowed to live so long.

Vandegrift told Colonel Twining it was time to execute the limited offensive to the west. "I'm sure the enemy will be reinforced again and renew the attack, so I want to catch him off balance and do some harm while we can. I'd like to attack along the coast but also position two or three battalions upstream on the Matanikau, undetected if possible, and hit the Japanese in the rear while they're occupied with our opening thrust. It would be nice to spring a trap and bag a number of them. I'll put Colonel Edson in charge of the operation."

Twining appreciated the way Vandegrift always "suggested" or said he "would like to". There's the MacArthur method and there's the Vandegrift method. There was no doubt which he preferred.

General Kawaguchi commanded fewer than 2,000 men still able to fight, remnants of his and Oka's outfits, the naval troops who operated Pistol Pete, and a handful of original Henderson Field occupants who'd been chased off seven weeks before. But he too was making plans with his ragtag force.

"Move a few companies off to the west," Kawaguchi told Kai Suzuki. "Have them camouflage themselves well. The Yankee devils may use small boats to raid our rear. I must not allow them to repeat the success they had with this tactic on the northeast shore while we marched to the attack."

Plunkett thought Able Company would be in reserve, but a change in orders sent them into the line, beside one of Edson's Raider companies again.

Plunkett's platoon got orders to take a small hill. "Daylight attack, thank God," he said. "The Japs think we hate fightin' at night. Hell, they're right. But I'll bet they do, too, after the ass-kicking we gave 'em on Bloody Ridge."

They pushed off, but it wasn't long before a Nambu machine gun on the hill soon enfiladed their sector, holding up the south flank of the advance.

"Terrain's bad," Plunkett said to Lieutenant Gates. "Lousy visibility. Lot of trees and vines, hard to tell 'zackly where they are. We should spread out thin all across the front and give 'em some recon fire. Get more of 'em to shoot back, expose themselves."

"Good, sergeant. See to it."

After Plunkett positioned the platoon, he called out, "Nine-trees, Delgado, lay a few potshots on yonder hill."

Minutes later, the enemy machine gun and several rifles clattered away up there in the brush.

"Okay, Lieutenant, it worked. We got 'em pinpointed."

"Frontal would be suicide," Gates said. "I'll call in artillery."

Gates is getting better at this, Plunkett thought. "Right, sir," he said, taking the lieutenant's binoculars. A moment later he said, "Also, looks like we might got us a little gully off there to the right." He handed the binoculars back. "We oughta patrol that, see if there's a way to flank 'em there."

Gates scanned the hill. "Okay, sergeant."

"Carmichael," Plunkett called. "Got a job for you." While he gave Kenny Nielsen's old squad its assignment, Gates called co-ordinates to the gunners of the 11th Marines. "Pour all you got on that ridge, boys," he told them.

Carmichael's squad had been gone less than ten minutes when howitzer shells started working their way across the hilltop. The enemy gun fell silent.

"Goddammit, I wanted to get them Japs," Scupper Harris snarled when the squad tramped back to the company.

"We coulda done it," Carmichael said. "Gone right up that draw and hit 'em in the side."

Despite this small Marine success, the famished Japanese fared better elsewhere, pinning down the initial strike at the river with heavy fire. Although some outfits succeeded in crossing downstream they weren't able to close the trap. These develop-ments forced Edson to try an amphibious end-run behind the Japanese. Kawaguchi had guessed right about that. He was ready.

Edson's company landed safely, but a few hundred yards inside the jungle it was battered by well-concealed guns. He lost sixty men.

The battle was not a victory for either side, just another bloody brawl. At the end of it, Kawaguchi was ordered back to Rabaul for interrogation.

"This is likely the end of my career," he told Suzuki that night before boarding a destroyer from the Tokyo Express.

Claudia thought most of the patients in the ward were sleeping. Under dim blue light, she and another nurse and a doctor circulated among them, checking a clipboard here, an IV drip-bottle there. Random snoring broke the hush.

John the Baptist was running a fever. There was a chance one of his wounds was infected.

Claudia thought Kenny was asleep as she paused and gazed at his bed.

She wore no perfume but Kenny knew she was there. He always knew. He was glad she'd stopped and was about to say something, but she moved on. The other nurse had left the floor.

Two beds away, a Navy doctor caught Claudia by the arm.

"Claudia, I've got some good scotch in my room and---"

"No," she snapped, her voice brittle as thin ice. She tried to shake his grip.

The doctor pulled her close and tried to kiss her but Claudia jerked her head to the side. His nose collided with her ear. He clutched at her breast. She pulled away in a rage.

"How many times do I have to tell you, Commander, keep away from me."

The suddenness and strength of a third voice startled them both, shooting from the darkness like a bullet.

"The lady said no."

Trying to look dignified, the doctor turned toward Kenny.

"You misunderstand, young man," he said coldly. "You saw and heard nothing here, understand?"

"Hear this, doc." Kenny was on his feet, the first time he'd done that without help. "Leave that lady alone, do *you* understand? Scram the hell out of here this minute."

The doctor started to say something. Must have thought better of it. The word dangled unspoken. He turned and left.

Claudia was a statue for several seconds, both gratitude and anger boiling within her. Then she went to Kenny, squeezed his hand, gave him a peck on the cheek and said, "Get to bed, Sir Galahad, you're not supposed to be up," and slipped into the shadows.

Kenny stood transfixed for what must have been a minute, his cheek tingling with the ambrosia of that fleeting little kiss. His body glowed. It was one of the best moments in his life.

But in his sleep that night, the same dream haunted him. At first he was patching paper targets at New River, covering the bullet holes with masking tape. Then the holes began to ooze blood. The targets changed into Japanese faces and he kept on trying to tape them. Something else crept into the dream. It was that strong, muscular leg, bent at the knee, caked with mud. It began to move. Looked as if it might get up and take its owner somewhere. It was as sinister to Kenny's subconscious as the bloody target-face.

An hour later, Jake Weaver, the war correspondent, sat in the O Club having a drink with the libidinous doctor. His name was Commander Kepple. Dr. Kepple was relating his version of the encounter and twice he used the term "obstinate bitch." His account left out a key detail or two.

"Idealistic young fool. Gets shot at once or twice on the island and he's pumped full of patriotism. I'll show him what happens to an ignorant foot-soldier who tries to show up an officer. An insubordination report on his record will take care of him."

Weaver stared at his glass, his hand moving it in slow, small circles, making the ice rotate. Then his eyes looked directly into Kepple's.

"Sir, I wouldn't do that if I were you. That boy's gonna get the Silver Star. Maybe y'all didn't know that. Could be embarrassing for you. No point in raisin' a ruckus just 'cause he stood up for a nurse he's prob'ly got a crush on. I'd just swallow some pride and let it pass."

Kepple knew Weaver was right. And hated him for it.

■

CHAPTER 31

CINCPAC HIMSELF, Admiral Chester Nimitz, was coming. Vandegrift's immediate superior, Vice Admiral Ghormley, never got off his ass at Nouméa, but the No. 2 man in the whole U.S. Navy, Nimitz, was flying to Guadalcanal to see for himself.

Vandegrift was gratified but he also feared a dressing-down because he held so little of the island. He hoped he wouldn't have to justify his strategy.

He'd just received another annoying message from Admiral Turner advocating various offensives. Vandegrift was sick and tired of hearing from Terrible Turner, who didn't know an infantry tactic from an anchor chain. Worried that the Commander-in-Chief, Pacific, might make similar demands, Vandegrift rehearsed his viewpoint with Bill Twining.

"I don't like the defensive. I've always been a fighting officer but this is a whole new type of campaign. Our objective here is simple: keep this airfield in U.S. hands. To do that against an enemy who can attack us by sea and air whenever he wants, we have to keep him off balance and interrupt his lines of communication and supply with limited attacks. What would you do in my shoes, Bill?"

"Just that, sir, and make the perimeter as strong as we can."

"Exactly. We don't have the manpower to occupy the whole island and it would be pointless anyway. I hope Chet Nimitz sees it that way."

After the admiral arrived, Butch Morgan went all out, roasting some wild boar shot by one of the men. The *second* Marine on Guadalcanal to do so.

While Morgan cooked, Vandegrift took the slender, red-cheeked Nimitz to the hospital, where he chatted with the wounded. The surprise visit seemed to do wonders for their morale.

Later, in a small ceremony witnessed by General Geiger and three colonels, Nimitz awarded Vandegrift the Navy Cross for "exceptionally meritorious service under fire, capturing all objectives and destroying opposing forces."

When they were alone, Nimitz, his pale blue eyes a startling counterpoint to his sunbaked face, said, "When this is all over, we'll write a new set of naval regulations. I'll want your suggestions. What you've experienced out here is all new to us. The British said amphibious warfare wouldn't work, but you've proved them wrong. The amphibious attacks we'll make in the next year or two on the road to Tokyo will really make old Winston Churchill sit up and take notice."

"I'll tell you one thing right now for those regs," Vandegrift said. "Remove all mention that a captain who runs his ship aground faces a fate worse than death. We've had far too many timid sailors out here."

Vandegrift meant Admirals Fletcher, now sacked, and Ghormley. He hoped Nimitz understood that. The admiral must have, because he said, "I've overridden that directive about the Navy not supplying you. It's difficult but essential." Then he astonished Vandegrift. "I'll want you in charge of the landing on Bougainville. Put that in the back of your mind for now."

Bougainville! It was at the top of the Slot, halfway to Rabaul. Guadalcanal was still in doubt and this man was planning attacks others would have thought impossible.

Nimitz seemed to catch his surprise. "Archer," he said, "this is just the beginning. We're going to capture the Gilberts, then the Marshalls, and after that the Carolines or the Marianas. This is all top secret, of course."

With Europe getting top priority, the U.S. Navy barely had the ships and planes to support Guadalcanal, but Nimitz was planning a grand counterattack to sweep the Japanese out of the

Central and South Pacific.

CincPac leaned forward over his glass of bourbon and said quietly, "This is not to leave these walls."

Vandegrift nodded conspiratorially.

"I'm sending Ghormley home. He's not aggressive enough for this job. I'm going to replace him with Bill Halsey, a real fighting man."

Before he boarded a B-17 for the flight to Nouméa, Nimitz said the Marines were doing a fine job here. He promised nothing about supply and reinforcements but Vandegrift knew there was tacit understanding on that. And he was ashamed of presuming he would have to explain his strategy. He'd been thinking too small.

It had been raining hard and the big bomber couldn't make it into the air. Vandegrift and air chief Geiger held their breath while the plane carrying Nimitz slithered to an uncertain halt just before the trees at the end of the muddy runway.

"I hope Halsey's as good as Nimitz thinks," Geiger said, scanning the clouds. "If he's such a fighter, name me a fight he's been in. He got to the Coral Sea too late for the battle, and I hear he missed Midway with dermatitis."

When the rain stopped and the field dried a little, Nimitz finally got airborne.

Kawaguchi reached Rabaul sick, weak and convinced he was finished in the army.

He was interrogated by a senior staff officer, Colonel Haruo Konuma, who was known as one of the aggressive young officers who hated defeatists and wanted older officers like Kawaguchi pushed aside. Kawaguchi vowed to be unflinching and forthright about the problems on Guadalcanal. Let the cards fall where they may.

But Konuma surprised him. "You have suffered much and the difficulties on Guadalcanal are great. We clearly under-estimated the time it would take the Americans to mount a serious counterattack. We need officers with first-hand experience there. I will recommend to his excellency that you return and command one of the units in the new attack."

Colonels holding generals' careers in their hands. A return to Starvation Island. It was too much for Kawaguchi to think about. He just wanted food and sleep.

In his crude, pagoda-style hut at the Bougainville airstrip, Kimi Otomo read his orders. His three dive bombers were to fill their tanks to the brim, attack the American field one more time, then return all the way to Rabaul. From there, liberty in Japan before reassignment to New Guinea.

A furlough to Japan! His twelfth mission over Guadalcanal would be the last, and then two weeks of precious leave to see his wife and children.

He felt a sense of failure that he and his comrades still hadn't taken that island. It was the first time he'd been reassigned before an objective had been achieved. Was the 11th Air Fleet admitting defeat? Of course not, it was just that his dive bombers could be better used on New Guinea. Still, Otomo was a finish-the-job type and he was troubled.

He missed his wife Kaneko more than ever. He gazed at her photograph for a long time. Her small graceful neck, the curve of her jaw, her heart-shaped mouth and delicate nose. It was a face shot, cropped at the shoulders, but he envisioned her small, buoyant breasts and the curve at the small of her back. What exquisite pain to think of those things. *Soon, my love, soon, I will be with you again. It makes me so happy.*

The doctors had started Kenny off with ten-minute walks and increased the dosage each day. He got only an occasional ache in his chest and it was the pain of healing---tissue growing and rehabilitating itself. He wasn't ready for an all-day hike in the jungle with a field pack, but he felt his strength growing. He could stay on his feet for an hour with no ill effects. Once he walked a half-mile to Luganville village and spent an hour gazing at the houses and shops there, a fascinating mixture of French and Melanesian.

His conversations with Claudia grew more frequent and relaxed. He desperately hoped she liked him as much as he did her. Neither mentioned the Dr. Kepple incident. Kenny occasionally saw him moving about the patients' ward, but the doctor always gave him a wide berth. Fine.

Then the orders came.

Kenny sat beside John the Baptist's bed.

"You're red-tagged all the way to San Diego, Bap, and I'm heading back to the Canal. Figures. The naval hospital in Dago can fix up that bad lung in no time. I hear they're expanding that hospital all over Balboa Park. You'll probably become an instructor at MCRD or something. Me? I guess what's left of my old squad will be waiting for me."

"Kenny, you did everything you could for the squad. Don't blame yourself for the ones we lost."

"Easy to say, Bap. I dream about 'em sometimes."

"I'm sorry for all the grief I gave you. About . . . you know. I've reached the conclusion that God forgives me for killing the enemy. I've prayed on it a lot. It was His will. I had to do it for you, for all the guys out there with me. Am I making any sense?"

"Yeah, I know what you're saying. I think the corners are still on that conscience-box of yours. We did what we had to, all of us. We're just tiny cogs in a big machine."

". . . *And forgive us our sins, as we forgive those who sin against us . . . .*"

"What's that?"

"It's been an honor serving with you, Kenny. You saved my life. I'll always remember that. You're a great shipmate. I hope we can keep in touch."

"Yeah, sure."

An hour later, Claudia stopped by. Kenny was sitting in a

chair beside his bed, reading a book from the hospital's small library, Jack London's *Call of the Wild*.

"How are we feeling today, Kenny?"

"We? Have you been ailing, too?"

"Oh, funny. You're not only a writer but also an editor?"

"Sorry. Sometimes I can't help myself, but it does strike me funny the way you nurses always say 'we'."

"It's a habit, I suppose. Hospital jargon. But enough about my quaint speech patterns. I'm about to go on break. Join me for a cup of coffee?"

"We think we could do that."

Claudia jabbed him on the arm.

Soon they were sitting together in a quiet corner of a room used as a lounge for recovering patients. Claudia was drinking coffee, Kenny a Delaware Punch.

"How much longer will you be here?" she asked, touching his hand. A warm tingle slithered up his arm, through his chest and down to his groin. Good thing she couldn't read his blood pressure right now.

"I don't know exactly. My orders read, 'When your recovery and transportation availability permit'."

"I hope that's not too soon. I . . . " She looked directly at him. Those hazel eyes swallowed him up. "I enjoy our talks."

"Me too." Kenny took a sip of his soda, broke the eye contact. "I'll bet you've struck up friendships with lots of fellows who've come through here."

"No. Only you."

That flustered him. "What I mean is, medical care is one part of healing, but so is individual attention. You know, personal interest, keeping up morale."

"That's true, and I write letters for those who can't use their hands, read to them, patch a shirt, and so on. But--" She touched his hand again. Wow, the glow. "--But you're the only real friend I've made. I've, well, I've never talked this much with a man before. You see, Kenny, you've helped *me*."

"Gosh, I have?"

Claudia smiled.

Kenny thought for a moment. "But why? Why haven't you talked this much with a man before?"

Claudia pulled her hand away. "It's getting late," she said. "My patient needs his sleep."

In his dreams that night, Kenny was crawling up that tortuous hill again, and also patching targets at the New River rifle range. There was a bamboo spear in the dream, too.

Admiral Yamamoto did as he'd promised. His Combined Fleet protected the transports bringing General Hyakutake to Guadalcanal with his 17th Army headquarters and its artillery, plus the entire Sendai Division. This latest beefed-up Tokyo Express was now near Bougainville. Yamamoto wanted the Americans run off that accursed island on X-Day.

But before the Americans could be driven out or Hyakutake even landed, another disaster befell his countrymen on that accursed island.

Vandegrift attacked the Matanikau again and this time he sprang his trap. With bridging supplied by Stinky Davis and his engineers, two battalions crossed the river upstream and got in the rear of the enemy garrison before the main attack struck along the coast.

With artillery and the Cactus Air Force joining in battering the encircled Japanese, it was a massacre. Sixty-five Marines were killed but the Japanese lost many times that.

Able Company was part of the attack. Scupper Harris alone claimed seven Japanese. Harris had gotten into the habit of cutting a notch in his gunstock for every enemy soldier he killed. With twenty notches on the stock, he was running out of space.

*   *   *

The next day, Vandegrift had lunch with Colonel Thomas in the command post. For once, they were caught up with their paperwork. Butch Morgan provided Spam sandwiches and a pot of chili spiced with a dash of captured *wasabi* powder.

"Jerry, it's a real shame the militarists have taken over in Japan," the general said, in a reflective mood.

"It sure is. A lot of people will die before we can put out the fire these maniacs have started."

"I've always admired the ingenuity of the Japanese," Vandegrift said. "I've always believed that the United States and Japan would emerge one day as the leading powers of the world."

"You mean that, sir?"

"A year ago I did, yes, before the military junta started their senseless Pacific war. Stringing along with Hitler was their big mistake. Yet somehow, years from now, I believe it will happen yet."

"Stronger than the British Empire?" Thomas wiped some chili from his lip.

"The British Empire is on its last legs. We're propping them up all over the globe. Alone, they didn't stand a chance against the Nazis, but now with the Russians and us at their side, they'll squeak through. The British will be flat broke and hard pressed to hang onto their colonies when this is over. Ireland pulling away was just the beginning.

"No, I think these industrious, resourceful little Japanese will pull themselves up again after we knock them down. What are we going to do, blast them to bits and then occupy their home islands indefinitely? We may have to do the former, but not the latter. Neither civilization would stand for that. You and I may not be around to see it, but I still believe the two of us eventually will lead the world. When that day comes, we'll have to cooperate and work together for the good of all."

Thomas pursed his lips thoughtfully. It was probably something he'd never considered.

In the communications hut, the radio crackled and came to life. It was the coastwatcher on New Georgia. The industrious, resourceful little Japanese were on their way.

Kimi Otomo led them.

After this mission Otomo was going home for two weeks! That glorious thought seemed to carry him along without help from the airplane.

Columns of cumulus towered above Florida Island and once again he drank in the tropics' spectacular hues and shades of green, white, gray and blue. It was hard to realize that two powerful nations were at war. From 12,000 feet as he approached Sealark Channel, the only signs of it were a smoke plume from a wrecked transport off to the right, somewhere near Tassafaronga Point, looking small and insignificant, and a few innocent puffs of AA smoke in the sky over the airfield. From his altitude, one had to look closely to see these tiny smudges on an otherwise tranquil panorama. It was all a matter of perspective.

He turned to the business at hand. Providentially, he saw no planes climbing to intercept. By now, his little group was so well-rehearsed in this process that he didn't need to give the other two fliers any signals. Otomo was the first to push over and dive. Then came crew No. 2, then 3, like obedient ducklings.

Again the orange tracers came up toward him, floating slowly at first, accelerating faster and faster as they got closer, then vanishing in blurs on each side of the speeding plane. The metal shrieked, the diving flaps whined like sirens, the rush of air whistled at the canopy and as always G-forces crushed against his face.

As the ground rushed up, Otomo released his bomb, pulled back hard on the stick and blacked out for a second or two. When he came to, he was leveling off.

He pulled up and had just begun his climb, only 1,500 feet above the ground, when the plane shuddered in the grip of an explosion.

■

CHAPTER 32

KENNY GOT THE WORD. A B-17 would take him back to the Canal in the morning. He and Claudia were strolling again in the flower garden above the sea. Neither one said much, just gazed at the picture-postcard sea of blue and green. For Kenny it had lost its luster.

He'd always loved visiting his grandparents' farm near Champaign. The fresh air and sunshine . . . searching for four-leaf clovers in the pasture . . . sheltering from cloudbursts in the corn shed, counting the seconds between lightning flashes and thunder claps. . . feeding the cows and hogs. . . gliding in the porch swing and listening to Cubs' games on the staticky wooden Philco in the parlor, the "ooooooom-BOOM" the fans called in unison as foul balls slid down the net above the backstop and dropped to the field. The same melancholy he had felt when those visits came to an end gripped him now. Something good was ending.

Kenny came out of his daydream when Claudia reached out and took his hand. Holding his hand! Not just touching it--holding it. This was no time to be daydreaming about Grandpa's farm.

"Would you write me?" he asked.

"I'd like that. Will you write me too?"

"You bet."

Silence again.With great clarity now, Kenny saw that the Coral Sea had regained all its brilliance. In fact, the world had never looked so bright.

For her part, Claudia was thinking, I really do trust this guy. All my instincts say I've done the impossible, found a good man. And now he's going back to the war. Are these few good days all

I'll ever have?

"Claudia."

"Yes?"

"I'd like to kiss you."

No man ever asked permission before. "What took you so long?"

He put a hand behind her neck and gingerly drew her face to his. Their lips brushed. Tentatively. The kiss grew deeper. The touch of his mouth felt surprisingly nice to her. And honest.

Otomo's plane rocked. The ear-splitting bark of the AA shell exploding. A horrifying shout howled through his earphones. Had to be Asakawa's death scream. The controls went softer than mush. Behind him the plane was a mass of flames. He'd never felt such heat, scorching the back of his head.

He did the only thing he could. Shoved the canopy back, un-snapped his harness, banked the plane so sharply it stood on a wingtip, and simply tumbled out, well aware of how little altitude he had. As the rush of air slapped him, he glimpsed a cluster of men down below. Were they Japanese or Americans? Had he crossed the enemy's lines?

He tugged on the cord. Was he even high enough for the parachute to open? The answer came in less than a second. Thanks be to Buddha, the chute billowed open. The sharp jerk of the shroud lines wrenched him.

He thought he heard cheering down on the ground. Saw the plane sheer into the jungle and erupt in a ball of orange that gushed above the canopy of trees. Had one good swing beneath the chute before he hit. He rolled with the blow as he'd been taught and seemed to be okay except for a shallow pain in one leg.

Plunkett saw it all. The platoon was only fifty yards from where the Jap had landed.

"Son of a bitch," Scupper Harris shouted, "son of a bitch." He jumped up and bolted toward the enemy pilot. Plunkett jogged along behind him. He saw Scupper Harris flourish his souvenir sword in his right hand and his service .45 in his left.

The Jap flier untangled himself from his harness. It looked like he was trying to stand up and raise his hands in surrender when he saw Harris, Plunkett and the others dashing toward him.

Was Harris swinging a sword like a windmill gone mad? Plunkett realized that fool kid wanted to decapitate the Jap. The sword swiped wildly toward the man's neck. He ducked the blade and shot a kick-boxer's blow to the kid's beltline.

Harris groaned and doubled over in pain. Plunkett knew why the pistol hadn't fired. His hands hadn't been able to carry out two dissimilar functions at the same time. The enemy pilot grabbed the pistol and fired it point blank into Harris' chest. A hole the size of a fist exploded out his back like a burst watermelon.

Plunkett emptied most of his rifle clip into the Jap. Four crimson holes materialized on his flight jacket. He fell forward on Harris. The two toppled to earth and came to rest in something very like the missionary position.

It happened so fast, Plunkett thought. One second Scupper Harris is about to murder a prisoner and in the wink of an eye both men are dead—although it seemed to him that the Jap fell in slow motion. His inner eye would always see the head jerk to the right, the hand lose its grip on the .45, and the Japanese eyes lock onto his, Plunkett's, almost as if to say "nice shot," all before striking the ground.

Otomo, in that nanosecond of time while his body had reacted in one fluid motion to kick this man and seize his pistol, had envisioned his wife Kaneko and their home in Nagoya. From the corner of his eye, he'd seen another American on him, a huge one, with many others close behind. *Be merciful, beloved Buddha, this is my time to die.*

"Dumb-ass stunt to pull," Plunkett said. "Fucker hadn't even had his nineteenth birthday. Maybe he's with his pappy now. Wade, Carmichael, take him over to the morgue tent."

Plunkett's head hung. He walked away. "Somebody dig a hole for the Jap," he called over his shoulder.

Darkness blanketed the ward. Kenny sat on his bed, feeling at once wonderful and terrible. Claudia Chase was the best thing that had ever happened to him--and he was returning to Guadalcanal in the morning. Part of him wanted to stay right here forever with this marvelous new lady friend and hated the idea of going back to that hell-hole. But another part yearned to see his buddies and do what he could for his outfit. Able Company was home.

And then Claudia was there. Most of the patients were quiet if not sleeping.

"Don't go back," she whispered, touching his arm softly. "Please. You've already done more than enough. I could put something on your records. Pneumonia, or--"

Kenny got up and faced her. "Don't go back?" he murmured, as much to himself as to Claudia. Could he really not go back? He stood silent for a long moment.

"No," he said at last, "I have to go."

"But why?" Sounding betrayed. "*Why*, Kenny?"

"I just have to, Claudia. It's hard to explain. But when you see what those guys do for each other when the bullets and the mortars are crashing all around, when the whole damn world's blowing up, all they have is each other. It's the holiest thing I've ever seen. I have to go back to them."

"Holy? That doesn't make sense." Exasperated. "I thought I meant something to you."

"You do! Look, I kept that old lecher off you, didn't I?"

Heads turned in several beds.

"Who asked you to? I can fight my own battles."

"Everybody needs a little help sometimes."

"I don't." And Claudia walked off.

"Claudia, wait . . ."

She was gone. Kenny stood there with a heart full of hurt.

General Kawaguchi was back on Starvation Island.

Since he knew the island, he led his commander, Lieutenant General Hyakutake, ashore at Tassafaronga Point. The Tokyo Express unloaded all night, the cargo including scores of 155-millimeter howitzers.

Kawaguchi had an instinctive dislike for the surly martinet. It was unnerving being back on this terrible island where he'd lost so many good men. Knowing that his superiors considered him a loser hurt even worse. As he guided Hyakutake along the beach toward army headquarters, the clanging of cranes and winches offloading supplies sounded like nails being driven into his coffin.

But by dawn, he saw that Hyakutake's confidence was shaken. He'd met sick, emaciated survivors of that bloody ridge and learned the results of the recent disaster at the Matanikau. The problems of movement and supply proved greater and the jungle denser than he'd ever imagined. Already he'd sent a wireless to Rabaul asking for more help, even though he had 10,000 men on the island.

The battle plan had been to attack along the shore, crossing the Matanikau to take the airfield by the easy coastal route, backed by the massed artillery. But patrols found the Americans much stronger than expected in that sector west of the field, so Hyakutake changed the strategy. X-Day would have to be postponed. The Sendai Division and Kawaguchi's regiment would march through the jungle behind Mount Austen and attack the airfield from the rear.

Kawaguchi was aghast. He was being ordered to return to the same ground on which he'd been so badly beaten before. The Americans had made a fortress of the airfield, he told Hyakutake, with large supplies of men, food and weapons. To successfully storm this alien fastness was nearly impossible with the available forces. Their only hope was in concentrating them all and attacking in force along the coast.

"Nonsense," Hyakutake snapped. "My plan will not fail. You will do your duty."

After leaving the command post, Kawaguchi's operations officer said, "Excellency, we have seen what it is like down there. He is making a great mistake. Dispersed piecemeal in the jungle we can only fail again. We should not split our forces. The Sendai Division is the army's best. We must consolidate and strike together."

Kai Suzuki must have realized how far he'd strayed from propriety. "Excellency, I am so sorry for my rudeness." He bowed deeply.

Kawaguchi managed a wan smile. "You'll make a fine general some day, Suzuki-san." *If you live.*

"My Dear Mildred,

"It's a strange war out here. For the first time in my life I'll have an Army regiment under my command. It arrives tomorrow and I'll gladly take all the help I can get. It's from a division which I shouldn't name through the mails.

"My knee is feeling better all the time. The tramping around this island has got these old legs in pretty decent shape. Of course I'm driven by jeep a great deal, but I insist on doing much walking. Whenever I set out on foot, Corporal Smith, my orderly, accompanies me with a 12-gauge shotgun. Ever since those three enemy soldiers got through and charged the CP, Smith has taken it upon himself to be my personal bodyguard. Honestly, Mildred, I was never in real danger.

"I'd be lying if I didn't admit it's a tough and sometimes unhappy life out here, as in the case of poor old Frank Goettge, but one day the nation will learn what an important task it is.

"Another old friend, Roy Geiger, is here, commanding our little air force. His men are getting quite run down, flying several tough sorties every day, and sometimes at night with only flashlights and burning oil drums to mark the runway. As you know, Roy is in his

fifties and a naval aviation pioneer. Well, he took up an armed bomber the other day, flew over Point Cruz and attacked the Japanese, just to set an example and boost morale. It was a wonderful gesture and a great bit of generalship.

"After getting nothing for three weeks, four of your letters arrived the other day. I can't tell you how much those letters mean to me. I'm keeping well and pray that you are, too."

Vandegrift received his first non-Marine Corps help on October 9th with the arrival of a regiment of the Army's Americal (America New Caledonia) Division. The existence of the Cactus Air Force made it possible for Admiral Turner down at Nouméa to be more aggressive in his efforts to protect and supply Vandegrift. The beleaguered but reliable air umbrella had enabled most of his transports to get through. The supply line was starting to stream toward Guadalcanal.

He soon learned this was true for both sides. A scout plane spotted a group of enemy supply ships near Shortland Island, escorted by three heavy cruisers and two destroyers. Admiral Turner still had the protective force for the Americal Division in the vicinity, so Vandegrift knew there'd be a fight. It took place the next night.

Plunkett and two squads were trudging back from a night recon, crossing a ridge, when they heard the rumble of guns and saw distant flashes out on the black sea.

"Looks like them sailor boys are havin' themselves another shootout," Plunkett said. "Take a seat, girls, and watch the show. Carmichael, put a sentry on each end."

Billy Ninetrees sat beside Plunkett. "I wonder how Nielsen is doing," said the usually silent Pawnee, "and if he will be back." Plunkett knew 'Trees had great respect for the departed sergeant.

Plunkett slurped some water from his canteen. "Aw, Nielsen'll be back, and prob'ly bossing all of us around 'fore you know it. He's big medicine, isn't that what you people say?"

"Oh, *please*." Ninetrees winced. "You think he will get a field commission?"

"Prob'ly. Second Loots are droppin' like flies, and Kenny's the smartest guy in the whole company."

"What if he doesn't come back?"

"He'll be back." A giant flash out in the channel. "Man, will you look at that!"

The next day, Colonel Thomas gathered all his dispatches and pieced the battle together for Vandegrift.

"The Tokyo Express caught a big surprise this time," Thomas said. "For once we attacked them on their own terms--at night."

"Good. Norm Scott commanded, didn't he?"

"Yes sir, I'm told that Admiral Scott gave his task force some concentrated training in night combat. He was patrolling north of Cape Esperance and west of Savo when his radar found the Jap column heading directly toward him.

"Both sides slugged it out for several minutes, then the enemy commander ordered a cease-fire, maybe thought he was shooting at the supply column he was there to protect. We kept firing. By the time the Japs corrected their mistake, cruisers *Aoba* and *Furutaka* were floating funeral pyres.

"A magazine exploded on our cruiser *Boise*, but some good damage control and firefighting saved the ship. By zero-two-hundred, according to our intercept, *Furutaka* was on the bottom of Ironbottom Sound, along with a destroyer. We lost only a destroyer."

"Very good news, Jerry."

"It wasn't a total victory, though, sir. While the battle occupied our ships, the enemy transports completed unloading their men and supplies at Tassafaronga Point."

"Good Lord," Vandegrift exclaimed. "More men to pound away at our perimeter. Out here, it seems every silver cloud has a dark lining."

* * *

In the morning, Kenny stared intently at the reflection in the mirror as he shaved. Who was that guy? Dark circles under the eyes betrayed the fact that he'd slept very little. The wound on his chest was healing nicely. The scar looked like the letter J. Why did I ever say that? he admonished. How could it all go smash over that one little thing?

He washed off the Burma Shave, rinsed the razor beneath the tap and then slipped into a clean new utility blouse.

Ten minutes later he stepped out the double front doors of the hospital and shambled down the four concrete steps, small valleys worn in them by years of use. His seabag swung over his shoulder. The jeep was waiting. The driver, a sailor, honked and waved. So this was it. He was going back.

He stood there a moment, staring blankly at the jeep.

"Kenny, Kenny, wait." He turned. His prayer was answered. Claudia was there.

She was in uniform. Beige skirt and belted jacket with a brass USN on the collar, prosaic black shoes. He'd never seen Claudia in anything but her white smock. She looked awfully good in that skirt. She approached slowly at first, almost shyly, then ran down the steps and pressed herself against him, her arms tightly ringing his back.

"I'm sorry," she said.

"Me too." He kissed her forehead. "I can say some pretty dumb things." The sailor let out a loud, rude whistle. An enlisted man embracing an officer. But Kenny didn't give a damn. "Will you still write?"

"Of course. You too?"

"You bet."

He kissed her lips.

Claudia leaned back in his arms. "You'd better get going then. You don't want to miss your war."

Reluctantly, he pulled free, took one last wordless look deep into her eyes, and turned toward the jeep, the tropical morning looking a little brighter. He tossed his seabag in the back and hopped in. He turned his head for a last look, but Claudia was gone.

■

CHAPTER 33

THE B-17, *SHOO-FLY PIE*, lumbered into the air. Kenny crawled into the empty waist gunner's bubble to look out. As the plane banked to the left he saw the receding airstrip, the shoreline, the coral reef and, for just a moment, the tiled roof of the hospital and the palms and banyans in the courtyard. Then the wings leveled and it was gone. The fleeting look at the place where Claudia Chase lived and worked was bittersweet.

The four Pratt & Whitney engines toiled in loud harmony as the bomber climbed to the northwest, bouncing now and then on a patch of turbulence. Kenny knew his buddies in A Company would give him a bad time about his clean new utilities.

His fellow passengers were two Marine officers, a Navy commander, and five enlisted men. The latter, like himself, were going back to their units on Guadalcanal after recuperating at Espiritu Santo. Kenny had no idea about the officers' assignments. Everyone was quiet, each man keeping company with his own thoughts. It was cold up here. He savored it, knowing the heat of the Canal as he did.

Kenny was more full of hope than at any time in his life and yet in the silence of his heart he was troubled. He wondered if Claudia would really write. What reason had he to doubt her? Well, that was natural, he answered himself. Jacqueline Lundquist, his high school sweetheart who moved away and stopped writing, crossed his mind. So did Nathaniel the Spaniel. He'd loved that dog but it went and vanished. As everything good in his life always had.

Even when Claudia was at her sunny best, there was still a trace of darkness there. He knew he loved her, for the first time in his life loved a woman as much as he had his mother. But he also knew that he might never have her love unconditionally. There must be a door to something bad in her past that she just couldn't close.

He wondered what his mother would think of Claudia. He felt her soul hovering nearby, concerned that her son was going back into combat.

Hell, you think too much. Get some sleep.

Almost two hours later, he climbed into the gunner's bubble when Guadalcanal hove into view. At first it was a distant lump in the sea. As it grew larger, the mountains took on distinct shapes. The island looked beautiful, if you didn't know better, a piece of jade on an elegant blue background. A rainstorm blurred the eastern part, beyond Taivu Point, but the rest stood out clearly.

The pilot flew across the heart of Guadalcanal and passed east of Henderson Field, to avoid AA fire from the Japanese around Tassafaronga Point. Kenny glanced at his watch. Oh-nine-forty. The enemy bombers would be on their way down from Rabaul by now, still many miles to the northwest.

Two small smoke trails snaking up from the north shore, staining the sky no more than a lumber mill would, were the only visible signs of war. Kenny could make out tiny wrecked trans-ports at the root of each plume. Those burning ships and the tiny gray scar that was Henderson Field were the only visible signs that thousands of soldiers were trying to kill each other down there.

Kenny was rapt. He had traveled very little by air and since he couldn't remember one detail of his departure from this place, the return had his full attention. The plane made a wide counterclockwise turn over Sealark Channel, whose swells danced in the sunlight like hundreds of diamonds. As the turn widened, he saw the Cow Pasture, the grass fighter strip the Seabees had built just south of Henderson. The bomber descended for a left-hand approach and landing. And then the plane was on an east heading, dropping fast, lined up on the field. Florida Island materialized in the distance and, much closer, the lump of coal that was Savo Island.

Then there was a bump and they were down. Kenny Nielsen was back on Guadalcanal.

The company had changed bivouacs while he was gone. It was set up now on a knoll beyond the Lunga west of the airfield, Hill 62, Turner's Tit.

"Will you look what the cat drug in?" Plunkett said when Kenny hopped from the back of a jeep, seabag over his shoulder. "I thought you was smart. But here you are, right back in this lovely war. If you really had brains," he said with a giveaway grin, "you'd've never set foot on this rock again."

"Nice to see you, too."

Hoagy Carmichael, Billy Ninetrees, Connie Keugeman and Skinny Wade gathered around--the old gang from August 7th was smaller now. There was much handshaking and backslapping. Kenny noticed a couple of tents.

"The Navy finally got some tents to the Canal?"

"Yep," Keugeman said. "Hey, you get laid down in Santo?"

Kenny blushed. "I was in surgery for cryin' out loud."

"Not for three weeks you weren't."

They gave him all the dope.

"Red Mike's the new CO of the regiment," Plunkett said. "Yep, Colonel Edson hisself. Hunt got packed off somewhere. Rusty Gates made captain and took over C Company."

The new platoon leader was a Lieutenant Ruffin. "I already got him in training," Plunkett said.

"Now we'll call the platoon the Ruffin Readies," Kenny said.

Plunkett groaned."Them surgeons down there sure didn't take out your corn bone."

Pretty soon Ruffin came up, accepted Kenny's "reporting for duty, sir," and reached out for his orders.

"Welcome back to our charming island," he said. "Heard good things about you, Sergeant. Your old squad is yours."

"Thank you, sir." God, he hadn't saluted anybody in quite

awhile.

Kenny was genuinely sorry to hear about the death of Scupper Harris. That reaction surprised him. He always thought he would dance on Scupper's grave but that's not how he felt now.

He shared the news that John the Baptist was going all the way home, and he cringed when Plunkett told him the Old Man himself was going to review the troops and present him the Silver Star.

Even Captain Brush came by to welcome him. "Glad to have you back from *Buttons*, Sergeant. Looks like they took good care of you."

"Buttons, sir?"

"Yeah, Buttons, the code name for Espiritu Santo. You never heard that?"

"No sir, they kept that a secret from me." They could sure use some help in the Code Name Department, he thought. "But, aye, aye, sir, they took very good care of me."

At last Kenny sat in a hole with Carmichael, getting his new utilities muddy. When he opened a can of C-ration chicken noodles, he knew he was back.

X-Day was postponed because Hyakutake's altered attack plan needed more time, but the big battlewagons arrived on Ironbottom Sound on schedule. Coordination between army and navy had always been even tougher for the Japanese than the Americans.

The fast battleships *Haruna* and *Kongo* passed Savo Island and were off Guadalcanal at midnight, loaded with incendiary and armor-piercing shells, ready to wipe out the American garrison with a killing barrage. These World War I battle cruisers had been modernized in the 1930s and now bristled with five-, six- and fourteen-inch guns.

Just before 1 a.m., Washing Machine Charlie dropped flares over Henderson Field and the big guns began raining incendiary shells on the Marines. With Charlie in the sky and a naval gunnery officer talking to the ships from Mount Austen, accuracy was a cinch. Within minutes, huge fires were visible and the skippers knew they were scoring on the airfield. Having lit up their targets, they switched to armor-piercing shells and the bedlam on the receiving end grew even worse.

The ground quaked as if doomsday itself were here. Marines set new records for tunneling deep in the ground. Fuel and ammunition stores went up in flames. The unlucky men were killed, the lucky ones merely had their eardrums burst.

The shelling impartially rocked the command post as well as the foxholes.

General Vandegrift came into the message center, where Colonel Twining was manning the telephones. "Jesus, sir," Twining muttered, "we've never seen anything like this before."

BROOMPH!

"That one sounded exactly like a freight train barreling down the tracks," Twining said.

Vandegrift knew the coconut logs over their heads and the sandbags at their sides weren't much protection against these monstrous shells.

Another loud blast, another concussion hammering their ears.

"My God, that didn't sound like anything," Twining said. "No warning at all. How do you explain that, sir?"

Vandegrift said, "The newer fourteen-inchers on their battle-wagons must propel shells faster than the speed of sound. They arrive and detonate before you hear them. Frightening."

"Sure as hell are."

To Vandegrift, the ground quivered like Jell-O.

Then, after nearly thirty minutes, it stopped. Outside, he heard Marines calling to their buddies and checking for damage. There must be plenty.

"I don't know how you feel," Twining told him, "but I'd prefer a good old-fashioned bombing or an artillery shelling."

Another blast drowned out Vandegrift's reply. When the sound died away, he said, "The battleships must have reversed course for another firing leg."

At A Company's bivouac, Kenny hugged the side of his hole, ears ringing, head throbbing. The earth trembled as if it too were afraid. Why the hell did he ever come back? He thought he'd experienced the worst there was, but this set a new criterion for terror, even though he figured he was west of the target zone. He didn't think it possible, but he was as frightened as he'd been on that first patrol almost two months ago. One near-hit lifted him off the ground, light and helpless like a sheet of paper in an updraft. Gravity dumped him back like a pancake. Claudia's face appeared in his mind's eye. I have to live. God, please let me live.

The assault lasted more than an hour, the ships working back and forth offshore and firing until their ordnance was gone. If General Hyakutake had been able to coordinate his attack with the hell of this unprecedented naval shelling, the American position might have collapsed that night.

Dawn found a battered and splintered Henderson Field. Maimed airplanes lay scattered like broken toys, trees were charred kindling, and the remains of supplies and buildings were strewn at random. The severely cratered runway needed major repair. Half the Americans' ninety planes were destroyed and precious little aviation fuel remained. Some of that was ablaze and would burn throughout the day. By some miracle only forty-one Marines had been killed. General Geiger, who figured the Japanese gunners had used the Pagoda as an aiming point, ordered the little command post torn down.

"How we doing this morning, Marine?"

Claudia gave John the Baptist a smile and started pumping a blood-pressure cuff on his arm.

"You knew Sergeant Nielsen pretty well, didn't you, John?"

"Yeah, swell guy."

"Tell me, what's he like?"

"A smart cookie, miss. He'd've been a college man for sure except his father didn't have the money. I'll never forget him. He saved my life, you know."

Claudia laughed. "So you've told me many times." She noted the blood pressure on a clipboard--one hundred over sixty--and unfastened the wrap.

"So he's smart and brave. What else?"

"Gosh, I don't know. Great sense of humor, always makin' jokes. He's just a nice guy. Never wants to hurt your feelings. You could always go to him with your problems. Funny, he was easy to talk to, but still kind of a loner."

Interesting, Claudia said to herself. Kenny a loner? She remembered him saying he'd dreamed of this hospital building the night before the invasion, although he hadn't even known of its existence. She wondered what that could mean.

"He lost his mother," the Baptist was saying, "and I don't think he was close to his dad or his brother. Honest, miss, I hate to leave him, to go home I mean. I lost some friends out there and, well, it feels like I'm walkin' out on those guys. 'Always finish what you start' is the way I was raised. Isn't there some way I could go back?"

"Afraid not. You're going to be fine and live a long life, but first you need to get that lung infection fixed up by specialists back home. You're fortunate. You're out of danger now. You should thank your lucky stars."

"I guess. Say, how come all the questions about Kenny?"

Claudia smiled and left. She prayed for Kenny that night and believed that John McKenna did, too.

Tokyo Rose's broadcasts were relayed by a high-power transmitter on Truk Island. They usually came in clearly after dark, although staticky if there were storms around.

"No sleep on Guadalcanal last night? Too bad. The burial

parties of the 1st Raider Battalion and the 5th and 7th Marines were very busy today, weren't they?"

"That bitch," said Hoagy Carmichael. "How does she know so much about us?"

"I've some nice music for those of you who are still alive. Enjoy it while you can. Here's the Benny Goodman Orchestra with a Gershwin favorite, *I've Got Rhythm*. Hey Marine, wanta dance?"

"Dance?" Plunkett grunted. "Hell no, baby, I want some sex-you-all intercourse."

"Where the devil does she get all those good platters?" Kenny said.

He and Plunkett went over to a nearby rock and sat by themselves. "You know, life has gotten awful cheap out here," Plunkett said.

"Down at Santo I spent a lot of time thinking the same thing. How it loses all meaning after you've killed a lot of the enemy. You get so it doesn't bother you much. What happens to a man when killing another man doesn't mean anything?"

"'Zackly what I'm sayin', Kenny. The Japs are brought up different. For them, it's hep to die for the Emperor; better to kill yourself than surrender, that kind of stuff. They have this --what's the word, mystical?--outlook. Think the Emperor is a livin' god, fer cryin' out loud. Now that's one way of arrivin' at life bein' cheap. We get there more direct. We just get worn down and hungry, tired of constant danger and fear, and the more we fight and kill the bastards the less it means. Kinda like we get vaccinated against feelings."

"You're a philosopher, Plunk."

"Ain't no such a thing, but it worries me, what all this does to a man. I wonder if we can undo it and get normal again after all this is over."

"I wonder too. We'll never be able to share the real truth of our experiences with people back home." Kenny sighed. "Meanwhile, hell, the war has to be fought."

Plunkett slurped some coffee from his aluminum cup and quickly spit it out. "Stuff's too thick to drink and too thin to plow.

Oh, damn right--after Pearl Harbor?--the war's gotta be fought. Hirohito's gotta be stopped, and Hitler, too. But after we cork 'em, the big shots'll kiss an' make up and go back a-tradin' again. But what about guys like you and me who had to come to this hell-hole and do what we did? Will we hate the Japs the rest of our lives?"

"Maybe.You're right about one thing anyway, Plunk."

"What's that?"

"Life has become very cheap out here."

■

CHAPTER 34

THE NEXT DAY Kenny trudged down to the news placard at Kukum to check the World Series results, chalked on the blackboard there. "Hot dog, the Cardinals beat the Yankees, four games to one," he said. "The Cubs woulda beat the Yankees, too."

"Yeah, but the Cubs weren't in it, Sergeant, the Cards were."

Kenny turned. Standing at his shoulder was the war correspondent he'd met at Espiritu Santo.

"Well, hi, Mr. Weaver. How long've you been on this rock?"

"Jake, the name is Jake. Mr. Weaver is my father." The reporter laughed at his little joke. "Four days now. Some shelling we had last night. They always that bad?"

"No sir, Jake, that's the worst I've ever seen. If I never see another like it, it'll be too soon."

"I guess it was your welcome home party. You know, I was in the big Long Beach earthquake in '33. Covered it for the paper. The old ground shook pretty good, buildings came down, cars were overturned, but it was nothin' like last night. Knocked me right off my feet. "

"Don't tell me you tried to stand up in the middle of that."

"Not for long, Sergeant, not for long . . . You're a Cubs fan, hey? I'm a Cardinal fan myself and I'm here to tell ya they're the best--Walker Cooper, Enos Slaughter, Marty Marion and this new Musial kid. I got five bucks says they'll finish ahead of the Cubs again next year."

"Five bucks? You play for high stakes. You know how much I make a month?"

"Make it whatever you want, then. I s'pose you want odds?"

"I wouldn't make a bet on next season if I was a millionaire. I figure half the guys in the majors will be drafted by the time the '43 season starts. This is gonna be a long war."

"Sure enough," Weaver said. "The Nips figure if it takes us this long to take an island, we'll be less than halfway back to the Philippines by 1948 and fixin' to quit."

"I got news for you, sir. The Marines will take every island faster than the one before. The Japanese will run short of ships and planes long before we do. They've used up a lot of them right here."

"B'lieve you're right about that." Weaver pulled out a pad and scribbled something. "Say, I'm gonna cover the ceremony Saturday when you get your medal from the general."

"You must be pretty hard up for a story."

When Kenny returned to the bivouac Plunkett told him volunteers were being sought for a raid on Pistol Pete. "D-2's got a line on where their artillery's dug in, across the Matanikau. Gittin' up a little posse. Whatta you say? I'd love to silence some o' them bastards."

When Kenny hesitated, Plunkett added, "You can't figure on livin' forever. Got your will made out?"

What the hell, he thought. I'm back. Might as well be useful.

Next morning, an intelligence lieutenant known as Gaucho Kirby led six men hauling a rubber boat, Kenny and Plunkett among them, toward the Matanikau.

The tramp through the jungle seemed almost routine to Kenny, as if he hadn't been away. He carried a bolt-action rifle instead of the heavy Browning Automatic as he passed beneath towering trees. The massive roots and the persistent insects were no longer curiosities, just familiar old stimuli. It occurred to him now why the Japanese attached little cloth flaps to the backs of their forage caps--to keep the sun and the bugs off their necks.

Within twenty minutes, though, his body reminded him how out of shape he was. Muscles grown soft during his convalescence screamed in protest. He breathed in deep, open-mouth gulps.

Remembering that he'd volunteered for this mission, he questioned his sanity. Yeah, he thought, come to think of it, I would like to live forever. Get together again with Claudia. Find a job writing for some newspaper. Maybe have kids. It was bad enough getting shot at by Japs in the perimeter, but sneaking behind their lines like this, Jesus, this was total insane shit.

To brush away those thoughts, he turned to his old mind-out-of-body trick, letting his feet slog on by themselves with no conscious help from the brain.

Reaching the muddy Matanikau, they piled in the boat and paddled across. After scrambling up the other side without drawing fire, Gaucho Kirby whispered, "Everybody down, we're getting close." They melted into the undergrowth and waited. Kenny couldn't hear a thing but the familiar jungle sounds. Apparently they'd got this far without being seen.

Kirby waited another five minutes to be sure, then led the tiny patrol toward a small saddle in a ridge which D-2, battalion intelligence, had doped out as an enemy artillery position.

It was only 300 yards from the river but each hundred yards took half an hour. The forest was that thick--plus Kirby was being extra cautious so as not to be discovered. No routine jungle march this. Kenny and the others were so careful they didn't even let a twig snap. Once his thoughts drifted to Claudia but the danger of the mission quickly slapped him back to the here and now.

When they were within twenty yards of the spot, Kirby sent Kenny ahead as a scout. He crawled along the edge of the depression, scratching and tearing his new dungarees.

Soon he encountered a pile of dry kunai grass. Why dry? Must have been hacked down and used to camouflage something. His heart hammering, he parted the dry grass and came face to face with two 75-millimeter pack guns, smaller than the Pistol Petes but oiled and ready to blast away at Henderson Field.

Kenny waved the others forward. Soon the patrol was at work removing the breeches. Then a shock. Glancing into the gulch below the gun position, Kenny saw several Japanese soldiers snoozing beside a small cave and a crude shack.

He tapped Lieutenant Kirby on the shoulder and pointed them out. The others noticed. They crouched and worked as fast and quietly as they could. They were almost done when Kenny spotted a small piece of brown-painted metal through the foliage in a similar hollow some distance to the north. With hand signals, he advised Kirby he would scout out this possible gun. Kenny crawled at least sixty yards, knew he was now far inside Japanese lines. Butterflies swirled in his stomach. When he reached a pile of lifeless kunai grass, he found that it hid two more guns, also well-tended and ready to fire.

He was dismantling the breeches when his sixth sense kicked in. The hairs on his neck froze. Somehow he knew he was being watched. He looked north. Beside a small native hut sat two Japanese soldiers--staring directly at him. They pointed at him and chattered in Japanese.

Kenny calculated his options. If he ran, he would alert the whole enemy detail. His entire patrol could be wiped out. He knew it was hard to distinguish between the U.S. and Japanese uniforms after they were dirty and torn, and the Marine green was bleached out by sun, rain and sweat. He nodded at the enemy soldiers, finished removing the breech blocks, smiled again, and carried them away as casually as his nerves allowed, never looking back. Trying to make his body seem small, he'd never felt so freakishly tall in his life. Had he really made them think he belonged there?

He reached the others at the first gun position, still amazed that his bluff had worked. They were about to start back when a gunshot crackled, then another. It hadn't worked after all.

Plunkett said, "I'll stay behind and cover while the rest of you haul ass for the Matanikau." Kirby started to argue, but Plunkett said, "Goddamn it Loot, git movin'."

"We'll wait at the river three minutes, no more," Kirby said, leaving Plunkett behind with a .45 and a new M-1 that he'd cadged from the Army.

The six reached the river and dumped the breech blocks in the water, a din of small-arms fire ringing in their ears. Kirby studied the sweep hand of his watch while one of the others pulled the rubber boat from its hiding place and set it at the edge of the water.

"Get in," Kirby ordered. "Two-fifty-five, fifty-six, fifty-seven. . . ." The firing decreased in volume. Occasional shots could be heard individually. Kenny agonized. Had he seen the last of his surrogate father? "Fifty-eight, fifty-nine, three minutes. Let's go." Kirby climbed into the small boat. So did the others. Kenny got in last, his heart reeling.

They were halfway across the Matanikau when Kirby said, "Look at that big bastard run. I never saw two tons of sergeant move like that."

Like a polar bear in faded green, Plunkett burst from the bushes, dived into the water, and began churning through the current. Kenny sighed a whoosh of relief and reached out for Plunkett's hand.

■

CHAPTER 35

"YOU KNOW, I can't stand powdered eggs," Vandegrift told Colonel Twining at breakfast. "In 1927 we were anchored opposite a powdered egg factory in China and the stench was terrible. Please don't tell Butch Morgan. Good old Butch does the best he can. Thank goodness he was able to cook up a slice of ham."

They discussed the dispatches, the juiciest being the official announcement of Ghormley's reassignment and the appointment of Bill Halsey as Commander, South Pacific. Although he'd been tipped off personally by Admiral Nimitz, Vandegrift was still cheered by the news. Halsey was supposed to be a man of action.

Vandegrift reflected that Guadalcanal had gone from being a forgotten island, "a mistake," to the most popular tourist spot in the South Pacific. Now in late October all the brass wanted a look. The next day the commandant of the Marine Corps, General Thomas Holcomb, would show up.

His would be one of the first landings on Cactus' new Marston mat, the steel-mesh carpet that hardened the runway. After the big shelling, the hard-working Seabees had repaired the runway and laid the mat in record time.

Holcomb was a good strategist and Vandegrift was eager to get his opinion on how he'd placed his defenses.

Next day, after giving Holcomb a full briefing, he showed his boss the entire perimeter, now arranged in five sectors. The 5th Marines held Sector 5, which stretched from the sea west of the Lunga, facing the Matanikau, through a line of hills and jungle toward Bloody Ridge.

That night, after a dinner of tinned stew and Japanese crackers, Vandegrift poured glasses of bourbon. He soon got the chief's blessing. "I don't see how you could cover any more territory with what you have," he said. "You've done a good job."

"Very glad to hear you say that, sir. Kelly Turner thinks otherwise."

"Terrible Turner can stick to his goddamned cruisers. Tomorrow afternoon, Archer, I fly to Nouméa to meet with the new theater commander, Bill Halsey. I'll say the same to him about what you're doing here.

"You've been saddled with a damn dirty job. Ghormley and MacArthur thought it was a mistake, that it would fail. MacArthur wants to fight the Japanese all by himself, hog all the headlines. You and your men are doing just fine, just fine."

"Thank you very much, sir."

Minutes later, a radio dispatch arrived from Halsey, ordering Vandegrift to accompany Holcomb to the conference at Nouméa. "Holy smoke," he exclaimed. Leave Cactus while the issue was still in doubt?

Kenny and six others received medals from the generals in a ceremony the next morning outside the CP.

Kenny didn't consider himself a hero, wasn't interested in medals. He had never expected to lay eyes on the commandant of the whole Corps, much less be decorated by him. He'd washed and patched his uniform, but still felt shabby in front of these generals. At least the others' uniforms were just as tattered.

Lieutenant Ruffin had the whole platoon in attendance, standing at smart attention. Kenny could feel their eyes on his back.

He was third in line. When Holcomb came to him, he read from a piece of paper, "Under fire, twice pulled wounded comrades out of positions in which the enemy had them enveloped. Also, helped to allay an enemy attack on the command post, disabled enemy artillery heedless of danger while patrolling behind their lines." Holcomb lowered the paper and ad-libbed, "And performed a number of other fine jobs over and above the call, I'm informed."

He smiled at Kenny and reached out to Captain Schwenke for the medal. As he pinned it on Kenny's blouse he said, "Sergeant Nielsen, it gives me great pleasure on behalf of our grateful nation to award you the Silver Star for gallantry in action."

Tears formed in Kenny's eyes. Damn it, he hadn't wanted that to happen.

Just two miles away, Kawaguchi and the other Japanese generals were busy planning the new attack, now postponed a second time till the night of October 23.

The pompous Hyakutake did most of the planning. He would make the main assault himself southwest of the airfield with his Sendai Division. In support, Kawaguchi's regiment would attack the right flank, the south end of the ridge behind the airfield. To the north, a diversionary attack of battalion size would be made across the Matanikau. All three would be coordinated, pulling the defenders to the flanks and enabling the Sendai Division to drive through in the center. With luck, Kawaguchi would also break through.

So the next day, Kawaguchi found himself tramping southeast along with his regiment, over the same route he'd taken a month before in his retreat from that gruesome ridge. He was surrounded by the men of three infantry battalions and three mortar and machine-gun battalions. And, he felt, the ghosts of the hundreds of men who'd died under his command last month. In fact, several men reported seeing skeletons.

The march was scarcely easier this time. The trail through the jungle had been improved by some strenuous manual labor and was well hidden from American patrols and aerial reconnaissance. In places, though, it remained so narrow the men had to walk single file. Each one carried an artillery shell in addition to his own gear.

Nearing the airfield at last, Kawaguchi surveyed the ridge and its spurs off to his left. A black awareness struck him. He had no more chance of taking those heights with a night frontal assault than he did before.

He remembered from September that flatter country and an easier route to the field existed east-southeast of the ridge, where they'd almost broken through the Marine Parachutists. That would mean another day or two of hiking and another delay in General Hyakutake's timetable. Already having trouble getting the Sendai Division in position, he had postponed the attack a third time, to the 24th.

Kawaguchi had expected to be relieved after his previous defeat. He knew he was on shaky ground. But he also knew the chances of closing a vise on the Americans and taking the airfield would increase if he circled around to that better ground.

He'd received word that same day that Japanese troops to the east had beheaded some Catholic missionaries. Why did some hotheads in the army commit such offenses?

Kawaguchi's natural rebellious streak took over. He would not carry out an attack plan that was senseless. That night he radioed Hyakutake and insisted on more time. He was rewarded with a verbal explosion. "No more delays," Hyakutake thundered. "Carry out your orders."

"Then I will make the night attack with the one battalion that is in position," Kawaguchi answered testily.

"You will follow orders precisely," Hyakutake shouted. "You will attack with your entire regiment."

"That will be impossible tomorrow night."

Hyakutake hung up. Kawaguchi pictured him fuming and storming about his camp.

That night, he and Major Suzuki did what little they could to speed up the positioning of their troops in the dark.

"I don't see how it's possible to attack the ridge at *any* point with our entire force tomorrow night, excellency," Suzuki said. "The men can only move so fast in this terrain. They are worn out."

"Please do not address me as excellency any longer, Suzuki-san." Kawaguchi's eyes were as flat as the Kanto Plain. "One way or another I am finished."

He was right. Hyakutake called back in a calmer voice and ordered him to report to the Sendai Division command post. He was sacked. Hyakutake ordered Colonel Toshinari Shoji to replace him as commander of the right flank.

Kawaguchi handed the headset to the stunned Shoji, who quickly protested. "It is not the Samurai way to change commanders on the eve of battle." Kawaguchi knew that only infuriated Hyakutake more.

Kenny knew something was up. A lookout on Bloody Ridge saw smoke rising from campfires on the forested foothills of Mount Austen. Then Plunkett spotted a Japanese officer scanning the American positions with binoculars.

The 5th Marines were dug in on their knoll, 900 meters south of the sea, about halfway between the Lunga and the Matanikau. Able Company was situated slightly higher than the jungle flats beside and in front of them. Considerably understrength, Kenny's squad had received only two replacements since Bloody Ridge and had the very non-regulation total of only seven men.

"How come we're never put in reserve?" said Hoagy Carmichael. "We been in the friggin' line forever."

If possible, the day was hotter and more humid than usual. Enormous pillars of cumulus assembled and reassembled themselves. The men improved their holes and their fields of fire and worked on the double row of barbed wire. Beyond that, a trip wire was concealed in the undergrowth. Pistol Pete--there were dozens left despite Kenny's raid--periodically flung shells over their heads toward Henderson Field.

A friendly patrol passed by in the afternoon and shouted out its account of a firefight with several Japanese.

Then an attack took place off to Kenny's right, just beyond A Company's sector. It looked like a Japanese unit of battalion size accompanied by *Chi-Ha* medium tanks. They struck to the north, along the beach.

Colonel Spike McKelvey's battalion was over there, with good support. The 11th Marines' howitzers, pre-registered on all the likely points of attack, hammered at the enemy column. Within minutes most of the tanks were blasted and burning. One wallowed into the surf and flooded out. Between the artillery and the Marines' mortars and machine guns, the attack fizzled. The steady hammer-beat of weapons receded to individual sounds, then only the occasional isolated rifle shot.

Then the rains came, an unrelenting tropical downpour. Trails became quagmires. Foxholes filled with water. Kenny's squad tried to keep dry with shelter-halves and ponchos. They failed. In the heavy rain, nightfall came early. "A real toad choker, ain't it?" Plunkett said.

General Vandegrift wasn't there. He was 700 miles away at Nouméa. He'd been ordered to accompany Commandant Holcomb there to meet with Admiral Turner and the new ComSoPac, Bill Halsey. It was the first time Vandegrift had been off Guadalcanal since the invasion in August.

Halsey, whom Vandegrift knew was called "Bull" only in the newspapers, questioned him about his needs and promised he would do more than Ghormley to meet them. Vandegrift fidgeted as the meeting droned on and on. His Vandegut told him he should be on Guadalcanal.

The storm subsided, started in once more, then let up again. At about ten-hundred, rifle fire began cracking. Kenny and his buddies were caught by surprise. Three Marines fell. Screams of pain and anger pierced the soggy air.

Kenny knew that somehow, despite the battalion's listening posts and sentries, enemy troops had gotten into the low jungle on their left flank.

These Japanese hadn't started out by burning a flare and they weren't recklessly charging like their predecessors. They advanced cautiously, firing from behind fallen trees and lava outcrops. "Looks like they've got only rifles and one submachine gun, nothing bigger," Kenny said. "Still, they've got us pinned down, the whole company, looks like."

Then Billy Ninetrees pegged a grenade that took some of the sting out of the attack.

The clouds opened up again. "Can't hardly see a thing," Kenny said, water dripping from his helmet. "Least the Japs can't either."

They were too close for Captain Brush to call in artillery. Stalemate reigned for half an hour.

Then one of the Japs charged from less than forty feet away. How had he ever sneaked that close before running out of cover? A bullet pierced his chest but didn't stop him.

Plunkett jumped up to face him, leveling his .45, but the wet pistol jammed. The man reached Plunkett. The big sergeant took a gash in the forearm parrying a bayonet thrust. Weighing nearly twice as much as his adversary, Plunkett separated him from his rifle with a football block, then grabbed his head with his slab hands and twisted it almost 180 degrees. Simply broke his neck. A tongue dangled from a stunned and exceedingly dead face. Plunkett tossed the limp soldier in the general direction of Australia and ducked for cover, holding his bloody arm.

"Incredible," Skinny Wade whispered. "If there weren't Japs all around, I'd give him a standing ovation."

Soon, effective shooting by Kenny on the BAR and Skinny Wade on the light machine gun, plus more well-thrown grenades, took some more fight out of the enemy.

Lieutenant Ruffin sent a squad to flank the Japanese on the left, where there was a thick stand of trees. Kenny was glad it wasn't his squad. They were exhausted.

The men Ruffin committed eventually succeeded. Muddy and bloody, they took the knoll. At the cost of another Marine's life.

* * *

On the Japanese side, Hyakutake's Sendai Division had the stage all to itself. The diversionary strike along the coast to help his main attack had been launched too soon. It had failed completely. Farther south, his firing of Kawaguchi had made no difference-- Colonel Shoji hadn't been able to get the regiment to the line any faster. Still groping in the jungle, it couldn't attack the ridge.

The rain stopped yet again and the men of A Company got word that the Japanese had broken through in several places, but mostly they were thrown back while the artillery chewed up their positions. Kenny wrapped Plunkett's arm the best he could, knowing the slash would take many stitches. Then he and his buddies took time out to take a piss and nibble on cold rations-- those who had any appetite.

They spent a bleak, sleepless night. Plunkett got himself sewed up at an aid station and came right back.

Toward dawn a runner came with a message from Battalion that an enemy unit had broken through on the left. Baker Company was pinned down. Plunkett's platoon was ordered to wheel to the south and bail them out. Even Plunkett grumbled, "What the hell. Ain't there no reserves nowhere? We gotta weaken our line for this shit?"

Then, getting over it, he called out, "Saddle up, children, the foot cavalry's goin' for another walk." A platoon of zombies, Kenny's ravaged squad among them, moved out.

Through streaks of dying storm an eerie dawn crept in. Birds sang and a breeze sprang from the mountains as the little column tramped off. The sky glowed an odd pink. Mist rose from sodden valleys. A light sprinkle fell. Kenny thought the island was weeping at the horrors committed on its surface.

■

CHAPTER 36

AN HOUR LATER they found the besieged Baker Company trapped in a small clearing, enveloped on two sides, taking crossfire. Men hunkered in holes or behind logs. Kenny saw three bodies sprawled in the open. Irregular gunfire filled the air.

From behind a clump of pandanus trees, Plunkett and Lieutenant Ruffin sized up the situation. Plunkett lowered his binoculars and said, "Kenny, take your squad over there to the right. Jap guns in those trees yonder, see? Flank 'em or get behind 'em if you can. Take 'em out."

"Right." Kenny motioned to Ninetrees, Wade, Carmichael, Keugeman and Manny Slocum, one of the new replacements. "Let's go, guys."

It took twenty minutes of belly-crawling to reach a spot beside a fast-flowing stream. Through vines and ferns, Kenny saw four enemy gunners on the opposite side. A machine gun, a mortar and two riflemen. They peered over well-placed logs, taking inter-mittent shots to keep heads down. American heads, trapped in the clearing below.

Kenny's men were at a right angle to them. He was pretty sure they'd arrived unseen. "We've got a little better field of fire over there," he whispered, nodding toward a small knob above the stream forty feet away. "'Trees, come with me. The rest of you, fire like mad when we start shooting. Pour it into 'em."

Kenny and Billy Ninetrees crawled to the knob. It took forever. Kenny's heart thudded in his chest and the BAR weighed more than ever. *How does Ninetrees do it? Moves so quietly. Moves like a ghost.*

Ninetrees got there first. Kenny slithered into position two yards to his left. "Yeah," he whispered, "we can see 'em good from here." He unfolded the bipod, fast and quiet. "You take the machine gun. I'll spray the others." He leveled the BAR and sighted. "You ready?" Ninetrees nodded.

They fired. All four enemy soldiers jumped, twitched and sprawled. The rest of Kenny's squad blazed away, too. Chips flew from logs. Bodies tore. Limbs splayed. It was over in seconds.

"Hold your fire," Kenny shouted. He pulled himself up into a crouch, gazing across the stream at their victims.

And his world disintegrated.

Three enemy soldiers--where the hell had they come from?--stood around them, rifles aimed. Dogged little men in slouch hats and patched uniforms. Kenny saw no stripes of rank but one of them seemed to be the leader. He stepped forward, motioning "hands up" with his Arisaka rifle. A mustache bristled as he said, "Sullenda, Joe. Sullenda. You got cigarette, Joe?" He stared at Ninetrees with coal black, curious eyes.

Captured? Kenny had got himself captured? And one of his best men, too. Some Marine he turned out to be. His heart stopped, he was sure of it. He always knew he'd get killed some day on this rock--but captured? And what the hell had happened to his other men, off to the left?

He sank into black despair, queasiness crawling in his stomach. A vision of wearily hacking at stone year after year in a Japanese quarry appeared in his mind. He'd never see his little brother again, or North Prairie Street. Or Claudia. She'd been right after all. He never should have come back, should have let her fake up something for his medical chart.

He'd probably be shot right here when they found out "Joe no got cigarette." Neither he nor Ninetrees smoked. Nearby, a bird screeched.

Sitting at a desk in the corner of the nurses' lounge, Claudia Chase jumped. A shiver of fear squirmed through her brain and down her spine. What was that? she wondered. What just happened?

Her breathing was just about back to normal when a voice behind her said "Hi." She jumped again.

"Didn't mean to startle you," said Peggy Stratton. "What are you doing there? Looks like you're writing a letter. You're actually writing a letter?" Sometimes Claudia hated Peggy's sarcasm. "Who to, your mom?"

Claudia looked up, twirling a fountain pen between her thumb and first finger. A wood-bladed fan revolved above them. "Uh, no. That guy, if it's any of your business."

"That sergeant you're sweet on? Nielsen."

"I wouldn't say I'm sweet on him, but he's a very nice man. The first true gentleman I ever met."

"I saw you two holding hands in the courtyard, sneaking off here and there in the moonlight. You're sweet on him all right."

"Oh, go on."

"I'll say this, he was good for you. What a difference he made in you, never saw your face so bright. I'm glad you're writing him. That's one to keep in touch with."

"Yeah, yeah. But look, Peg, should I say 'Dear Kenny' or 'Hello Kenny' or what? I wouldn't want him to get the wrong idea."

"You worry too much, Claw. Say 'Dear'."

"What if he took that to mean 'Sweetheart' or 'Honey'?"

"Worse things could happen."

Claudia frowned. "I don't want to sound forward, but not distant either."

"Definitely say 'Dear'."

"What about the closing? I can't say 'love'."

"You two kissed, didn't you?"

Claudia hesitated, finally nodded.

"And you want to see him again somehow, somewhere, don't you?"

"I think so."

"You *know* so. You're really fond of the guy. He'll get a furlough some day." Peggy shrugged and turned. "Want some coffee?"

"No thanks, I've go to finish this up."

Five minutes later, Claudia read the letter for the third time.

Dear Kenny,

"I hope this finds you safe and well. How is the malaria? Surely by now the quinine I slipped you (quite illegally, you know) has run out. But do take your atabrine. Please take good care of yourself. I wouldn't want to treat you for any more wounds, but I certainly enjoyed our visits together. As I mentioned, you're one of the finest men I've met. I'm sorry I snapped at you that night.

"Things are the same here, only busier. Unfortunately, we've seen quite a few of your fellow Marines. We've overflowed the old building. There are two annexes now, round ugly tin things called Quonset huts.

"I hope that we will meet again.

"God bless you,
Claudia Chase"

She read it a fourth time, then crossed out her last name, folded the letter and sealed it. She kissed the envelope, but not before rubbing off her lipstick. Couldn't have him getting wrong ideas. She still wondered what had made her shudder like that a moment ago.

Someone grabbed Kenny's arm. Hurled him at the river. The burbling water rushed up fast. Kenny met it with an enormous splash. Next thing he knew, he and Billy Ninetrees were being swept away by the cold current.

Kenny heard shots. This wasn't like swimming at Lake Storey back in high school. This was for his very life.

He was so damned heavy with his utilities and boondockers, plus a grenade cluster strung around his shoulder. The trick was just to somehow stay afloat, let the strong current do the rest.

Soon he lost his helmet, then his grenades. Rocks, vines and branches swiped at him as he rushed along. He swallowed water, coughed, tried not to panic. He caught a glimpse of Ninetrees just ahead of him, swimming much stronger than he was. That dog-gone Ninetrees, he did this. Shoved himself and me both in this stream.

Could he make it? He was a good swimmer, but 'Trees had always beaten him whenever they'd raced at Camp Lejeune.

They swept into a swirling rapids. Corkscrewed over some rocks. Kenny's dungarees tore. Some skin, too. *Aaoow*. Felt like his ribs had been flogged with the claw end of a hammer. He went under.

No, the answer was no, he couldn't make it. Would drown here and now. Couldn't see, couldn't breathe, lungs screaming for air in a silvery twilight of boiling water. So damned heavy. How come he couldn't get back to the surface?

Maybe he should rest. Just slide down to the bottom of this river and rest there for a bit. Yes, that's it, rest awhile.

His mother stood before him with her little "you're a good boy" smile, just as she had on that evac plane to Santo. She'd never looked so small, standing there with her hands folded in front of her waist. Tiny and yet large. Small and large at the same time.

"Thank you for cleaning out the garage," she seemed to say, even though her lips weren't moving. "But you can't rest yet, Kenny. You've more work to do. You can't rest yet, Kenny. Can't rest, Kenny. Can't rest. . . ."

He bobbed up. Coughed up water and gulped some precious air. Caught sight of Ninetrees again. Rest on the bottom? Jesus, that was dangerous thinking.

On they rushed. How could he keep his arms stroking? They were made of lead. Push on, push on somehow. Got to keep going.

Past the white water now. The current growing weaker, not quite so fast. Soon much slower. Gliding into a calm spot at last.

Then Ninetrees had his arm. He felt himself being dragged onto the bank. Didn't have the strength to crawl all the way out. Coughed more water from his mouth. He just lay there, waist and legs still submerged. Tried to fill burning, empty lungs. His legs wouldn't work.

Pretty soon, Ninetrees tugged him up the slope into jungle shade. Kenny shivered for awhile. He hugged himself and rubbed his arms. Eventually he stopped trembling. He sat there a long time, his mind working no better than his legs. He watched a column of big red ants marching past his dripping-wet boondockers.

Finally, Ninetrees said, "This is a tributary of the Matanikau or the Lunga. I knew that if the water could get out, so could we."

That was about the longest speech he'd ever heard from Billy Ninetrees. God bless him. Saved my life.

Kenny touched abraded skin above a bruised, aching rib. It felt like it had been scraped with a file. He had no idea where they were. He was lost, completely lost. But alive. And not a damn POW. He thought about his weapon. Hated losing that BAR to the enemy. At least it was almost out of ammo.

Ninetrees pulled a compass from his soaked utilities, shook off drops of water, and studied it.

"This way," he said, pointing. "Able Company is this way."

Now how the hell does he know that?

■

CHAPTER 37

NINETREES WAS RIGHT. It took that impassive Indian exactly one hour to find the outfit. Now, reunited with the others, they trekked on together. Ninetrees was supporting Hoagy Carmichael, who'd taken a .30-caliber slug through the calf.

Kenny could barely support himself, his fatigue beyond anything he'd yet known. He'd have to think about all this, thank 'Trees for saving his life, later. Later.

What was Plunkett saying? Sounded like, "Had yourself a nice refreshing swim, did you, while the rest of us was killing Japs?"

They slogged on. "When we stop to rest I'll tell you something I heard about you an' me," Plunkett said. Kenny thought about saying, "Yeah, what's that? Tell me now," but he didn't have the energy.

When they got back, feeling a bit stronger, he pulled his little squad together to rehash the action. Where the hell had they been when he and Ninetrees were captured?

Skinny Wade looked down at the tips of his boots. "We headed for the platoon," he explained, "when we saw you cleaned out the gun nest. Hoagy was hit, you see. When you didn't catch up pretty soon, we came back, all but Hoagy. Found three Japs standing there staring at the stream. Had a little firefight. Got 'em all, I think."

"Good, but you shouldn't have all headed back without us. That was wrong. Should've sent one guy with Hoagy."

"I know," Wade said sheepishly. "Sorry, Kenny, won't ever happen again . . . God, I was glad to see you guys show up."

"No more than me, pal."

Kenny dismissed everyone but Ninetrees. He took him aside and said, "Great work, Billy. I can never thank you enough. . .

What I can't figure is, why didn't those Japs just shoot us?" Kenny remembered them gaping curiously at Ninetrees. They'd probably never seen an Indian, never seen an American soldier with tawny skin so much like their own.

"A screaming cockatoo distracted them," Ninetrees said. "They looked away, so--"

"That's when you saw your chance and took it."

"I shoved us into the water when they looked away. Didn't stop to think."

"Good man, Billy."

Then Kenny went to Lieutenant Ruffin and urged him to put Ninetrees up for some appropriate medal.

Anxiously rubbing his forehead, Vandegrift was on his way back. "I hate to be off the island when there's an enemy attack." He shouted at his aide, Ray Schwenke, to be heard above the PBY's engines as they clamored at the morning sky.

"Admiral Halsey certainly wouldn't have called you down there if he'd had any way of knowing," Schwenke said. "I'm sure General Geiger and Red Mike handled it okay."

"A bad time to be away from my command," Vandegrift repeated. "First time off the island in eleven weeks."

At least Halsey had promised to do all he possibly could to bring him more supplies.

Vandegrift had learned by radio from Geiger that a patrol had captured some of Hyakutake's documents. Among them was a complete plan for the surrender ceremony. It was to take place at the mouth of the Matanikau and it even indicated where Vandegrift was to stand as he yielded up the island and all his Marines to Hyakutake.

Vandegrift was irate. "If we've driven them off again with loss, it will be time to go over to the attack. I want to pursue them, cross the Matanikau in force, drive Pistol Pete out of range, do them some real damage. Kick their ass. Pardon my French." He realized it was the first time Schwenke had ever heard him use a vulgarity.

* * *

Depressed, disgraced, awaiting transportation off the island, General Kawaguchi sat on a canvas stool at the Sendai Division command post. He heard the reports as they came in. Heavy rains had disrupted communications and the ability of troops to reach their attack points. Disorganized and exhausted, they had attacked, failed, fought off counterattacks, regrouped, attacked, and failed again. All night long, each attack weaker than the one before.

At last Kawaguchi heard that Hyakutake was withdrawing the survivors, vowing to re-form and try again the next night. The fool.

Kawaguchi's longtime aide, Major Suzuki, muttered, "You were correct, excellency, when you said we should have concentrated our forces and attacked along the coast, supported by our artillery. The Sendai Division is bleeding to death in the jungle."

Kawaguchi stared into space and said nothing.

At his bivouac, Kenny was cleaning and field-stripping his new weapon, a Springfield rifle. At least it weighed a lot less than that BAR he'd lost. Well, he thought, it's November. Been on this damn rock nearly three months. Seems like three years. He squirted some oil on a cloth patch and worked it up the gun barrel with his ramrod.

Before long, Plunkett came over and named Kenny and four others to go with him on a small patrol, northeast of Mount Austen. A missionary said the Japanese had set up a strongpoint out there someplace in No Man's Land.

Once again, the foot cavalry trudged off. Kenny tried to picture Claudia. He wished he were meandering through the hospital grounds with her, holding hands and talking, talking about anything at all. Maybe in a day or two she'd be nursing Hoagy Carmichael, who'd been hit that morning. Lucky Carmichael.

The farther they got from their bivouac, the more cautious

they became. Crouching and moving silently was second nature. From walking Indian file, they switched to the diamond configuration of patrol. Jungle-rot stench filled Kenny's nostrils and the equatorial sun made a white furnace of the sky. He moved stealthily through a low, shell-pocked area, cleared by explosions and fire. A few disheveled clumps of wild flowers somehow had survived.

Back in dappled light under the canopy of trees, something made him glance obliquely at a monkeypod tree. Then he looked ahead again. Two more steps. Hold on. Something wrong. His eyes flashed back to the tree. A brown face, not entirely hidden by leaves. Too late! A rifle fired.

Kenny's right index finger went to the trigger. He fired that old Springfield as fast as he could. Others did the same. A small enemy sniper, measled with red holes, skidded face down from limb to limb, as if in slow motion. Leaves and small branches were affixed to his helmet and much of his body for camouflage. His bloody head finally bumped to a stop on the tree's spidery roots.

Almost before the echoes died away, Kenny saw that Plunkett was down. He sprang to his side. A small hole in the chest leaked blood. Kenny put down his rifle, pulled out his green handkerchief and pressed it against the wound. He put his other hand under his friend's head, cradling it like a baby's.

Plunkett's breath came slow and ragged. Kenny started to say something when his hand felt a sudden change in the big head. It was different, heavier. A gush of air rattled from the mouth. The eyes froze, staring sightlessly into infinity.

The man inside that body, his good friend, was no longer there. And he'd left without a word. Not, "Write Miz Tillie for me," not anything. None of that stuff you saw in the movies.

Tears blurred Kenny's eyes. He leaped up, grabbed his rifle, jabbed it at the nose of the dead sniper and fired a round, obliterating the face in a spray of bone and flesh.

He tossed the rifle down. Clenched his fists. "Shit shit shit. Damn it, God, why'd you let this happen? Abandoned the best man we had. Why? Why?"

Someone's arms wrapped around him. "Easy now, Kenny." It was Skinny Wade. "Easy now." Kenny unstiffened a little. "Nobody can hurt him anymore," Wade said.

But I'm gonna hurt. Forever and ever.

Just above Hadley Plunkett's head a large white jasmine blossom gave the scene a ludicrously lovely fragrance. Kenny knew he would always hate the scent of jasmine, would associate it with that terrible moment forever.

Later, Kenny wouldn't even remember hiking back to camp, though he and Manny Slocum had carried Plunkett's body, wrapped in a poncho, back inside the perimeter. He didn't do another decent thing that afternoon.

He wanted to be alone the rest of the day. The rest of his life. This was as tough as when his mother died. He didn't know if there'd ever be a way out of this realm of contrition and despair he'd fallen into.

He knew he should help the burial parties, but he didn't. He didn't do his share to tidy up the bivouac, either.

Lieutenant Ruffin must have understood. He left him alone. He could afford to, because the sector was quiet, all the action southwest of Bloody Ridge.

Kenny slouched away from the field kitchen, his eyes as hollow as old bamboo. He'd put very little on his mess tin. Wasn't hungry.

He reflected on Plunkett telling him he should patent his idea for recording telephone messages. The big guy firing toward Kenny but actually killing an enemy sniper. And breaking that Jap soldier's neck with his bare hands--Kenny would never forget that.

He knew that Plunkett's badgering him about using four-bit words and reading books had really masked regret that he hadn't been better educated himself.

Other memories surfaced. How cool Plunkett had been on that first hike to the Matanikau, when the virgin patrol drew fire and Lieutenant Gates verged on panic. His contention that Gates did ninety percent of what he told him and that the other ten "ain't worth worryin' about." Saying, before Gaucho Kirby's raid, "You can't figure on livin' forever." Missing his wife's fried chicken.

Kenny suddenly remembered that Miz Tillie was expecting. Poor old Plunk would never see his kid. He tossed his food into the mud. Why am I alive, he thought, when so many are dead? Including the best friend I ever had. Plunkett saved my life a couple of times, but when the chips were down, I couldn't save his.

It was remorse he was feeling, and loss, but most of all guilt.

He tried to pray for Plunkett that night, but decided he wasn't on speaking terms with God. Instead, he went through Plunkett's things, found a bottle of liberated Japanese sake. Drank too much of it.

■

CHAPTER 38

KENNY DIDN'T DO a damn thing the next day. A sake hangover only made his anguished soul ache all the more. His stomach seesawed like the old *McCawley* on a rough sea; his tongue was sandpaper. Some black coffee and water helped a little, but not much. It was fifteen hundred before he could finally eat some food.

That night on his bedroll he relived a moment from seven years ago. He'd brought home his best report card ever, all A's except for a B in geometry. His mother smiled that little smile and gave him a fifty-cent piece which she'd obviously secreted from their meager grocery money.

Already weak with the cancer, she said, "Kenny, you're a fine boy. I'm so very proud of your school work. But now you'll have to start doing even more around here. I get so tired. I'm sorry my meals aren't what they used to be."

Kenny accepted the four bits but spent it on potatoes at Stanley Oberg's store. He put them in the larder while his mother was napping.

He'd done the right thing then. He couldn't do anything now.

In the morning, shaving in front of a tiny mirror wired to a tree, Kenny didn't like what he saw. "Enough," he said. "What the hell's the matter with you?"

He decided to go see Lieutenant Ruffin and apologize. Ruffin called him into his dugout and spoke first. "Platoon sergeant, it's time to get to work."

"Sir?"

"Nielsen, you're my new platoon sergeant. Hadley Plunkett was a fine shipmate. Continuing the splendid work he did, that's the best way you can honor him."

Holy smoke! Take over the whole platoon? "Aye aye, sir. I'll do my best, Lieutenant."

"I'd like to promote Ninetrees to take over your squad, but my superiors wouldn't like it, an Indian commanding white boys."

"Do it, sir, he's one of the best we have."

"I don't know."

"Do it, sir."

"I'll get some heat."

"Do it. Edson will back you."

"Bossing me around already, hey? Oh, what the hell, I'll probably never get captain's bars anyway. . . Okay then, we have replacements to assign, squads to re-form. . . ."

A week before Thanksgiving, correspondent Richard Tregaskis was strolling alone near the cemetery at Kukum at twilight when he saw a sergeant bending over one of the new wooden crosses, his Kabar knife in his hand.

Tregaskis watched silently, concealed behind trees. When at last the sergeant shambled from the graveyard, Tregaskis went over and read the inscription in the last light of day.

> *And when he goes to heaven,*
> *To St. Peter he will tell,*
> *Another Marine reporting, sir,*
> *I've served my time in hell.*

Tregaskis made a point of finding out who he'd seen carving that epitaph. The next day, carrying his notepad, he visited the 1st Battalion, 5th Marines.

Watching him approach, Kenny thought, What does this beanpole want?

"I'm Dick Tregaskis of the International News Service," the beanpole said. "I saw you carve some words on a grave marker last night."

"Me?"

"I've heard quite a bit about you, Sergeant. Got a minute?"

"Got a lifetime," Kenny said.

"Yeah, so it seems. In spite of all the fighting and the work, it's mostly down time, isn't it?"

"There's either too much time or not enough. Sometimes you've got the crap scared out of you and other times you're bored to death."

"I understand you won the Silver Star for gallantry under fire."

"I'm no hero. You should be talking to Manila John Basilone of the 7th Marines. There's a hero."

"I already have. Basilone killed eighty Japanese in that night attack last month."

"Then he's sixty-three or -four ahead of me."

"You also have the Purple Heart and came right back here from the hospital. Moreover, Lieutenant Ruffin tells me you're a great platoon sergeant."

"Oh, I've got 'Ruffin Ready' trained. He does ninety percent of what I tell him. The other ten isn't worth worrying about."

"Ha. Yes, armies are run by good sergeants. I've heard that before."

Kenny noticed the poised pencil. "But please don't write that. Keep that to yourself, what I just said about the lieutenant."

"Don't worry. Where you from, Nielsen, someplace in Illinois, isn't it?"

"Right, Galesburg."

"I've heard of it. Carl Sandburg's birthplace, right?"

"That's right."

"Lincoln and Douglas debated there, too, didn't they?" The correspondent's glasses slipped and he pushed them back with the middle finger of his left hand.

"Yes, at Knox College. You've been there?"

"Nope, that I haven't. Tell me about it."

When the correspondent blinked behind his glasses, he looked like a stork, but Kenny liked him. This was doing him some good, keeping his mind off Plunkett. "Well, they got the biggest maple trees you ever saw. In the summer they make shade you can really savor. Nothing like a cold lemonade under a maple tree on a hot day."

"Shade you can savor. Good line. You're a writer yourself, I understand."

"Me, nah. Worked on the school paper is all."

"Well, that's writing. You got a wife or sweetheart you write to from the Canal?"

"No wife."

Kenny stopped abruptly and Tregaskis let it pass. "Tell me something about Guadalcanal that I don't know," he said instead.

"Well, it's the last battle the Springfield rifle will ever fight. The old boy's really going out in style."

"I believe you're right. Can I use that?"

"Sure, if you want. Don't need my permission."

"What I mean is, I'll quote you. What do you think about the war?" Tregaskis added.

"What do I think about the war? This fucking war?"

"Right, dumb question. Let me tell you what I think, Nielsen. I think the Japanese have shot their wad here. They've given us hell day and night for four months, air force and navy both, mounted several big attacks, all turned back. I know there's a lot of tough fighting ahead for men like you, but there's no doubt in my mind who will win. I think we've broken the back of Japan's offensive right here on Cactus. Oh, it may be a long time before we 'gain the inevitable triumph so help us God,' to quote the President, ha ha, but he's right, you Marines will. Maybe Guadalcanal should be put in that song of yours. The shores of Tripoli have nothing on this place. I can't tell you how impressed I am with what you've done here."

"The Japanese, too," Kenny said. "They're some of the toughest buggers I ever saw. Fight like hell even when they're starving to death. . . . Hey, I just thought of something else about Galesburg. The guy who invented the Ferris Wheel was born there. He was an engineer, built it for the World's Fair in Chicago, 1893 or '95, somewhere in there. Name was Ferris, of course."

"You learn something every day."

Figuring he'd bored the correspondent, Kenny changed the

subject. "On this campaign, I agree with you. It's like when you're trying to open a package wrapped tight in cellophane. Sometimes it takes awhile for your thumbnail to rip open that first little piece. But once it does, the rest tears away in a hurry. We'll do for Tojo what Wellington did for Napoleon."

"Now *that* I'm going to quote. Say, I heard something very interesting about you, Sergeant."

"What's that?"

"Jake Weaver, one of the other correspondents--I believe you've met him--saw your name on a list of field commission nominees."

"What?"

"That's right. Two names from your outfit on that list. Yours and a fellow named Plunkett, I believe."

Again a long silence from Kenny. I'm on the Mustang list? he thought. And Plunkett was, too? This guy doesn't know poor old Plunk is dead.

"Me an officer?" he said at last. "No siree."

This guy's been through some tough times, Tregaskis told himself.

Suddenly their ears were treated to some beautiful whistling. The spirited tune sounded vaguely familiar, but Kenny couldn't name it. He turned. The whistler was new squad leader Billy Ninetrees.

"One of Brahms' Hungarian dances, right?" Tregaskis asked.

Ninetrees nodded agreement without missing a note. They fell silent for a minute, seemingly mesmerized by the surprising music floating through the rainforest.

"Tell me, Sergeant, what's it like in combat? How do you handle the fear?"

After a long pause, Kenny said, "You just do what you have to. If you screw up, your friends die." Another long silence. His eyes got watery. "And if they screw up, you die. It's not bravery." Tregaskis scribbled away.

"What would you like to do after the war?"

"If I get *through* this war, I guess I'd like to settle down with a good woman, maybe do some newspaper work like you."

"I truly hope you do both. I can give you some leads, editors to talk to you, that kind of thing. You know, Nielsen, besides my regular columns, I'm writing a book on this campaign."

"What's it about? The main idea, I mean."

"Just a story of the campaign, written chronologically, what I've experienced, what I've seen, what you fellas have been through."

"Whatcha gonna call it?"

"I don't know. Haven't come up with a title yet."

"What about *Guadalcanal Diary*?"

"Not bad. I'll have to think about that."

■

CHAPTER 39

KENNY HADN'T BEEN the one to carve those words above Plunkett's grave, "Another Marine reporting," and so on. No one seemed to know who had. Tregaskis, seeing Kenny sitting there, had drawn a wrong conclusion.

Nevertheless, Kenny felt drawn to the spot. He sneaked down there every now and then because it made him feel close to his lost friend. He was back again the next day at twilight.

He'd been sitting alone in the little cemetery for several minutes beside the grave, relaxing his mind. It was still and peaceful under the cocopalms, as good a place as any, he thought, for Plunkett to lie, if he couldn't be back home in North Carolina.

Several minutes passed before he found himself saying, "Well, Plunk, to tell the truth I'm kinda scared. I don't know how to be a platoon leader, more than forty guys to worry about. I'm putting 'Trees in charge of my old squad and thinking about moving Skinny Wade over to lead Second Squad. Wade's made sergeant now. Carmichael will get a squad, too."

Carmichael's leg wound hadn't been too bad. He'd been patched up and returned to duty.

Kenny felt a whisper of air wash across his face, although there wasn't a hint of breeze in the still, muggy grove. His spine tightened. What was that? Had he heard a voice?

"That's fine."

There. Again.

Kenny thought he'd heard a faint voice, as if filtered through a bulkhead. "What's fine? Who said that?"

"That's fine, givin' squads to old Wade 'n' Hoagy. I'd do the same." Kenny's forehead went cold. Was it Plunkett? "An' spread them replacements out even among the squads. Don't bunch them green ones together. But you know that, I don't have to tell ya. You're gonna be fine."

"I don't know--"

"You're gonna be fine, kid. You're plenty smart. Trust yourself."

"Plunk, Plunk . . . ." He heard nothing more. It was perfectly still.

Before long, the chill passed from his face and he grew warm again. Had he actually heard Plunkett's voice? Nah, he must have imagined the whole thing.

He sat there for several minutes, feeling placid and drowsy. Gradually he began to realize, to his surprise, that he didn't feel quite so sad about Plunkett's death.

Well, this old island is awash in ghosts, he thought. Maybe I've just been talking to one.

At last he got up, said, "So long, Plunk," and started hiking back to the platoon, *his* platoon. He knew he had to get back before it was fully dark. Wouldn't do to get shot by one of his own sentries. Such things happened.

He knew he would never tell anyone about what he'd just experienced--or thought he *might* have experienced.

In the distance, the bugler began playing Taps. The somber notes drifted through the trees and fell on Kenny's ear like little teardrops.

■

CHAPTER 40 - ONE MONTH LATER

"**WHAT ARE YOU** doing there, Bill?" Vandegrift shouted over the howl of the C-47's engines.

Colonel Twining had drawn something on a notepad.

"An idea I had for an insignia. The division's never really had one." He handed his sketch to the general. "The stars are the Southern Cross."

Twining bit his lip while Vandegrift studied the drawing.

"And your numeral 'One' of course needs no explanation." The general continued to scrutinize it, then said at last, "I like it." Uncapping his fountain pen, he scrawled the initials "A.A.V." in the upper left corner. "Approved, Bill. Have it made up when we reach Brisbane. Order 20,000."

Twining beamed. "Wherever they send me, sir, I'll never forget those splendid bastards we brought to Cactus. They're so worn down and exhausted, a lot of them couldn't make it up the cargo nets yesterday. Sailors had to climb down and help them, did you notice?" Twining didn't mention that the sight brought tears to his eyes.

Vandegrift shook his head. "Those troops were given an awfully dirty job, Bill. I'll always think of them with gratitude." He gazed out over a pearly blanket of clouds. "Well, imagine, the war's been on for a year. Did you honestly think we'd live to see December 1942?"

"Yes, I was pretty sure we would, sir."

"Or to see me turn that island over to the Army? I think General Patch can finish up what we started very nicely."

"I think you mean 'mop up,' sir. We did the real work. Weakened the enemy, smashed his attacks, ultimately drove him well beyond range of Henderson."

"We taught the Army a lot in the last four months, didn't we? But that's our role. We're the amphibious specialists. We land in the top of the first, seize the initial objectives, score some runs in the middle innings, then let a relief pitcher come in and finish up."

"To continue your baseball analogy, sir, the men of the division have certainly earned a hot shower and a few innings of rest in Australia. With a couple of months to square away, they'll be full of piss and vinegar again, ready to hit New Britain or anyplace else they need us."

"I hope these scrawny devils can fatten up a bit first. I'll bet they eat up all the ice cream on the continent in less than a week."

"They'll create quite a beer shortage, too, sir."

He wasn't quite ready for a big and civilized city like Brisbane. Not after four months on the Canal. He caught himself glancing about tensely, looking for Japanese snipers in second story windows. He was off the rock and yet he wasn't.

With its river bridges and all, Brisbane reminded him a bit of Peoria. Except for the eucalyptus trees and hordes of soldiers milling about in Australian and American uniforms. It was all so strange after the adrenalin rush of combat.

Hot--it was summer down here--but not as hot as the Canal. He couldn't get used to clean streets and pretty policewomen in the intersections around King George Square directing traffic with white-gloved hand signals. Limestone churches and shady parks, electric trams squealing about, toting their loads of people here and there, as if there were no war anywhere.

In a friendly little café, he'd devoured a big bowl of ice cream, very rich, more cream content than you got back home. "Icy cream" they called it here.

Kenny chewed on all these thoughts as he waited his turn in line at the red phone box. Finally the door swung open and an Aussie soldier pushed out, his wide-brimmed hat pinned up rakishly on one side. "You're next, mate," he said with a broad grin.

It took Kenny a moment to figure out which coin to drop in the slot, then which number to dial.

"Is this the long distance operator?" he asked the voice.

"Trunk calls, yes."

"Ma'am, I'd like to place a call to the U.S. Fleet Hospital at Espiritu Santo in the New Hebrides."

"Quite. And the party you wish to ring up?"

The memory of those sweet kisses three months ago came fresh and bright, like a favorite old song. "Ensign Claudia Chase, Nursing Section."

"Right you are, then. And whom shall I say is calling?"

"Second Lieutenant Ken Nielsen."

"Lines bloody busy at Christmastime. This may take a bit."

It would give him time to think. He wasn't sure what he was going to say. He had some leave. Maybe he could hitch a ride to Santo on a military plane.

■

AFTERWORD

This work of fiction is faithful to the major events on Guadalcanal as they took place during the Second World War. All the Japanese and American admirals, generals and colonels are real and behave as the historians say they did in 1942.

With apologies to the real men who served in A Company, 1st Battalion, 5th Marine Regiment, all members of that company as described here are fictitious, with the exception of the officers Hunt, Brush, Gates and Ruffin. The 5th Marines didn't hold part of the line in the Battle of Bloody Ridge, but readers will understand the writer's need to place Nielsen and Plunkett in that action.

General Vandegrift's written citations to his men have been abridged but not altered in substance. Some of his letters home are genuine, others invented to illustrate what must have been in his mind. Vandegrift was awarded the Medal of Honor for his leadership on Guadalcanal and later became commandant of the Marine Corps. His eyesight continued to fail and he was virtually blind when he died in 1973.

In February of 1943 the last Tokyo Express evacuated the surviving Japanese troops. About 12,000 were taken out but more than 24,000 others remained to sleep forever on Guadalcanal. The American dead, 2,200 Marines, soldiers, airmen, and sailors were moved in 1949 to cemeteries in the Philippines and the U.S.

The Imperial Fleet lost so many ships in the Solomon Islands battles that it didn't seriously challenge the American Navy again until the Battle of the Philippine Sea in mid-1944.

Major General Kawaguchi was sent back to Japan, placed on reserve, and ignored for the rest of the war.

The troopship *McCawley*, which carried Marines to Guadalcanal, was crippled by a Japanese torpedo bomber off Rendova Island in the central Solomons in July 1943, then mistakenly sunk by an American PT boat.

Richard Tregaskis was regarded as one of the foremost press

correspondents covering the campaign.

In 1955, Red Mike Edson, the troubled hero of Tulagi and Bloody Ridge, took his own life.

Iva Ikuko Toguri D'Aquino, "Tokyo Rose," was convicted of treason in the U.S. and served six years in prison. Gerald Ford pardoned her on his last day as President in 1977.

That same year, Great Britain knighted Jacob Vouza, the courageous native scout and honorary Marine sergeant major who "did it for the king."

* * *

BIBLIOGRAPHY

Frank, Richard B. *Guadalcanal: The Definitive Account of the Landmark Battle* (Random House, Penguin), 1990.

Hammel, Eric. *Guadalcanal: Starvation Island* (Crown Publishers, Inc.), 1987.

Hoyt, Edwin P. *Guadalcanal* (Stein & Day), 1982

McMillan, George. *The Old Breed: A History of the First Marine Division in World War II* (Infantry Journal, Inc.), 1949.

Morison, Samuel Eliot. *The Two-Ocean War* (Ballantine Books), 1963.

Toland, John. *The Rising Sun: The Decline and Fall of the Japanese Empire* (Random House), 1970.

Tregaskis, Richard W. *Guadalcanal Diary* (Random House), 1943.

Twining, General Merrill B. *No Bended Knee* (Presidio Press), 1996.

Vandegrift, General A. Archer. *Once A Marine* (Ballantine Books), 1946.